I AM THE ALPHA
THE MOON FORGED TRILOGY: BOOK I

AJ Downey   Ryan Kells

Second Circle Press

Published 2015 by Second Circle Press
Book design by Lia Rees at Free Your Words (www.freeyourwords.com)
Cover art by Cover Your Dreams (www.coveryourdreams.net)

ISBN: 978-0692460887

Dedication

To RTN, you did it, I'm proud of you. This one is for you in so many ways. – *AJ*

Dedicated to Lia for encouraging me from the beginning to actually write this story and to AJ for giving me the kick in the ass I needed to actually do it and for giving voice to Chloe – *Ryan*

The Moon Forged Trilogy

1. I AM THE ALPHA
2. Omega's Run
3. Hunter's End

Contents

Prologue
Chloe

"Good-*bye* Girl, I'll catch you later," I rolled my eyes at my best friend Tabitha and we parted ways in front of Twist, a swanky club in lower Manhattan. It was pushing on toward three in the morning and I was worn out. It'd been a night of dancing, drinking, and just too much fun. I breathed deep the crisp, fall night air and heels clipping sharply against the cracked sidewalk, jostled my way past the corner and to a clear spot of curb.

"*Taxi!*" I shouted cleanly, hand upraised and one of the yellow cabs slid up in front of me. Wow, that had been way easier than I'd thought it would be. I tried to slip across the vinyl seat, the backs of my thighs sticking where my short skirt didn't cover. *Ew, gross.* I rattled off my address which was only forty or so blocks away. I could have walked it, but not in these heels after dancing all night!

The cab I'd hailed pulled smoothly into traffic and I sighed. The cabbie didn't care to make small talk and I didn't either. I was already planning on a nice long shower and my nice soft bed. I couldn't wait for them, in fact. My makeup felt like it was sitting on my face like a painted mask and I was ready to be clean and to sleep. I'd had a blast though, and I was all smiles when we pulled up in front of my brownstone, well, *my dad's* brownstone.

He was a CPA for the city's elite and had been thrilled when his little girl had chosen law; he hadn't been so thrilled when it'd turned out to be criminal law with an emphasis on prosecution, but we'd come to an agreement of sorts. It wasn't perfect but it was getting me what I wanted, which was a degree in criminal justice. He didn't need to know the particulars.

He'd wanted me to be a defense attorney, where the money was at, but a degree in criminal law was a degree in criminal law. He didn't need to know I'd crossed my fingers behind my back when I'd made the promise to go defense versus prosecution. Once I was graduated, I could do what I wanted. It wasn't the first thing my father and I disagreed on and it probably wouldn't be the last.

I paid the cabbie and took the stairs at a sharp clip, letting myself into the brownstone and powering down the alarm. I sighed out and dropped my keys on the table by the door, ditching my fashionable, small clutch alongside them.

"God, I just want out of these *shoes*," I groaned to no one in particular. I relished slipping the heels off my feet and digging my toes into the plush carpet as I took the stairs two at a time. I was being exceedingly lazy, stripping as I headed towards the bath, letting my clothes fall as I made my way across my bedroom to the private bathroom. I wouldn't leave them, I would just pick them up *after* my shower. It was a tiny, illicit little thrill since Dad would have blown his top to see the mess I'd left strewn across the floor on my way across. I was in my twenties and he still treated me like I was eight, the curse of being an only child, I guess.

The water sluiced hot and delicious down my skin as I stepped into the spray and worked the pins out of my French twist, my red hair foaming around my face until I got it wet, the vibrant, fiery locks turning deep auburn as they soaked to the ends. I shampooed, conditioned, scrubbed myself free of makeup, and rinsed in record time.

Thank God for being clean! I wanted nothing more than to pick up and crawl into bed. I shut off the water, grabbed the first towel and wrapped my hair. I dried off quickly using another and shrugged into my nightgown, satin and lace and a cream that complimented my coloring. I liked sexy night things. Even if I were too damned busy with school for anyone to see them, they weren't really for a prospective boyfriend, they were for me.

I slipped the matching satin robe over my shoulders and let it hang open. Some hand cream that smelled like peaches and a brisk rub of the towel on my hair and I could get rid of it with the rest of the dirty laundry down the chute in the hall.

I sang to myself softly, one of the songs from the club and snapped out the bathroom light. I walked out into the bedroom and stopped short, a short, startled scream escaping my mouth. I pressed my hands to my chest, over my heart as if to contain it and blinked, willing it to be a shadow, and it was, or it appeared to be.

It'd looked like the shadow of a man, standing just outside the French doors to my balcony. The shadow of a man, standing just outside *my bedroom...*

Chapter 1

William

I hated New York. I hated cities period, always have and I always will. The stinking, noisy, clinging press of humanity rushing about their meaningless, insignificant lives as if whatever they had to do was the most important thing in the world. They were missing the point.

It was here, in New York, that I nearly died so many years ago. And of course, it would just have to be here, that I would have to come to bring sanity back to my family. And it would all end with *her...*

I watched her through the windshield as she called for her cab, my hands gripping the steering wheel so tightly that an audible creaking sound filled my car. She was shorter than I'd expected, adorable really, but it *was* her. She definitely matched the picture. I wasn't sure how I felt about the fact that my initial assessment from that photo of her had been dead on. She was just as hot in person as she was in the pictures.

Seeing her now, I realized I would tower over her by more than half a foot. She had vibrant red hair that glimmered copper fire under the street lights and eyes that looked like they were a light color, but from the distance I was at, I couldn't really tell. I knew from the photos that they were blue, though. A vibrant blue like a summer's midday sky.

When the cab pulled away from the curb I started my car and pulled into traffic behind them. I held back a few car lengths. I didn't expect the cabby to be looking for people following him but with who her father was? She might be. I couldn't be certain, so I used every trick I knew to stay out of sight, to blend in. I'd had plenty of practice with *that* over the years.

In the end, the cab pulled over outside of a two story brownstone to let her out. She paid the man as I cruised by and I drove around the block until I could park just around the corner from her place.

At just after three in the morning there wasn't a lot of foot traffic in such a quiet residential neighborhood, not a whole lot of parking either. Still, I was in luck and everything worked out for me as I walked around to the back garden wall of her building and looked up. The room, *her room*, lit up in a blaze of light from the inside. The room *with the balcony* that butted up *right against* a large old tree. This was almost going to be too easy!

I grinned and glanced around, unable to believe my luck so far. Everything was falling into place *just so* and I was incredibly nervous that luck wasn't going to hold. It was amazing to me that the household would be so unguarded despite the identity of the people living in it. There wasn't a soul in sight either way down the street and I couldn't see any cameras. I leapt the low garden wall easily and crouched down beneath the balcony, at the base of the tree.

A moment later, when I was sure it was clear, I jumped, the tense muscles of my legs propelling me up, through the air, until my hands just cleared the bottom of the balcony ledge and I was able to grab on. I didn't even need the tree but it provided great cover from the street or any night owl neighbors across the way.

I pulled myself up and over, the sound of a shower running inside easily drowning out the whisper of my coat sliding over the railing as I dropped onto the balcony. The French doors were locked but that was easily dealt with, all I needed was a credit card for the old latch. I jimmied the lock and slipped into the room, my bare feet making no sound on the plush carpet.

The scent of her filled the elegant bedroom. Sweat, makeup, alcohol and the tantalizing odor of summer peaches. Queen sized canopied bed to my right, desk to my left just next to the French doors that'd let me into the room. The bathroom lay directly ahead of me and through the half open door I could just make out her silhouette through the frosted glass of her shower door. My body moved of its own accord for a moment, taking a half step toward the bathroom before I stopped and forced my focus back onto more important and immediate concerns.

I moved as fast as I could, firmly keeping my attention away from the bathroom. Her closet was easy enough, drawers as well. I pulled out a few different things, not paying significant attention to what but I made sure there were full outfits, at least. These were thrown roughly and hastily into an overnight bag that I found hanging off the back of a chair and the whole lot was tossed over the railing on the balcony and into a flowerbed down below. The sound of the shower shut off and I shut the balcony doors with barely a whisper, leaving me on the outside.

She was singing when she came out of her bathroom, and I distinctly heard her short scream as she obviously caught sight of me, or at least my shadow. I leaped into the branches of the tree that grew next to the building, silently cursing myself.

Dumbass, dumbass, dumbass, I swore mentally. *How could you be so careless? Father taught you better than that.*

I held still, waiting for her to scream again or to go for the phone to call the police, either action would require I move extremely fast. Instead, she did the opposite of what I expected, she cautiously opened the doors and stepped out onto the balcony. I was hidden well and I knew it, so I held still and waited for her to go back inside.

I was tempted just to take her right there, but the area was too well lit between the streetlights and the lights in the bedroom blazing away like they were. If she made enough noise before I got to her, someone could and would easily spot us. It was too dangerous, too half assed, and it was better to wait... to wait until she was in bed and I had the cover of darkness to aid me. Another thing my Father taught me? That I should spend more time considering all the angles if I wanted to stand a chance. That I needed to be more patient.

She spent several more minutes outside with me. She looked around the balcony, even going so far as to lean over the railing to look down and out over the garden wall. She was trying to check out the street below, there was no one there, of course; the culprit was above her. As with most people, she never thought to look up. I had to smile to myself, then she really gave me something to smile about. When she straightened up hands flat to the stone railing, I had an exceptional view straight down the front of her slinky sleepwear, her arms bracketing her lush tits and squeezing them together for me. *Oh, that was nice!* A wave of heat ran through me and I forced it down with a ruthless determination. Now was not the time, nor was she the person. Jesus. I settled in, disgruntled with myself and forced myself to be patient. I waited for her to return to her room. My luck held out, she went inside and she hadn't spotted her bag down there. I let out a slow breath, relieved I was still on track and finally, after what felt like hours, the woman turned out the lights and got her ass to bed.

Still, I waited. It took time for her to settle in and to stop fidgeting. I mean, fear is a powerful motivator to keep someone from settling down right away and I'd caused her quite a jolt. But as the minutes wore on, she calmed down, the rustling of her unrest stopped and so did her random mutterings which were just that side of inaudible to me, damn it. It would have been nice to know what she'd been muttering about. The scent of peaches lingered in the air behind her even now, for all the time it took for her to settle in. I waited for it to dissipate completely before I made any kind of move.

The air outside was still, crisp and cool, edging toward chilly, and though she had been startled by the brief glimpse she got of me through her curtains, she had left her balcony doors, not only unlocked but slightly ajar. They would have been no barrier to me even if she had locked them, but I found it convenient that she still obviously felt so safe and secure in her own home.

This was one of my favorite parts of the hunt. The moment just before the kill, or the capture in this particular case. She wasn't asleep. Almost, but not quite, her breathing hadn't deepened enough, the cadence was wrong for true sleep. My patience had run out though and so I moved with the silence of a shadow, slipping down from the tree and through the open door. I stood, for a moment, looking down at her. She lay on her back, the light robe tossed to the foot of her bed. Her night gown clung to every curve of her in a thoroughly distracting manner where her blankets didn't cover her body. I was pretty sure she wasn't wearing anything else under the nightgown.

While I waited, I watched, taking in every minute detail. Admittedly, I stood there with a raging hard on growing in my jeans while I did it. I was waiting for that moment, that one precise moment that was one of the sweetest sensations in the world. The moment she realized subconsciously that she was being watched, that the predator had found her and it was already too late.

The thing about the human mind that so many people have forgotten is that not long ago, on an evolutionary scale, human beings were ruled far more by their instincts than their rational minds. And to this day, in the back of their brains it still resides there. That instinct, that fight or flight reflex that lives on in the primal, animalistic, part of the mind. That part of deeply ingrained humanity that you all try so hard to push down and suppress. The instinct. The sixth sense that tells you when you're being watched. That tells you when you're being hunted.

She didn't disappoint me. Her eyes snapped open and locked on mine. In that very instant I moved, lightning quick, my left leg came up and I leaned over, letting my leg fall heavily across her middle. My left hand covered her mouth as she opened it to scream and my right slipped under the blankets, up her leg, and beneath her nightgown. It landed directly on the juncture between her thighs. I smiled a very unfriendly smile. I was right. No underwear. I was also intentionally being a prick, watching the fear unfurl in those pretty blue eyes. I put pressure on her pubic bone, pressing her ass into the yielding mattress beneath her and leaned in close.

"Don't scream… and if you value your life? Don't bite me either. There are things swimming around in my blood that you *really* wouldn't want in your system," I grinned at her and I knew it was intimidating. I wanted it to be. "You're going to have to pay for the sins of the Father, Little Huntress," I breathed.

She struggled, of course. They always do. She screamed, of course, they always do that too, but my hand over her mouth kept the noise from being any kind of audible, and there was no way she would be escaping my grip. I was far stronger than I looked and her slight build was no match for my larger one. She threw her weight around anyways, as much as she could but she weighed all of a hundred and ten pounds soaking wet and with my hand between her legs, the leverage I had kept her from doing much, if anything, but kick her feet ineffectually.

I waited, calmly, until she had worn herself out in her struggles. Her fists beat at my shoulder but she was unable to move me. Eventually she fell still. Her breath coming hard and fast, nostrils flaring and relaxing rhythmically.

For a wonder, there were no tears. I'd expected tears. Usually people cry when they're as afraid as she seemed to be. Or maybe she was angry. Come to think of it girls cried *more* when they were angry. Whatever the case, she hadn't tried to bite me, so there was that.

I looked down at her, acutely aware of the weight of her breasts against my leg and the pleasant warmth of her body beneath me. Without thinking my fingers moved between her legs, going for an even more intimate touch than I already had on her, but I quickly stilled them. That wasn't why I was here.

"You're not going to scream if I take my hand away, now are you?" I asked, calmly.

There was nothing for a moment as she glared at me, but then she shook her head, just slightly.

"Good girl," I took my hand away from her mouth and wiped her saliva on the sheets next to her.

"Who the fuck are you?" she snapped as soon as my hand was away. "What the fuck do you want?"

"Who am I?" I grinned at her again, I couldn't help it. That was always one of the first questions asked. Who was I? Did it really matter if they knew who I was when I was usually about to kill them? Would it make any difference to them to know who had them at his mercy?

"You don't really need to know who I am," I said. "Not right now at least. As for what do I want? Oooohh... now that, *that*, my dear, is a much better question." I jumped into the air, turned and came down straddling her waist faster than she could track it or react. I grabbed her wrists as she shrieked and tried to hit me and I pinned them to the bed above her with one hand, re-covering her mouth with the other. I leaned down until we were practically nose to nose.

"What I want, little girl," I growled, my voice deepening and taking on a rougher quality. "Is to save my world. My life that *your* family, *your* father destroyed! Now keep your mouth shut!"

She blinked and shivered for a moment before she nodded. I took my hand away slowly and she spoke, hesitantly. "My father is an accountant, what could he have possibly done to—" She cut off mid-sentence as I threw my head back and let out a short, quiet laugh.

Amazing! Impossible even. She didn't know? She had no idea what her father did? She had no idea who she was living with, what kind of monster her daddy was. Huh.

"You don't even know what Daddy Dearest does for a living, do you?" I crowed, my voice returning to normal as I pushed back the change.

"I told you, he's an accountant—"

"He's a murderer!" I snapped. "He killed my father. He destroyed everything! And now, he's going to lose his daughter. I'm going to take her from him, just like he took my father from me."

I leaned over and snatched the belt from her robe. The thin garment went flying but I had what I needed. I used it to tie her hands together at the wrists while she babbled incoherently at me. I didn't listen to her. Rage battered at my will to hold it back and I couldn't afford to kill her. Not yet. I needed her.

I slid to the floor and hauled her up by the wrists. I ducked and threw her over my shoulder and with four long strides, I was out of the room. I didn't stop my momentum, leaping fluidly over the balcony railing to the garden below.

Behind me I heard a loud whoosh of air as my shoulder was driven into her stomach on our initial landing. All the breath was driven from her lungs and any protestations she'd been spouting suddenly ceased. I didn't care, it only helped me really. I grabbed the bag I had packed for her and strode forward, letting us out the back gate. I kept walking, making the final strides around the corner to my car.

I wrenched open the back door, threw her and the bag inside as she dry heaved, trying in vain to force her battered lungs to inflate. I gave no quarter, spared no pity and slammed the door shut. I paused for a moment, watching her through the tempered glass as she struggled to breathe before making long strides around the sedan to get into the driver's seat. In less than a minute I was pulling out onto the road and heading for the nearest entrance to the I-80 West. From one coast to the other, we were heading for Seattle.

Chapter 2

Chloe

Oh my God, he was crazy. He was fucking crazy! I tried valiantly to pull air into my lungs but my body just wasn't having any of it. Tears leaked out of the corners of my eyes, hot and stinging, which pissed me off. I was not going to cry. No, fuck that. My father's daughter didn't cry. No, the tears were definitely not from emotion. They were purely from having the wind knocked out of me, a physical reaction. I worked hard to draw air but it so wasn't happening.

Damn it!

Where were we going? Where was he taking me? How did he make that jump? How had he not broken anything? So many questions, no way to get any answers. I was drowning on dry land, no ability to pull air, I was panicking; my body struggling, my mind not far behind and finally, *finally,* I sucked in a breath.

I coughed, violently and struggled, trying to get into a sitting position, to flag someone down to get help.

"I wouldn't," he drawled from the front seat in a threatening tone. I looked up into the rearview mirror. Deep brown eyes, intense, brooding, and *very* unfriendly were illuminated by the headlights from the oncoming traffic. I met their reflection with a grim resignation. I had nothing on him size wise. Nothing at all. I was stuck.

My breathing was returning but it hurt, I knew I would be bruised, but I could live with that. I could probably live if he raped me, even if the thought did make me ill... but if he actually physically took me away? Out of the city? No. If he took me away, I knew the odds. I knew the likelihood of what happened next. If he took me away I couldn't live with that, I *wouldn't* live, statistically speaking. If he took me, rape would be the least of my worries. If he took me away he was going to kill me and I wouldn't, couldn't go down without a fight.

As soon as I could draw full breath I struggled into a sitting position. I was about to let loose and start screaming when he *growled* at me. It was unlike anything I had ever heard before, an animal sound emanating from his very human throat. It caught me so off guard I forgot about the whole screaming and making a fuss that I was supposed to be doing. He knew it too! The bastard jerked the wheel and slammed on the brakes and I was thrown back down below the level of the windows. My head connected sharply with the tempered glass on my way down and I cried out, my hands tied and useless in front of me, though I desperately tried to stop myself from colliding with anything else.

He jerked the car's shifter into park and got out, the crisp fall air swirling into the car's warm interior in his wake. The back door opened and I kicked out. He cursed and grabbed my ankle and I screamed. I screamed and howled and I kicked out with my other foot and connected solidly with his chest. Predictably, it didn't do a damned thing for me, except piss him off.

He grunted and dove into the back seat, over the top of me, his large hands curving around my tied wrists. He was between my thighs and I gasped which I choked off into a whimper. His black jeans may have been two sizes too big, his belt working overtime to keep them up, but there was no amount of fabric in the world that would disguise the hot, solid length of his erection which pressed solidly at the apex of my thighs.

"You keep struggling, I *will* rape you, just to make a point," he threatened. I blinked and he grinned savagely, his teeth very white and almost sharp looking, nestled in his dark blonde goatee.

"Where are you taking me?" I asked and hated how breathy it was.

"None of your business, either behave, or I'll put you in the trunk."

I turned it over in my mind. That had possibilities, I could break out a tail light or pull the emergency... I gasped and suppressed a moan as he squeezed my wrists so hard, I swore the bones in them ground together.

"You're hurting me!" I cried.

"That's the idea, Little Huntress, you going to calm your shit?"

"Oh my god, fuck you!" I spat, "Why should I cooperate with you? Why should I help you *kidnap* me?"

He leaned back a bit, actually considering the question before meeting my eyes again. "Because I'm not the only one interested in finding you, and they aren't nearly as nice as I am."

I stilled, confused, but that didn't stop me from considering the implications behind his statement.

"I don't understand..." I said and he scowled.

"You don't need to, you just need to do what you're told," he shook his chin length, dishwater blonde hair back, out of his face.

"It's not in me to go down without a fight," I told him. He smiled and it wasn't a nice one.

"While as much as I would like to find out what it's like for you to," he cleared his throat, "Go down, we've got a long drive ahead of us. Now you can either lay here, real nice and quiet, or..." he gripped one of my fingers and bent it back painfully, "I can start breaking little pieces off. Your choice, Little Huntress."

He wrenched on my finger until I cried out, "Okay! Okay! I'll be good." Oh my god it galled me to say it. I was no match for this asshole physically though. Even if I did manage to hurt him, it would have to be bad and there wasn't anything I could do with just my body to incapacitate him. I needed a weapon and there, predictably, weren't any back here.

"Good girl," he praised me mockingly before he let my hands go. He ground his hips and by default, his cock, into me suggestively once, and raised an eyebrow to get his point across. I closed my eyes and turned my face and he chuckled darkly, a menacing sound, before he backed off of me and out the door.

I was so fucked. He retook his place behind the wheel and put the car back into gear. I sniffed.

"You are such an asshole," I muttered and my captor barked a laugh.

"You would know, being the daughter of that piece of shit. To break your word is disgusting. To give a false promise in order to get closer to someone?" He shook his head, the disgust clear in his voice. "Your father has a debt to pay and only blood will settle it."

"My father is a goddamned accountant! A CPA for Christ's sake! I have no idea what kind of crazy you've got going on in there but you have the *wrong person!* You have to have the wrong person!" I turned away, refused to meet his glances in the rearview.

Why were the good looking ones either taken, gay, or crazy? I found myself wondering. It was true. He wasn't half bad to look at. Handsome face, long straight hair half way between his chin and shoulder and those shoulders were enough to drool over. If we'd been in the same bar or club I wouldn't have hesitated to talk to him.

He continued to drive and he didn't speak anymore. I didn't try to engage him in conversation either. We had to stop sometime, for gas or food or even for him to take a piss. When we did, I would figure something out. I *had* to figure something out. I closed my eyes, weary. This is not how I'd planned on my evening ending, not at all.

Chapter 3

William

My throat hurt. Multiple times in a single evening she'd made me growl and I couldn't keep doing that for long, it would do damage, take time to heal. And the fact she made me growl? It fucking irritated me. That growl was not designed for human vocal chords. If she kept pushing my buttons like this I would do some serious damage to my voice, and that damage took a while to heal, sometimes it became permanent.

I had made sure to fill up the tank before I'd taken her but I would have to stop eventually and I didn't like the chances that she would throw a grade-A hissy fit in the back and draw attention to us when we finally did. I needed to figure that out sooner rather than later because on top of my throat hurting, I was hungry and I needed to eat.

"Hold out your wrists." I said it so suddenly that it almost startled *me*, not to mention her. She jerked in the back where she was still laying down. She hadn't been asleep, but she had been pretending.

"Come on," I said, getting irritated again, "I know you weren't sleeping, hold out your wrists."

She was hesitant. Who could blame her? I'd attacked her in her home, kidnapped her from her bed, bruised her, threatened to rape her and then even gone so far as to threaten to mutilate her. It's no surprise at all that she would be hesitant, but I didn't have fucking time for this shit. I pushed back the rising tide of anger and breathed in and out slowly.

"Give. Me. Your. Wrists." I demanded slowly and deliberately. She held them up and I reached back and with one hand, jerked loose the knot I had made in the satin sash from her robe. I knew she had already tried the door handle discreetly. I'd heard it, but I was already one step ahead of her, the child lock was on. The back doors wouldn't open from the inside.

"Climb up front. Come here and sit down," I ordered her. For a minute I thought she would stay in the back but eventually she decided it would be better to move. She climbed carefully into the front seat, trying to keep as far away from me as possible but the sedan wasn't exactly roomy so I had to tilt my head slightly as her butt swung past me. Almost without thinking, I reached out and gave her ass a little slap.

She yipped and spun quickly into the seat, face flaming a brilliant red to match her hair. I didn't bother to hold back the laugh that bubbled out of me. You've just got to love the Irish, they wear their emotions on their faces. That fine skin did nothing to hide shame, embarrassment, or rage.

"Asshole," she muttered.

"Put your seatbelt on."

"Suddenly so concerned with my safety?"

"I'm concerned that I don't want to be pulled over because a cop noticed that you weren't wearing your seat belt. I could easily kill you before anyone managed to do anything about you being here. Come to think of it, I could kill them too… so don't argue with me, just *put your fucking seatbelt on!*" My volume had grown and my voice had deepened and by the last few words I was bellowing in a bass so low that it practically shook the car.

She put her seatbelt on, hands trembling so violently that she had trouble getting the latch to catch. I smiled at the small victory but it was drowned out by the wince. I rubbed at my throat. That *really* hurt. I needed to quit fucking doing that.

We were silent for a time. I paid attention to traffic, which was picking up as early morning crept on into mid-morning. She stared out the window, deliberately looking away from me but I could see the wheels turning. A sign caught my eye from the edge of the freeway and I changed lanes. Hitting the exit I reached behind me and grabbed a spare jacket which I dropped into her lap.

"Drape that across yourself," I ordered and stopped at the light. She obeyed without question but there was a curious look in her eyes, which I ignored as I pulled into a parking lot and slid my hand under the jacket. I was throwing her off base, which was a good thing.

"Don't say a word, or you won't like what happens," I warned.

She was stiff as a board, but nodded quietly as I slid my hand up the silky skin of her leg until it met the warm center between her thighs. She was clean shaven, I noted idly. I was tempted to mess with her seeing as she was such a pain in my ass, but I simply let my hand rest across her lips and hit the switch that rolled down my window with my free hand as we pulled to a stop.

"Welcome to Carl's Junior, may I take your order?"

The voice emanating from the speaker was unnaturally loud and grating, something I didn't appreciate but I nodded, even though they couldn't see me.

"Four of the Super Star burgers, please. Three large fries, make two of those cross cut. A large chocolate shake and a large Dr. Pepper." I glanced at her. "You want anything?" Her eyes were wide at my order but she nodded after a moment. Fear wouldn't stop her from eating, good to know.

"A steak burrito combo, with a coke," she said faintly and I relayed her order.

"Please pull up to the window."

I pulled up, reached into my inside pocket and pulled out a black credit card with gold lettering to hand to the guy at the drive-thru. He was a pimply faced teen and I noticed him give an appraising look to Chloe's barely covered torso. Can't say I could blame him, she filled out all that creamy satin and lace really nicely. Still, for some reason his admiration pissed me off and I growled at the guy, my fingers tightening almost possessively on her before I could stop myself. She gasped and shuddered and I quickly loosened my grip.

"Will there be anything else, Sir?" the kid asked after he handed back my card, the receipt, and our food.

"No, that's all, thank you," I ground out, tersely. I hit the gas and roared out of the lot, irritation rasping in the center of my chest.

She said nothing but began separating out the food. There wasn't room for her to spread out all of mine but she pulled out one of the fries and set it in between the seats and pulled out a burger which she held out to me with a shaking hand.

"Um... are you going to let go of me?" she asked and I realized I still had my hand resting between her legs. I nearly jumped, but I managed to calmly pull my hand out from under the coat and took the burger from her. I got onto the freeway and put my foot down, pushing the speed up until just under what I thought would flag police. Using my card hadn't been the best idea, they would be able to find me, but my dumb ass hadn't thought to grab cash.

I ate my food in silent contemplation of how I was going to make the rest of this work, all the while ignoring the girl's fragrance on my fingers.

Chapter 4

Chloe

"Eat," he commanded. Instead I continued my sightless staring out the window, my food growing cold and forgotten in my lap, which was thankfully, still covered by his coat.

"Don't touch me like that again, please." He stopped shoving food into his face and looked over at me. I could see him out of the corner of my eye but I didn't turn to look. I was embarrassed for one. I should have been pissed, I should have been afraid, and I *was*, all of those things and more, but the humiliating part? I'd been aroused, too.

I don't know what it was, if it was fatigue, adrenaline, or if maybe my hormones had gone wonky from the stress… I don't know what, but his hand between my thighs had turned me on a bit and that bothered me more than anything right now.

"Eat your food," he said again but his tone was different; not sharp, not angry… I think it had been the most normal sounding thing he'd said to me thus far.

"Who are you?" I asked, unwrapping my food with shaking fingers.

"Doesn't matter," his response was short but I think that had more to do with him shoving food in his mouth than it did with his being intentionally terse. He was eating like he was starved but at least he chewed with his mouth closed. I thought to myself, *if only his mother had gotten around to teaching him that kidnapping girls from their beds was a bad thing.*

I couldn't help it. It made me giggle, and once I started I couldn't stop, the giggles turned into laughter and he looked at me with those wide brown eyes and I noticed the deep amber colored flecks in them. Beautiful, or they would be if he weren't such a fucking weird maniac... Like I could talk, laughing hysterically like a crazy person as I was.

"What's your fucking deal?" he demanded and that just made me laugh harder.

"*My* deal? Oh that's rich, you asshole! I'm not the one kidnapping girls from their beds in the middle of the night!"

"Don't call me an asshole."

"Then tell me who you are, if I can't call you anything else, 'asshole' it is."

He threw the wrapper to his burger back into the bag and gripped the wheel of the car with both hands. A muscle in his jaw ticked as he gritted his teeth, but I simply stared at his profile. It really was a crying shame he was such a dick, because he really was handsome. Straight, dishwater blonde hair hung halfway between his chin and shoulder, just barely brushing the top of his coat. He had a full goatee that had been unkempt long enough that it was headed into beard territory but it added to his good looks, it didn't detract. Same with the long pale scar along his jaw, almost hidden by the beginnings of his beard. He had 'bad boy' written all over him without the benefit of his having kidnapped me, and a mouth that was made for sin.

He turned those brown eyes on me and in the full light of day the amber colored flecks in his irises stood out more, almost glowed with a fierce inner light. I arched a brow and kept my mouth shut. The decision was his on if he wanted to be permanently branded 'asshole' or if he wanted to at least give me an actual name.

"It's William," he said finally.

"William what?" I didn't mean for it to come out sounding so demanding but I was kind of glad it did. I needed to stand my ground with him. I couldn't keep letting him run roughshod over me.

"It doesn't matter," he grated finally, after some more silence and a tense standoff.

"William the Asshole it is then," I muttered.

"Just William, Little Huntress. Just William."

"Chloe," I demanded and he chuckled, rummaging around

blindly in his bag of food for some more.

"Whatever you say, Princess. What was so funny anyways?"

"I was thinking at least your mother taught you how to chew with your mouth closed, it's just too bad she skipped the lessons about kidnapping and hurting girls."

His hands tightened on the wheel and that tick in his jaw resumed at a faster rate. He cleared his throat, "My mother's dead," he said. "She died a long time ago." I looked out the window, the scenery swishing past as he kept a steady course on the freeway.

"Guess we have something in common then," I said solemnly. I saw him turn his head in my direction and I turned and met the look.

"My mom's dead too," I said.

He nodded, "I know."

The calm way he said it, with such assurance and something bordering on pity that it pissed me off. Wise or not, I lashed out at him.

"What the fuck do you think you know?" I snapped, "You don't know anything about me!"

"Chloe Young. Twenty-four years old, twenty-five next month. Only child of Mathias and Marianne Young. Your mother was killed when you were eight by a hit and run driver who was never caught. You're studying Law at NYU in prep to transfer to Harvard's Law school. You want to be a lawyer. Based on some of the papers you've turned in, your focus is on prosecution *not* defense. Your favorite color is lavender. You like to play pool and enjoy martial arts but never practiced much yourself beyond the one tournament you competed in as a yellow belt when you were ten. You took second place. You like to do things yourself but you're not too stubborn to ask for help when you need it. You have $10,327.58 in your checking account and your social security number is–"

"Stop, stop, stop, *stop!*" I shouted completely aghast. I was horrified, when he'd started talking my mouth had dropped open against my will. I couldn't believe the flood of information he rattled off so quickly. *I* didn't even know exactly how much money I had in my bank account! I hadn't checked it in a while.

"What the fuck! How long have you been stalking me, you fucking ass?" I demanded.

"Eat," he said and I reared back and let fly. I punched him, or I tried to at least. I hadn't even stopped to think what would happen if I punched the guy in the face while he was driving but I was too furious to think straight. It didn't matter though because his right hand came off the wheel and he caught my fist in a vice-like grip an inch before it would have touched him.

"You really, *really*, don't want to do that," he said in a low tone that sent all the rage I felt fleeing back to hide under a rock. A shiver of fear ran through me that I couldn't begin to explain. He knew so much about me, *too much* about me. Which meant that none of this was a mistake. He knew too much about my life, my *family* for this to be any kind of mistaken identity which means he really *did* mean to kidnap me. Oh my God...

I jerked my hand back out of his grip and he let me, otherwise I'm sure I never would have been able to break his hold. He didn't lower his hand, in case I decided to try to hit him again I guess, but I didn't. I didn't try. I shrank in on myself, trying to become as small as I could in the passenger seat. He waited a few moments before he put his hand back on the wheel and we descended back into an uneasy silence.

"Eat," he said again after about ten minutes and, with nothing really better to do, I complied, even though I wasn't at all hungry anymore. It was a while before he reached for more of his crazy amount of food. The fact that it had all long since gone cold did nothing to deter him and he rapidly put away every bite. For some reason, I found it supremely unfair that he could eat so much, and even began to wonder where it all went.

We drove for hours in silence. I didn't try to engage him in anymore conversation and he didn't try to talk to me either. Which was fine, even though I was dying to ask him like a million questions. I figured it was an exercise in futility so I didn't bother. I mean, he'd been so forth coming up to this point, am I right?

The sun was beginning its descent, completing its arc across the sky, sinking towards the tops of the trees when he pulled into a rest stop.

"We're stopping?" I asked, hopeful.

"You've been fidgeting for the last twenty miles," he said as if it was the most obvious thing in the world.

"Didn't really think you'd care if I had to pee or not," I muttered.

He scoffed a laugh, "I happen to like my car, I don't need you pissing on my seat, besides," he made a sweeping gesture with one hand, taking in the whole of my nightgown covered body with one motion. "You need to put on more than that. My self-control is good, but it's not *that* good."

I stared at him as he pulled up to the brick restroom out buildings and looked around. It was just us here. One lone big rig was parked on the other side, towards the freeway but it looked deserted. Past the bathrooms we were parked in front of there was a flat, wide expanse of grass. And beyond that? A steep incline and a whole lot of trees. William the Asshole reached behind the seat and hauled a bag over the back and dropped it in my lap.

"Packed you a bag, now let's go Princess."

He got out of the car and was around to my side before I could register that the bag I held in my hands was *mine*, from my room, I mean, from my closet.

He grasped me firmly by my elbow and I got out of the car feeling both hot and cold at the same time. I padded carefully across the blacktop and paver stones of the rest area and he pushed open the women's room door. I blinked a little dazed and went in, the door shushing shut behind me.

I quickly pulled it together and went through the bag. Jeans, tee shirts, a long sleeved, fitted blouse in blues and greens, a flannel print without the shirt actually being made from flannel material. It was just a light weight cotton. He'd packed copious amounts of both bras and panties, *loads* of them in fact, which with everything so far, did that really surprise me? William the Asshole was good looking, psycho and a Grade-A number one pervert. *Who I thought was hot.* God what did that say about me?

I went through everything in the bag, which was a surprising amount, looking and hoping… but no, no shoes. Damn. I wondered if it was an oversight or if it had been intentional.

"Chloe," he called through the closed bathroom door, "I'm going to piss, you can't run so don't try it."

I dressed with lightning speed. Bra, panties, jeans and a white fitted ladies tee. I pulled on the cotton blouse and snapped the buttons closed. I smoothed my damp palms over the tops of the thighs of my light blue jeans and stuffed my nightgown in the top of the open bag before I pushed out of the bathroom. I dropped the overnight bag to the ground and looked from the car to the woods. I may never get another chance, shoes or not, I had to try and so I bolted.

I ran across the grass and was dimly aware of a frustrated growl and a curse back behind me. I didn't dare look. I hoped against hope that I could and would make it to the trees; that I somehow would be lost among the foliage, my hair blending with the orange of the falling leaves.

The notion was ridiculous but the adrenaline was flowing, making my body buzz with nervous energy. I barely noticed my feet, I felt like I could run forever, but nothing lasted forever did it?

I reached the tree line, breath exploding out of my lungs in ragged pants, heart beating a fierce thrum in my chest, and the blood rushing in my ears. I risked a glance over my shoulder and poured on the speed. William was closer than I'd like, despite my head start. He was already midway across the grass. I plunged headlong into the woods, leaping over fallen branches and crashing through underbrush. Fallen tree limbs reached for me and it felt like the woods, well, like they were trying to trip me up, slow me down, like they were somehow in league with my captor. I whirled and stopped, looking this way and that, waiting, listening.

A blur of motion ghosted from one tree to another, and my brain tried valiantly to make sense of what I was seeing. It didn't make sense though, it was dressed like William, but it wasn't him. I mean it wore his clothes, his black jeans, at least. It looked like he had tossed his jacket and his shoes. Though it looked like him at the same time it appeared as if he'd bulked up, filled out and his skin…

it was darker somehow, it just didn't make sense!

Fear, I was hallucinating from fear. I had to be. A noise tore through the twilight. A sound like a giant dog would make and I jumped. I whirled and continued to make my way up the hill hands over feet, trying not to slide back down, trying not to lose progress. God I should have thought this through better.

I scrabbled up the side of the hill and pulled myself under an outcropping of rock and hid there. I fought to calm my breathing and my pounding heart. My ears strained against the silence, listening for something, anything... I waited huddled small and close, I waited to hear him thrashing through the leaves as I had done, waited for him to shout, but there was nothing.

Seconds ticked by, drawing out into minutes and my breathing slowed, returning to normal until finally I let out a pent up breath, slow and steady, my lungs deflating in minute increments. That which had been numb with adrenaline, began to come alive, my feet hurt, burning with a mix of cold and likely, cuts. I couldn't care about that right now, I wouldn't care and I didn't dare look either. My hands were filthy, and I'd torn a nail, but I was more concerned with if he would find me or if I had effectively hidden myself away.

"Did you really think it was going to be that easy, Princess? I told you, you couldn't run. I warned you not to try."

My shoulders dropped, my eyes slipped shut as my body and soul were weighted down with defeat.

"Come out of there, before I *drag* you out."

"Okay, okay! I'm coming," I said and I heard him sigh.

"You're bleeding, hurry up. I want to see where you're hurt, what you've done to yourself."

I froze for a moment. How did he know I was bleeding? I had barely been aware of it myself in my adrenaline fueled state. I crawled out from under the outcropping and his hands closed around my arm, hauling me to my feet, I cried out and staggered and he swore, with feeling.

"I got you," he said and I was up, off the ground, feet dangling. I hadn't even been close to getting away. Not even close. Defeat washed over me as he held me, one arm beneath my knees, the other curved behind my back as if I weighed nothing, nothing at all. It was driven home how horribly I was outmatched by him physically. He had been absolutely correct, I couldn't run, so why had I tried it?

"So stupid," I whispered, berating myself, cheeks flaming with humiliation.

"Yes, yes it was," he stated flatly.

Damn it.

CHAPTER 5

William

I guess I should have expected the escape attempt. I really should have. I'll be honest, this was my first kidnapping. Most people didn't remain alive long after they ran into me under such circumstances. I didn't usually have to try very hard to keep a corpse from running away. It just doesn't work like that, you know? I growled and bit off an oath that I'm fairly certain I can't repeat in polite company or Nan would've torn a stripe out of my hide… literally.

I'd thought we had started to bond there a little bit, Chloe and I, but I guess it was too much to ask for her to voluntarily stick around, considering she still didn't have the slightest clue of the danger that was out there. By far I was the lesser of two evils, but all she saw was the danger that *I* represented, which sucked. I sighed, I really hadn't expected her to be so damn clueless or half so plucky and determined. I really only had myself to blame for keeping her that way. This was such a mess in just so many different ways.

I shucked off my coat, dropping it to the ground and kicked off my oversized boots. The concrete beneath my feet was chilly but as I started to run I didn't even feel it. The air against my bare chest and arms was cool and refreshing instead of slicing through me to the bone as it had moments before. Anger swelled in my chest, rage beat at the walls I had carefully erected. I didn't have *time* for this shit.

The scent of peaches and fear tore through my anger, leaving it in tatters and my feet left deep gouges in the dirt as I left the manmade surfaces and picked up my pace to plunge into the trees after her. With every step my hunter's instincts to track, find, and rend flesh grew. I slammed a lid on the *'and rend flesh'* part and tried to stick to just tracking and finding her ass.

She didn't make it far before she cut herself. Her feet weren't tough and calloused like mine. They weren't used to the conditions and it wasn't like she took any care in her flight to watch her step. She was just so intent on getting away from me, and again, I couldn't blame her. I'd been a real douche-weasel so far.

Branches bent and cracked, leaves rustled and flew through the air in the wake of her passage and thirty feet from the rest stop's outbuildings I saw the first brilliant splash of red.

It was barely the size of a penny, gleaming wet against the muddied ground. The blood practically glowed with an intensity normally reserved for summer sunlight against closed eyelids and it was so not helping me suppress the predatory instinct that was fundamentally a part of me, that whole 'rend flesh' thing jumping out to the fore again.

The scent of her lingered still, in the air. Peaches and fear mixed with desperate pain and the coppery tang of her blood. God, it was touching off such a deep longing ache in me to drop to all fours and make a meal out of her that had absolutely nothing to do with sex. It took everything I had to lock those instincts down, to keep my focus, to stay…

Fuck! I lost her trail! I paused, swinging my gaze from side to side, scenting the air across my tongue and… *There!*

On a tree, two trees ahead and to the right, there was a brilliant swatch of indigo, the scent of her where she'd touched the bark in her flight past it. The further I got, the closer I drew to the tree, the stronger her scent until my eyes landed on another swatch of blood in the leaf litter. I followed it, tracking out from it in a spiral pattern until I saw another and another. The closer I drew to her the brighter each bloody footprint became, the color gleaming brilliantly to my senses.

The lingering scent of peaches and blood, such a strong and intoxicating mix, led me directly to her and it didn't go unnoticed by me that the longer she ran, the more blood there was in a trail for me to follow.

Stupid little idiot! She was going to get herself killed and I was the last person she even had to worry about! I fumed, the inferno of rage subsiding to an ember when I caught sight of the rocks, indigo emanating from the outcropping, billowing from the crevice, amorphous and wild like untamed smoke from a signal fire. That sparkling reddish hue painting the ground in the brightest swatch yet, just in front of the dark mouth of the little hollow she'd fitted herself into.

The gray wash of the world around me slowly faded, allowing a touch of normal color to bleed back in. The breeze which had been cool and refreshing, became almost painfully cold against my exposed skin as my humanity returned, rushing back to the surface.

"Did you really think it was going to be that easy, Princess?" I drawled as calmly as I could. A new hunger gnawed at my gut. A hunger that had little to do with burgers or fries but I had greater concerns on my mind. I could see her shoulders drop in the deep gloom created by her chosen hiding place.

"Come out of there, before I *drag* you out," I said as calmly as I could. She was caught and she knew it, there was no need to snap at her, but my impatience at the whole damned situation made me do it anyways.

"Okay, okay! I'm coming," she said, and I heaved out a quiet sigh.

"You're bleeding, hurry up. I want to see where you're hurt, what you've done to yourself."

Stupid little girl, she really should have known better, but how could she? My mind argued.

The deepening gloom around us was becoming oppressive and more difficult for my enhanced vision to pierce, she had to have been nearly blind in there. I couldn't understand what she thought she was going to accomplish by attempting to run like that.

She froze for a moment before she continued out and as soon as she was close enough I grabbed her arm and hauled her to her feet. She immediately cried out and raised one foot gingerly and I bit out a curse as I scooped her up into my arms. The little idiot, she really *had* managed to hurt herself.

"I got you," I said as gently as I could, I couldn't disguise the edge of irritation in my voice if I wanted to though. To be fair, I was almost more irritated with me and the situation than I was with her, though. Holding her close against my chest I turned to make our way back toward the rest stop and the car. She was quiet, too quiet for several heartbeats.

"So stupid," she whispered finally, cheeks flaming.

"Yes, yes it was," I said and started walking. I barely felt the branches and dry leaves beneath my heavily calloused feet.

"Can't exactly blame you," I admitted, "But running like that definitely wasn't your brightest move."

She gave a halfhearted shrug but said nothing. She shook slightly in my arms, whether out of fear, pain, or an adrenaline crash I couldn't say. Nor did I particularly care at that point, we'd wasted enough time with this foolishness.

At the car, I stooped and pulled open the passenger door. I twisted with her in my arms and set her on the seat with her legs hanging out, she was so short they didn't touch the ground. That wasn't a bad thing, it was super helpful in fact.

A quick inspection, which she suffered through silently, revealed no real injuries save the minor ones I expected. The bottoms of her feet were a mess of mud, twigs, crushed scraps of leaves and blood. The metallic scent of which rose heavy, cloying, and sweet around me. I bit the inside of my cheek hard enough to fill my mouth with a tiny flood of copper. The pain and the metallic taint of my own blood focused me, allowed me to concentrate. I needed to get some dinner and I needed to get some soon.

I rose and walked around to the trunk of the car, popping it with the key fob as I approached. I dropped my keys back into my pocket and dug around in the trunk's space for a moment. I grabbed one of the emergency protein shakes I kept back there first and shook it, cracked its seal and chugged it down. It tasted alarmingly like strawberry. *Just* strawberry. When these things tasted as advertised without any off flavoring whatsoever it meant your body needed it. For one of my kind, that meant I was way past time for food. We go too long without eating, we lose some of our control and eventually, the survival instinct kicks it into high gear, we shift and we hunt and when that happens? We aren't too particular about what or who is on the menu. It gets messy, fast.

I returned, kneeling beside her again, setting down a small first aid kit and several bottles of water before I took hold of her right foot and got to work. The cuffs of her jeans were filthy and had even frayed in a few places. I grabbed the material and ripped her pant leg halfway up to her knee. She jumped, startled, but said nothing. Pouring water over her foot I carefully cleaned it off using the scraps of denim as best I could. I probed gently at the few small cuts I found there. As I worked the muscle in her calf tensed and relaxed beneath her warm, silken skin and I bit my cheek again, studiously fixing my gaze on her foot instead of her toned leg when what I really wanted to do was let my eyes sweep over every inch of her. I redoubled my efforts at focusing on the task at hand.

"The damage isn't that bad, minor lacerations. No stitches. I'm going to clean and bandage your foot, okay?"

She didn't say anything but I saw her nodding out of the corner of my eye. She had her face turned to the side and pressed into the seat, so I set back to work. A few small pieces of gauze, a thorough cleaning and some stinging disinfectant later, I was able to wrap her foot. I was being as gentle as I could while I held the gauze in place, but she was stiff and ridged regardless.

We said nothing as I did the same with her left foot, which luckily had even fewer cuts but one of them was relatively deep as compared to the others. Still not bad enough for stitches, but it would hurt like hell later. She would be limping for a few days, at best. I'd been stupid in forgetting to pack her some damned shoes but when I'd realized my mistake I'd figured it could and would work to my advantage, maybe make her think twice about trying to run away. So much for that brilliant idea.

I dug around in the first aid kit for a moment, came up with a white oblong pill and held it and a bottle of water out to her.

"Here."

She looked up at me, eyes bright with unshed tears; the blue of them unbelievably luminous, before they focused on the pill in my hand.

"What's that?" she asked suspiciously.

"Vicodin, it's a little strong for the level of your injuries but it's all I have on hand. You can take it or not, up to you."

I know I was being short. I'm well aware of the issues I have with my temper and a total lack of patience. But she could have gotten herself killed with that stunt and I would be damned if she was going to get hurt on my watch.

I paused and shook my head roughly. *I needed her alive when we got to Seattle,* I reminded myself forcefully. That was all. It wouldn't do me any good at all to bring a corpse back and that was my *only* reason for concern.

I lifted her legs into the car, shut the door, and retrieved her bag of clothes where she'd left it before going around to the driver's side. I pitched the bag in the back seat and got in, putting on my seatbelt. I started the car then sat there and waited while she studied the pill in her hand for a moment longer before she shrugged and popped it into her mouth, washing it down with half the bottle of water.

"Seat belt," I said and she put her seatbelt on without argument. As soon as it clicked into place I pulled away from the curb and headed back for the freeway.

"Why do you know so much about me?" she asked some time later. The words were listless and so quiet I barely heard her. The Vicodin was obviously starting to take effect.

"Why me?" she asked when I'd been silent for too long.

I heaved out a deep sigh, unable to help myself and pinched the bridge of my nose between thumb and forefinger for a moment before putting my hand back on the steering wheel. "I told you," I said. "Your father killed mine. It only made sense to do as much research as I could on him."

She said nothing but her half lidded eyes were fixed on me so I sighed again. "It was a little over a week ago. Eight days, to be exact. My father died. He was killed. Murdered, in his bedroom, in his home. I'm no criminal justice expert but I can put two and two together and come up with four. Only one person visited my father recently. One person that my father had a long standing and bloody feud with." I glanced at her again and saw she was listening with rapt attention.

"Your father, Mathias Young, visited mine the day before he was killed with a certain type of weapon that Mathias is well known for. There's no one else that it could have possibly been but him."

"But he's just an accountant," she whispered and she looked so lost, so hurt and confused that it made me uneasy. It was the first time looking at her that I felt like a total tool. I gritted my teeth, determined to hold onto my anger. Anger kept me strong. Anger kept me from feeling sympathy.

"Your father is not an accountant," I growled, frustrated with her stubborn refusal to see the writing on the wall. "He never has been, he never will be. With how much I know about you, and about your family, can you honestly still think that I have the wrong person? Is it possible, just maybe, that I might know more about your family secrets than you do?"

She said nothing for a long time and I caught a glimmer of movement. I turned and jerked back but she was reaching a finger out carefully.

"What are you doing?" I asked her and she blinked, foggy from the too-strong painkiller. I should have snapped it in half. She was so damned tiny and the prescription was mine, meant for a person of my size and weight and then some because of my metabolism. That shit was little more than a couple of aspirin to me, but to her… I really hoped I hadn't just OD'ed her past just several hours of sleeping it off.

"It's really a shame that you're crazy, you know that?" she asked and she traced a gentle fingertip along the scar I knew resided along my jaw. Yeah, that Vicodin was hitting her like a fucking freight train but she didn't look like she was in any trouble from it.

"Yeah, why's that?" I asked genuinely curious.

Her hand dropped listless to the center console between us, "Because you can be nice when you try and no matter how incredibly sexy you might be, the crazy really detracts from that."

I laughed outright, "Is that right?" I asked, but when I glanced her way again her eyes were closed and her breathing was deep and even in sleep. It wasn't too surprising. She had gotten zero sleep the night before and the pain killer easily took care of the rest of her will to stay awake.

I sighed again, something I don't remember doing so often before I met her and focused my attention back on the road. The burning lump of coal I had felt in the center of my chest since Father's death was gone. In its place was simply a cold feeling of loss and regret and I found it harder and harder to stay angry at her over her father's actions. I didn't like that, I needed to hate her, I needed to want her dead and I needed to see her blood. The debt must be paid.

For now, I let her sleep, kept my eyes on the road, and put my foot down. I would need to stop for food, the protein shake just a temporary measure. I would also need to fill up soon judging by the fuel gauge, not to mention get some sleep of my own. Fuck, I was running out of time. My window of opportunity was closing and all too soon, there would be even more obstacles in my way. Her father would already know she was missing and he would never take that calmly. Not the Mathias Young that I knew.

As dangerous as that man could be, however, there were two others that terrified me even more and every time I heard the roar of a Harley Davidson motorcycle my pulse would begin to race against my will.

Chapter 6

Chloe

Light... bright and shining, causing my world to glow like fire. I squeezed my eyes shut tight and brought my hand up to rub them but a sharp metallic clack brought it up short. I tried my right hand much to the same result. I blinked rapidly several times and looked over, William looked back, a bemused expression on his face.

Fuck! It wasn't fair for him to look that good this early and it really wasn't fair that he had me handcuffed twice over. My right wrist was latched to the inside door panel of his car while my left, yeah, that he'd looped through the steering wheel, the other cuff around his own wrist.

"Really?" I asked incredulous.

"Really," he responded. I eyed his key ring hanging from the ignition. He grinned wider at me.

"What?" I asked.

"I know what you're thinking, and no dice Princess, the keys to the cuffs are in the trunk, well outside your reach."

I stared at him open mouthed. "*What?*" I shrieked, the sound sharp even to my own ears but the grimace on his face made it seem like I'd been pitched high enough to shatter crystal or something.

"Okay, one, don't ever do that high pitched bullshit again! And two, calm your tits, the object is to keep you from getting away and this was the best way to ensure that and make sure I'd wake up if you tried," he swore under his breath.

"You don't have to snap and yell at me all the fucking time, *you kidnapped me*, remember?" I stared at him, face bright with my own temper.

"Glad I filled up before bunking down," he muttered and then did something so horrible I can't even...

He gripped his thumb, the one on the hand that was cuffed and he *broke it* or dislocated it or *something*. The bone gave a sickening crunch, my stomach flipped and I scrambled for the door handle on my side but couldn't reach it with how he had me cuffed.

"Oh no, you had better not fucking puke in my car!" he cried and lunged across me, hooking the fingers of his mutilated hand and popping the door for me. I leaned out and gagged, sucking in heaving breaths of cold, clean, morning autumn air as I tried valiantly not to heave.

"You okay?" he asked a moment later and eyes watering with the effort it took *not* to throw up on an empty stomach, I nodded silently.

"Hey, look, come on look at me, over here," he said tersely. I didn't want to, I really didn't want to, I looked though, because after how things had gone thus far, I wouldn't put it past him to grab me by the hair and *make* me look.

"It's fine, see?" he held up both his hands with a flourish, like a shabbily dressed magician and wiggled his fingers and both thumbs, "Didn't even hurt," he said and for some reason it was just too much. I shut my mouth and shut the car door and shivered, but it had nothing to do with the temperature. I was *not* going to cry. Crying wasn't an option. My father's daughter didn't cry.

I was hurt, I was exhausted, I was scared and as much as we didn't get along all the time, I missed my dad. And this... this *asshole*, kept doing terrible and terrifying things, each one more horrible than the last and I just reverted to that hysterical little girl line of thinking. My brain went out to lunch without me and I resolutely shut my mouth, biting my lips together to keep from screaming. I stared out my window and tried to breath. In and out, in and out, in and out but I was pretty sure all I was going to accomplish was hyperventilating.

I could feel the tears slip free and that made me so incredibly angry. It wasn't *fair*. None of this was fair. I just wanted to go home, but there wasn't any going home and there wasn't any getting away from him and...

"Easy," his voice was gentle, almost soothing and I closed my eyes, my shoulders and back shook with the sobs that I may have not been able to contain but I *did* manage to keep silent. At this point, I would take any victory, no matter how small.

I heard William sigh and he swore softly, "Shit," as he started the car. We were pulled up alongside a deserted service station, and I glanced over at his instrument panel. Sure enough, full tank. He studied my face for half a second before I turned away from him, but it had been enough for me to see his brow furrowed, an expression of grave consideration or perhaps even concern painted across his handsome features.

Well as far as kidnappers go, I guess I can at least be grateful I didn't get an ugly one, I thought to myself bitterly, the humor was there but it was black as pitch and I couldn't even bring myself to smile this time.

William pulled out onto the deserted road and put the dawn at our backs. West, west, ever traveling west. I wondered how far we'd go until we stopped. Would we turn south? Would we turn north? I just wanted one *slice,* just one *sliver* of certainty in a whole world gone mad with uncertainty. At least for me.

"Where are we going?" I asked tremulously, and hated just how broken I sounded. I sounded used up and broken. William didn't answer me. I swept my fingers against my cheeks, swiping at the wetness there, the handcuff swinging from my wrist, gleaming silver and cold in the morning light. I sighed out, frustrated in so many ways.

"To find food," he said finally, tone gentle despite remaining intentionally obtuse, still, he wasn't being an overt dick right this minute, which I guess was something, and so I would take it.

"I have to pee," I told him.

"We'll stop soon, when we do, I'll get the keys and take those off but Chloe…" the way he said my name made me turn and look at him plaintively, "Don't run, Sugar. It's not worth it. I'll catch you, I'll drag you kicking and screaming and we'll be gone before the police can get there to make any difference."

I closed my eyes and nodded, desolation filling my heart. We drove on in silence and finally he pulled into the parking lot for a strip mall that held a bunch of bargain basement retail type places.

He shut off the car and looked at me.

"What size shoe do you wear?" he asked gently.

"Six," I said hollowly.

"Thanks for not arguing. I'll be back in a minute."

"I'll be here," I said sarcastically, rattling the handcuff against the door.

He disappeared and I stared out the passenger window. It was too early for anything to be open, I didn't know what he would do or how and truthfully I didn't really care. I was alerted to his return by the trunk opening, the clack of the mechanism letting go making me jump. He shut the trunk and came back, getting behind the wheel. He handed me a bag with two shoe boxes in it. I blinked.

"They were open?" I asked.

"One of 'em, yeah," he said and took a key to the handcuff closest to him. He released the cold metal from around my wrist and his fingers were warm and gentle where he rubbed out the mark left behind. I watched his hands, fascinated for the moment by the rhythmic motion they made against my skin.

William seemed to startle, realizing what he'd been doing and let me go. He cleared his throat and started the car, my right hand, my dominant hand, remaining cuffed to the door for now.

"Should find someplace to eat further up," he said quietly and I nodded. We were in some kind of muted, uneasy holding pattern with one another and it was so tentative, so fragile… I didn't want to break it. I was tired and I much preferred the nice William to William the Asshole and so for now I simply took the path of least resistance.

I peeked into the bag, a pair of running shoes and a pair of flip flops. Simple, nothing fancy, but that was okay. They were shoes where I'd had none before, which was something. I sighed and looked at my ruined, ragged jeans. One leg torn to the knee, the other mostly intact.

"Can you fix this?" I asked quietly, and he glanced over. He smiled, the first really genuine smile I'd seen since this whole ordeal began. It made him… human.

"Worried about the fashion police?" he tried to joke but I had no humor. I turned and stared out the window, silent instead.

"Yeah, I'll fix it for you," he said quietly and we lapsed into a short silence while he found us someplace to eat.

He parked at a little mom and pop diner that was mostly deserted at this hour, it being during the week and early like it was. He reached across me and unlocked the handcuffs while I studied the place through its windows. There were a few people inside, retirees by the look of it, so no help there. Not that I would want to put anyone else in danger. I sighed.

William came around my side and I swung my legs out the door, setting my shoe boxes on the floorboard my feet and legs had just vacated.

"How short you want 'em?" he asked and I used the blades of my hands atop my thighs to indicate. He raised his eyebrows at me and I looked at him plaintively.

"Okay," he said in an almost sing song timbre and he went to work, tearing the denim with an almost wet, sloppy sound. I marveled at the strength he possessed, I mean, he made it look so *easy*.

Within moments, I sat in his passenger seat in a brand new pair of cut-off shorts that were so short, they made my legs look long. An amazing feat on my five foot four frame.

"Was that a smile?" he asked me, and let his fingertips graze my leg. I nodded and tried not to think about the sensations that little, seemingly unintentional, touch left behind.

"Let me get you some socks," he murmured when I said nothing. He got my bag out of the back and rummaged for a pair. He propped my heel on his knee and stretching the sock wide, took care to get it on my foot without hurting me further. I swallowed hard.

"Why the change of heart?" I asked.

"What?" he asked, distracted by the act of getting my new running shoe on.

"You haven't been worried about hurting me up to this point, why are you worried about it now?" I asked.

He looked up at me, gaze intent and fixed on my own and

arched a brow, "You're cooperating. You try, I can try too," he said solemnly and I nodded faintly, not sure of what to make of that. I sniffed and flinched as he slid my heel home into the bottom of the first shoe.

"Sorry," he said, consternation in his voice. I let my bottom lip go from between my teeth.

"It's okay," I murmured and just like that, I think a small, and I do mean infinitesimal, truce had been declared.

It didn't stop him from waiting right outside the bathroom door for me to come out, nor did it stop him from ordering for me when I perused the menu a touch too long, but that was okay. I really wasn't hungry and my mind was just purely out of any decision making skills.

Our food came, William watched me for several moments as the waitress set down many, many plates and finally, he ordered me gently, "Eat," adding a belated, "Please," to the end. I nodded and picked at my food while he watched me, eating ravenously. He finished well before I did, but leaving, well it wasn't an option until he was satisfied I'd had enough. I was struck by the thought, *even in prison they can choose how much and how little they eat...* but again, I didn't want to argue or complain, he wasn't being rude, or mean, or harsh today, I wanted to keep it that way as best I could.

"Come on, we can't stay, we have to keep moving," he said quietly and guided me out of the restaurant by a firm grip on my elbow. Firm but not hurting. I stumbled along beside him anyways. My feet hurt, so did my stomach where he'd shoulder checked me while taking me. God, I was in such a mess.

He started the car and returned us to the highway, I didn't even know where we were, what state we were in anymore. I suppose it didn't really matter. I wondered vaguely if anyone was looking for me. My dad must have been out of his mind. He'd always been so over protective of me since mom had died, so demanding. Not loving, not my dad. No, no and did I mention no? That wasn't and had never been his style. Who knew? Maybe he was relieved I was gone. I'd never been much of anything except a disappointment my whole life.

I stared sullen and silent at the passing scenery while William drove, startling when he turned on the radio. I stared at it as he surfed the channels looking for something he liked and I realized, it was because I was curious. I mean, what *did* he like?

"What do you like to listen to?" he asked as if he'd plucked the thought right out of my head.

"I was just thinking the same thing about you," I told him truthfully.

"Rock, metal... sometimes blues or jazz depending on my mood. I even like a little bit of country from time to time," I blinked, I hadn't expected him to answer me, at least not so stark and honestly.

After apparently not finding anything that interested him on the radio he popped open the small compartment hidden in the center console and reached blindly into it, fishing around for a moment before he came up with a rewritable CD. The word 'Happy' was scrawled across it in messy writing with a thick, black marker, and he popped the disc into the CD player.

A moment later the music started and he started bobbing his head and tapping his fingers on the steering wheel. It wasn't until the chorus that he started singing along.

"Peel me from the skin, tear me from the rind," he sang. "Does it make you happy now? Tear me from my home, tear me from myself–" he cut off and turned the radio down when I suddenly started laughing.

"What?" he asked, sounding offended, "I'm not that bad a singer you know!" I couldn't help it. He seemed so hurt and offended that it was just hilarious and I burst out into even more uncontrollable laughter. He sat in silence and waited for me to get myself under control, which took a while. When I finally did I held my stomach, sore from my bruising and the laughing and looked over at him.

"No," I admitted. "You're not a bad singer, you just don't know the lyrics." I laughed a little more and he blinked, surprised. He looked at me, then glanced at the radio as if it held the answers he sought, then back at me again.

"Huh?" he asked, oh so eloquently.

"The song. It isn't 'tear me from my home.'"

"It's not?" he asked sounding surprised.

I shook my head. "No it isn't. The line is 'tear meat from the bone'."

"You're kidding," he reached out and restarted the song and cranked the volume up a bit more, head tilted to the side slightly while he listened. When the line he screwed up arrived again he listened intently and there was a dawning look of wonder on his face that almost sent me into hysterical laughter again.

"I'll be damned," he muttered. "You're right. How the hell did I never notice that before?"

"Couldn't tell you, but now I'm almost afraid to hear you sing more." He gave me a sidelong, confused look. "I'm not sure my stomach could handle it if I laughed like that for much longer," I sputtered and giggled for a bit while he cracked a smile.

"Alright, message received, Princess." He turned the music down as the cd changed from Mudvayne and moved over to something by Bruce Springsteen, definitely an eclectic mix, and for a few minutes we just listened, our truce seeming to grow ever so slightly in a sense of shared amusement.

"Why did you kidnap me?" I asked a minute later, figuring I might as well go for broke. I mean he did answer when I asked what kind of music he liked, and he didn't bite my head off when I laughed at his expense so maybe…

"I told you, your father killed mine and there's a debt that must be paid for that," he said and that muscle along his jaw began to tick, beneath that pale scar. I frowned and tried to remember if I'd really touched it or if that had been a dream.

"What?" he asked.

"Nothing," I lied, and he let me with a careless shrug of his shoulders. We lapsed into silence after that and he drove, leaving me alone with my thoughts, for which I was grateful.

Morning crept into afternoon, afternoon brought the sun in our eyes and a pair of wraparound sunglasses out of the little cubbyhole meant for such things above our heads. He slipped them on and it was very terminator-esque. I kept my smile secreted inside. I didn't know if it would pitch him back into being an asshole or not. He may have let me get away with laughing at his expense once but the mood was much more somber now. I tried the sun visor but I was too short for it to do much for me and so finally, I settled on closing my eyes against the glare, but I didn't sleep. I hurt, and I was tired, but I couldn't sleep.

Eventually, the sun sank below the horizon, the glasses went back into their spot and William hit his signal to get us off the freeway. I perked up as he traversed lanes towards the next exit.

"We're stopping?" I asked hopeful. I was sick of the car, sick to absolute death of it.

"Yeah, you've been good Little Huntress, I figure we can stop, and if you behave while I fill up, then I might consider stopping for the night," he flashed me a smile and I sighed inwardly, it looked like William the Asshole was back in part.

"Can I use the bathroom?" I asked sullenly as he pulled up to the pump.

"Yeah, let me get this started and I'll take you in," he said.

It was better than nothing so I waited while he got the gas flowing, listening to the clack of the nozzle going in and the subsequent rush of fuel in the tank did absolutely *nothing* for my bladder, but he quickly popped my door and I slid out. I shivered in the cool, autumn evening air and he was at my back, he radiated warmth and stayed close, by all accounts for the other patrons of the station he was just my overly protective and affectionate boyfriend keeping me safe in unfamiliar surroundings. Gag me with a spoon.

He waited outside the bathroom for me and walked me back to the car, but he let me stand and stretch while the tank finished fueling. It'd been a very long day and we'd gone God only knows how many miles.

"Get in," he said, pulling the nozzle from the tank and what could I do but comply?

He took us back onto the highway and I felt discouraged, I'd really been hoping we were going to stop for the night as he'd said, and just when I was about to open my mouth and say something about it, he hit his signal again and drifted off the next exit. He pulled into the lot at a roadside motel and all I felt was grateful. He reached over me and cuffed me to the inside of the door.

"Really?" I asked and it sounded exasperated even to me.

"Fool me once, shame on you, Princess. I don't give second chances," he searched my eyes, my face from inches away, so close we could kiss, before he pulled back to his side of the car, "I'll be back in a minute," he professed and then he was gone, the door clicking shut and I watched him make strides for the little glassed in lobby that held the front desk.

He spoke to the attendant, an older gentleman who looked past him curiously and nodded. He ran through the check in process and activated a key card for William and within a few minutes time he was back behind the wheel and steering us towards a room at the other end of the motel.

"Good girl," he uttered as he pulled us into a space and he shifted the car smoothly into park, shutting it off and regarding me.

"I really want a shower," I said and he nodded.

"As soon as I check the bathroom for windows it's all yours, wait here."

"Like I can go anywhere," I muttered and jerked ineffectually at the cuff holding my wrist to the door. He took my bag and another bag or two from the trunk up to the room. I huffed out a sigh the longer and longer he took, growing impatient with waiting. When he came back down he had a bag he replaced in the trunk of the car, wore fresh clothes and his hair was wet. Asshole.

He got into the car and leaned across me to unlock my cuff, he smelled clean, like men's soap and I swore there was nothing better than the smell of freshly showered man, which put me into an even fouler mood that I could and would even think along such lines about him, after everything so far.

"Come on, got fresh towels and things waiting for you," he said and came around as I got out of the car.

"Didn't have any place to chain you up there," he said softly, "Sorry for the wait, Sugar." I nodded, I mean should I really be surprised?

The inside of the room was a single queen bed, I guess I shouldn't be surprised by that either, except the sight of it made my mouth suddenly dry. The main light source was a dimly lit bedside lamp and what light poured from the bathroom.

"Laid your stuff out, go ahead. When you get out I want to change your bandages and have a look at those cuts."

"Sir, yes Sir," I mocked and gave him a snappy little salute. He snorted and laughed a little. I shut myself into the bathroom. My nightgown hung on the hook set in the back of the door. I didn't know if I liked that but I was almost too tired to argue. Truthfully, I'd about given up. He was going to do whatever he was going to do and damned if I could stop him. I mean, he'd proven that already so yeah. William in a decent mood was better than William the Asshole so I could live with the nightgown.

I pulled back the curtain to start the shower and froze. My body wash, I mean the same exact stuff I used, shampoo and all was neatly lined up waiting for me. I felt this odd and bizarre mixture of both touched and chilled. I glanced at the sink and yep, there was my usual lotion too. It scared me how well he'd had me researched if he knew these minute and intimate details.

I sat on the closed lid of the toilet and scrubbed my face with my hands. I sat for a good few minutes while the bathroom filled with steam before I carefully began pulling and picking at the bandages, taking them off, swearing softly and hissing every few seconds. A light knock fell on the door.

"You okay?" he asked, a quiet note of concern in his voice.

"I'm fine! It just... I just hurt," I said irritably.

"Take your time," he called out.

I took a long and luxurious shower and tried valiantly to beat back the lingering question, *would it be my last?* To keep it from ruining the whole experience, I mean, when things were this bad it was good to focus on the little things, right?

Finally, I was as clean as I would ever be. I'd gotten all the dirt out from under my nails and I was a prune and I guess it was time to face the music to a certain extent. I wrapped my hair in a towel and carefully patted myself dry with another. Swiping a hand through the steam on the mirror, I took stock of myself.

I was deeply bruised from just under my breasts to just below my navel. I had bruising around my wrists here and there too. My feet were battered, pathetically so, and I was pale, almost ghostly, my wet hair framing my face like spun garnet. I picked up the new hair brush with the tags still attached to the handle and pulled at them, discarding the paper bits in the trash.

I used the hair dryer on the wall that the hotel provided and took my time brushing and drying my hair. If I slept on it wet it would be untamable and I was just vain enough that if I had the time to do something about that, I would. Finally I couldn't stall exiting the bathroom any longer. I slipped on my nightgown, wished it covered more and gathered my dirty things, clutching them over my chest before I let myself out into the room.

William was standing just the other side of the bathroom door, as if he'd been waiting the whole time. He took my things from me and said, "Go sit, let me have a look at those feet."

He'd set the first aid stuff he'd need out on the bed with an almost military precision bordering on straight up OCD and I went over and sat down next to it, putting my feet up and leaning back against the headboard. William shoved my dirty things away and packed up the bathroom while I watched from the bed. He piled everything neatly by the door and turned to look at me.

"Stay here, I'm taking this shit down to the car, you try to run and I'll…" he trailed off and I heaved out an irritated sigh.

"Save it, please? I've learned my lesson," I said somberly and he searched my face, nodding.

"Good," he said before he went out, closing the door firmly behind him. He'd left some clothing out on the table, had gone through my things apparently and selected what I was going to wear, tomorrow. Awesome. Just freaking great. I pressed my fingertips into my eyes and lowered them just as he returned.

He looked after my feet, dabbing antibiotic ointment on the cuts and using fat rectangular Band-Aids on them. The good kind. The ones made out of cloth with the super adhesive. He'd probably bought them along with my shampoo.

"Take this," he said and held out a half of one of the pills from the day before. God yes, it may not be a whole one, which knocked me on my ass the day before, but I would do just about anything to sleep, to forget, even just for a little while. I took it, washed it down with the proffered bottle of water and turned on my side, away from him. Curling up, curling in on myself. He settled behind me on his back and I just couldn't help myself.

"Not afraid I'll bolt in the middle of the night?" I asked. He sighed and turned onto his side, one of his arms curving around my middle, he dragged me back into the curve of his body, except he was right over the bruising so I yelped. He immediately stilled.

"Sorry. Is that better?" he asked, his breath puffing warm against the back of my shoulder, along the curve of my neck. My breath stilled in my lungs.

"No," I was such a liar. There was something comforting about this, which was just so sick and twisted, I knew that. I mean I really knew that. *He'd kidnapped me!*

"Sleep, Chloe," William murmured and my eyes closed, the drug kicking in, though not as brutal as the day before. I closed my eyes and warm, held fast by my captor, I slept.

Chapter 7
William

It's interesting what the body will do while the mind is unaware. Some people walk, talk, or eat in their sleep. Some even have sex in their sleep. But while your conscious mind is dead to the world, your unconscious mind can, and will, find ways to tell you what's what.

When I woke, in the very early hours of the morning, it was to the feeling of something soft and warm pressed against me. I didn't open my eyes at first. I was still far from rested. I'd had almost no sleep the night before, choosing to drive as much as possible while Chloe still slept. I'd figured the more ground I managed to cover while she was unconscious, was just that many fewer miles that I would have to fight with her which had been a plus, but not without its own cost because *fuck* was I tired…

Maybe I could just keep her hopped up on pain killers until we got there? I thought to myself idly, but no, that would never work. I dismissed the idea and turned my half coherent thoughts to the first realization I'd noted upon rising into a state of semi-consciousness… Something soft and warm was pressed against me. What could that be? The scent of peaches that seemed to be a part of her told me the answer easily enough. Chloe. The smell of her was everywhere, surrounding me like a delicate cloud.

At six feet even I was considerably longer than her, and with her body pulled back against me, the top of her head just reached my chin and the gentle curve of her ass was pressed firmly against my groin.

Ah.

That was nice, and what I really should have noted first upon waking. With the realization there was no stopping the immediate physical reaction of my body as my cock slowly stirred to life.

Painfully so, as it tried to straighten against the confining material of my jeans. She stirred in her sleep and shifted her weight, unknowingly grinding her ass harder against me and I bit back a groan.

She's the enemy, dumb ass, I thought.

She's the daughter of the enemy, came the counter argument, unbidden from some further portion of my mind. *You know damn well you want her. You know what you'd love to do with her. So why fight it?*

Because she's still the enemy! Her family hunts and kills our kind!

Right. Keep telling yourself that. In the meantime you might want to get your hand off her tit before she wakes up.

Great. I was totally losing an argument with myself and had no idea which side was the angel versus which was the devil on my respective shoulders. I went to roll onto my back away from her, only to find my hand held fast and I blinked, surprised to realize that in my sleep my right hand had somehow worked its way under her thin lace and satin of her nightgown and the warm weight of her breast was cupped comfortably in my hand. I could feel the nub of her nipple pressed into my palm and the partial erection I had been working on suppressing? Yeah it exploded into a full blown hard on that had me wincing.

She had neglected to wear anything beneath the gown, perhaps out of habit? More likely because I hadn't thought to put anything out for her. I didn't think she was comfortable enough with me at this point to simply sleep in such a state of undress but... *Maybe she didn't think she had a choice, you've given her so many this far. Dumb. Ass.*

Fuck me and fuck this fucking nightgown! The entire garment had been pushed up by my arm to just below her breasts, leaving her completely naked from her chest, all the way down the length of her body. I admired her long, slim legs, for half a second too long before I remembered I needed to untangle myself.

My cock twitched in my pants and I fidgeted against the painful feeling until I had myself comfortably situated, pain *there* necessitated my *immediate* attention. When I stopped dealing with that, she moved again, pushing her ass back hard and the length of my dick landed naturally between the cheeks of her ass. I froze. All I would need to do was unzip my pants and I could so easily find her opening, slip into her, plunge to the hilt inside her…

Pulling *away* suddenly became an exercise of supreme will, but I managed it. I carefully worked my hand out of the top of her clothes and tried to pull her gown down without waking her but everything I tried caused her to stir in her sleep. I could just imagine the reaction if she woke to me pulling at her sleepwear so I finally just rolled onto my back and stared at the ceiling with her gown still bunched around her waist. Oh well, it was still better than it'd been.

I found the idea of sleep bordering on the impossible after that. The foggy lethargy I had felt when I first woke was gone, swept away as if by hurricane force winds and the only thoughts that could occupy my mind were memories of her breast in my hand and her ass pressed against me while the scent of peaches filled my senses.

I'd had an idea of what to expect when I first came looking for Chloe Young. An image built in my head based on the information I had read on her. The real thing was very different than I had expected, however. The fact that she appeared to know nothing of what her father did might have had something to do with that. I tried to ignore it. I'd been taught to ignore it, trained to ignore things like that. An enemy was an enemy and enemies were to be eliminated. Now I found myself caring for her injuries?

I mean, logically if she were injured she couldn't make attempts to run. But, logically, if she were injured worse, or if her feet became infected she could slow us down. I scoffed at myself quietly. I could try to rationalize, could try to justify it all I wanted but there was no denying the facts.

I didn't help care for her feet because it was the practical thing to do. I didn't help care for her feet to build a trust so she wouldn't try to run off on me again. I didn't buy her shoes and toiletries for any reason other than I was starting to *like* her, and I have a great deal of difficulty being an asshole toward people that I actually liked. There were so few of those in the world already, I couldn't afford to push them away by being a total dick.

Chloe had a backbone, she didn't take my shit, but she was a smart girl too. She figured something out, she didn't back down. Didn't shy away. Even after her attempt to bolt I could still see her trying to figure out a way to resist, to get away. I could also tell that she wasn't willing to put anyone else in harm's way to further her own agenda of achieving freedom. It was the diametric opposite of her father. I mean, I'm not going to lie, it was hard to believe that Chloe was the daughter of that ridged old bastard. Maybe she took after her mother? We didn't have anything on *her* except when and how she'd died...

Whether it was the erection I was still fighting to calm, the smell of her filling my nose, or the lingering effects of sleep deprivation, I couldn't tell you. But when the knock came at the door, interrupting my idle thoughts, I didn't take a moment to think. I didn't question, I didn't wonder: *Who the fuck would be knocking on the door of our motel room at half past three in the goddamned morning?* No, I just got up to go answer it.

I moved off the bed a little too quickly, which startled Chloe awake. I noted her hurriedly pulling down her nightgown out of the corner of my eye before I grabbed the doorknob, threw back the deadbolt and pulled the door to our room open.

Sloppy. Very sloppy. So incredibly goddamned sloppy!

The fist that slammed into my face was roughly the size of a cinderblock and pretty much felt the same with all the weight and force behind it. I mean, it belonged to three hundred pounds of bone and muscle all fueled by a hardcore animalistic rage. My nose shattered, blood spattering my front and I'm pretty sure two of my front teeth were knocked loose. My head snapped back so hard that I felt and heard several loud pops in my neck and pain radiated out across my nerve endings, through my shoulders and down my arms. The kind of pain that communicated in no uncertain terms that I was well and truly fucked.

I went flying back through the air, across the room, sailing clean over Chloe and the bed to land against the wall, sliding down it onto the ground in a heap. That fucking sucked. That sucked hard.

"You should know better than to steal from us, William." The voice was deep. Exceptionally so. *Darth Vader eat your robotic heart out*, kind of deep. I pushed myself up so I was sitting against the wall, using it at my back to support me while blood streamed down my face. I shook my head to clear it but all that did was set off white sparkles, flitting at the edges of my vision. I scrambled to my feet and over the bed, putting myself directly between Chloe and our visitors.

I towered over Chloe but the two men that entered the room towered over me to an even greater degree. Over six and a half feet tall each, they both wore oversized pants and boots like me. Instead of jackets though, they each wore white hooded sweatshirts with the sleeves torn off, mostly because sleeves wouldn't have stretched far enough to encompass their massively muscled arms. They wore no shirts underneath the open zip-up hoodies, and as they stood shoulder to shoulder between me and the door leading out into the night they tossed back their hoods in unison. I always wondered if they practiced that shit in a mirror somewhere to get their timing right.

Square jaws, high cheek bones, short cut hair spiked up in the front like a couple of Jersey Shore douchebags, they had eyes so dark they could have been black. They were identical twins, monstrous of size and the cold look in their eyes told me in no uncertain terms that the blood I had already lost would be the least of my worries in a moment.

"Chloe," I said quietly. "I'd like for you to meet my brothers, Romulus and Remus."

"Is kidnapping something of a family business?" She snapped. She tried to be angry, she really did, but I think she'd realized that we were in the middle of something seriously dangerous and fucked up. She didn't know that any attempts at her seeming nonchalance were totally ruined by the scent of her fear. I didn't want her to know that though. I needed her to be brave right now.

"Not exactly," I muttered, never once taking my focus off of the twins. "You might want to get your stuff together, put some clothes on or something while my brothers and I... talk." I noted that she was moving behind me, pulling on clothes before I could even make the suggestion and that, for once, she'd followed along with what I'd told her to do without complaint. Yep, the girl really did have some smarts, for all I'd been calling her stupid all this time.

"Give her to us, Baby Brother," one of the twins ground out, damned if I could ever really tell which was which. "Give her to us and we might just let you live through this. Father's death demands blood."

"And I will be the one to provide it, should it come to that," I grated.

Rom grinned, at least I was guessing it was Rom. "Little Cub," Yep, it was Rom. He was the only one that called me Cub like that. Derisive, insulting. "What chance do you really think you have? The two of us next to you? We're stronger. We're older and we're more experienced. We've killed many that have threatened us and you? You've killed none by comparison. The Pack will accept one of us as Alpha over you. Can't you see that?"

I was silent for a moment, reaching for that animal that resided inside me. Praying I still had the edge I would need to survive this.

"You might be bigger and stronger and have more experience than I do Rom," I admitted. "But you constantly underestimate me, and you always forget, I'm faster!" My voice deepened as I spoke and the two giants before me seemed to shrink as I grew. My skin darkened, covered quickly in short hair from head to toe as my fingers and toes grew longer, each tipped with a razor sharp claw. The bones inside my body cracked and shifted sickeningly as my body changed and my jaw mutated, pushing out into a short muzzle, mouth filled with two rows, top and bottom, of wickedly sharp teeth.

As the transformation finished I stood in the center of the room, seven and a half feet tall, stooped because of the ceiling, and I knew I looked like something out of a horror film. Behind me I could hear Chloe screaming, almost hysterically. I glanced over my shoulder at her, one gleaming amber eye meeting hers.

"Run," I rumbled and then I took my own damned advice. I ran, right at the twins with my arms held out to my sides to catch them, and hold them from Chloe. As I slammed into them I grabbed tight, digging my claws into whatever flesh I could reach and I kept going. The door and the frame around it, cracked and erupted in plaster dust and splinters. The second floor, thin metal railing of the open air breezeway on the motel did nothing to slow our progress as I carried them both out and through it, into thin air.

A single story drop doesn't leave a person a lot of time for thought, so action took its place. I pulled with my right arm and tucked in my knees. Just as Rom was about to hit I shoved hard. The force of my kick propelled him down and Rem and I were launched back into the air. A Jeep took the impact of Romulus' body, hood caving in and the windows shattered in a pretty spectacular explosion of glass. While that was going on, I grabbed hold of Remus with both hands and threw him toward the ground as hard as I could.

He landed, part way through his own transformation, head and shoulders first with a sickening thud that cracked the asphalt beneath him and with any luck, his skull right along with it. By the time I landed, lightly on my feet, both of them were standing and almost fully transformed as well. I'd always been able to shift faster than the both of them, but now, the advantage I had gained in size and strength vanished in the face of *their* hybrid states.

The twins were well known throughout the Pack for being two of the biggest, most powerful of us all. I was in trouble. Lightning quick they rushed me, low to the ground and all teeth and claws, bloody intent in their eyes as their toes dug deep lines in the blacktop. I leapt just as they reached me, desperate to keep out of reach. Just as I cleared their heads I felt long fingers wrap around my ankles, sharp claws dug into my leg and a hard tug sent me slamming into the ground. A pained howl ripped its way from my throat and I kicked instinctively. I caught a piece of one of them, not sure which, or what piece but whatever it was; it counted for something. The grip on my leg loosened and I managed to roll free.

I stood in the middle of the parking lot as human voices rose in the otherwise still night. Lights turned on in several of the rooms but all I dared focus on were my brothers as they circled me.

"Don't you remember this game, William?" Rom growled as they moved. "Father used it to teach us to fight."

"And you never were very good at it," Remus added. I kept my head on a swivel, swinging back and forth, feet moving in a tight circle constantly to keep them in sight as they moved. They were right though. I never did very well at this game. When your life is spent in constant battle you always want your opponents to underestimate you.

Without a sound Remus rushed me from behind. The same tactic as always. A feint from one of them to draw my attention and hide the real attack. I ignored Remus, and took the glancing swipe of his claws to my shoulder as I kept my focus on Romulus. When he rushed in I grabbed his extended arm, turned and threw him over my shoulder.

He let out a startled yelp as he crashed into his brother and the two of them went down in a tangle of limbs and claws. The revving of a car engine drowned out their growling roars and Chloe, beautiful Chloe, raced up in my car, the headlights cutting through the gloom.

She slammed on the brakes in front of me and I leapt, leaving the ground, and the tangled wolves behind. I latched onto the passenger side of the car, yanking open the door and by the time I tumbled into the passenger seat, I was back to looking human. The cuts to my shoulder and puncture wounds in my leg, which had been stinging annoyances at first, became painful wounds, burning like fire and had me groaning pitifully. My shoulder roared in agony as a series of blows landed against it.

"Ow, ow, ow, ow, ow! Chloe! Quit hitting me goddamn it!" I roared, doing my best to fend off her wildly flailing fist.

"Get out!" she screamed. Her eyes were wild, knuckles white on the steering wheel as she continued to hit me with her right hand. Her foot slammed on the brakes again, probably to try to force me out of my car.

"No! Don't stop!" I ignored her still flailing arm, leaned over until I was practically lying in her lap and reached down to shove my palm into the gas pedal. The car shot forward and she screamed, both hands now on the wheel as she steered. "Don't stop, don't slow down, just get us the fuck out of here!"

Behind us a pair of voices rose in animalistic howls that rapidly faded away as we sped off into the night. The twins' hunt had to begin anew.

It took a good half an hour to get Chloe to calm down. I wasn't surprised though, she had seen something rather disturbing. Something she had never been exposed to, and I whole heartedly believed that now. She didn't have a freaking clue about her father's true line of work. Luckily, she had enough sense not to try to stop again after her initial attempt to get me out of the car. She had also stopped trying to hit me.

She got back on the freeway heading east, back the way we came, but there was little I could do about that at the moment, so while I waited for her to calm down and start asking questions I pulled a bottle of water out of the glove box and downed two of the same Vicodin that I had been giving her. My ankle wasn't too bad, the four deep puncture wounds had already scabbed over. My shoulder was worse, but it was still healing nicely enough so I wasn't overly concerned. Of course with my metabolism the two pills did little more than a couple of aspirin would for a human. Still, something was better than nothing until my body could repair itself.

"What the fuck are you?"

Chloe's speaking surprised me and I glanced away from the road to look at her. She was a mess. The bruising on her wrists stood out sharply against her pale skin, her hair, a tangled wild mass surrounding a face that screamed she was still in shock. She was a whiter shade of pale, her eyes sunken, almost hollow despite how wide she held them. Her lips were pressed into a tight line, whether to keep from crying or screaming or both I couldn't say, but maybe I could head some or all that off at the pass. She seemed to operate better when she was pissed off.

"I would think that was fairly obvious," I said, laying thick the patronizing tone. "I'm a man that turns into a wolf like creature. You're smart, I'm sure you can put two and two together."

"That's bullshit," she snapped, some of that fire I first saw coming back, which was much preferable to the sad and subdued version of herself from the last day or so. "Werewolves? That's a fucking fantasy."

"We prefer wolf-kind, but you're more or less correct. Werewolf does fit the bill, we just don't like the term."

She took a deep breath. "And those were your brothers back there?"

"Not by blood. They're the biological sons of my adoptive father, the Alpha of our Pack. The man that made me wolf-kind in the first place."

She laughed, a high pitched, hysterical kind of giggle for a second before she bit her tongue or the inside of her cheek, pressing her lips closed again. I could smell the coppery tang from the small, self-induced injury. Hard to miss in the close confines of the car. My stomach clenched and it reminded me how much energy I had burned in my transformation. I needed to eat, but we needed to put more distance between us and the twins right now, more than I needed to fulfill the need to refuel. Food could wait.

"Are they the ones you were talking about?"

"What's that?"

"Back home, before we left. You said there were other people looking for me, and that they weren't as nice as you. Are they who you were talking about?"

I nodded even though I couldn't be sure if she could see it. Her eyes were locked onto the road, as if the highway's centerline were a goddamn lifeline, pulling her through the darkness. "Yeah. My brothers aren't exactly the most stable of individuals. I may threaten you, but they don't bother with making threats, they would just break your bones or slice your tendons so you couldn't run. They would drag you along by your hair, kicking and screaming for *real*." Subtle? Perhaps not. But I wanted to make sure she understood *exactly* the danger I had saved her from by kidnapping her. There was a method to my madness after all, even if it hadn't been altruistic at the start.

She didn't say anything for a few more minutes but when she did finally speak she was in better control of herself. Some more of the fire I saw before was growing back and she was less the broken girl I'd had to deal with yesterday. For some reason, that made me feel a little better.

"Answer me this, and no more fucking bullshit William, what the fuck have you gotten me into?"

"Honestly?"

"No," she snapped, acidly. "Lie to me, I really like that. Turns me on like you wouldn't believe."

I bit back a chuckle, "I haven't gotten you into anything, Sugar. Your dad did." She opened her mouth, probably to yell at me but I waved her off before she could get going. "I know you don't get that, I know you don't understand or believe me but just bear with me, this is going to take a little bit of an explanation."

She settled back in her seat, shoulders hunched angrily and knuckles white on the steering wheel but she didn't look like she was going to start screaming at me any time soon so I took a deep breath and launched into it.

"It's going to sound like something out of a movie or a TV show but I promise that what I'm telling you now is the absolute truth. There are wolf-kind in the world. Werewolves, loup-garu, whatever you want to call us. There are a lot of us, actually. Far more than you would guess. I'd be willing to bet that you've probably met a few in your life and never even knew it. By no means do we equal the human population, but there are a handful of us in just about every human community.

"Like real wolves, we tend to group into Packs. Most Packs are small, family units. Mom, dad, kids, uncles and aunts, that kind of thing. But occasionally, you get a large Pack. Large Packs are dangerous because the more of us there are, the more damage we can do if the Pack decides to get violent."

"Who makes that decision?"

"The Alpha." She gave me a sideways glance at that so I pushed on, "Again, like with real wolves, there's always an Alpha. One of us rules the Pack. All decisions and actions that may, in any way, impact the lives of the Pack must be vetted and approved by the Alpha. My father was the Alpha of our Pack and ours is the largest

Pack in all of North America, including Canada."

"And you think my father killed yours?"

"It doesn't matter what I think. What matters is what the Pack thinks. A weapon was left behind. A weapon only your father is known to use and he was travelling last week yeah? On business." I could see her turning that one over in her head. She dodged the question though.

"Why would my dad know anything about... wolf-kind?" She stumbled a bit over the name but I was somewhat pleased she didn't just call us werewolves, most Hunters went straight for the derogatory terms. They were assholes like that.

"Because he's a member of a different organization. The Hunters," I explained. She snorted out a laugh there but otherwise didn't interrupt. "I know. It sounds ridiculous. But wolf-kind have always been persecuted and hunted, wherever we've lived. Hunters find us and kill us without any thought for mercy or discrimination. Your father is one of the best in the business and is rather highly placed within the Hunters' ranks. We don't know exactly how high as no one has ever been able to penetrate their organization. They have tests to identify my kind."

"Multiple choice or short essay?" she quipped. I liked the sarcastic Chloe, she was funny. Now wasn't the time though, especially not about something so serious.

"Silver," I snapped with a frown furrowing my brow. "This isn't a joke, Chloe. I know it's incredible and sounds insane but it's the truth. Your dad killed mine. Or if he didn't, someone is trying to frame him. I'm inclined to think that it really *was* him. I think he's been trying to build up to something. There hasn't been a full forced hunt for wolf-kind in a long time. We don't know why. It's been kept to small skirmishes for the last few decades. I think your dad is trying to galvanize the organization into an all-out war with us."

She became strangely silent for a few minutes and suddenly hit the turn signal and rocketed off the next exit at speeds that even *I* found to be a bit reckless.

"What the–!"

"Shut up," she snapped. She turned onto a street and then into a gas station parking lot, slid the car into a space and pulled the brake after shifting into park.

"I'm not sure if this is going to make things better or worse," she started. "But I think there's something I should tell you." I said nothing but simply arched an eyebrow and waved one hand in a motion for her to continue.

"I've seen your brothers before."

That certainly got my attention.

"That's not possible."

"My dad works as a CPA. He really does, William, don't give me that fucking look. I've seen his work files, I've met a bunch of his clients. Whether he's a Hunter, or not, the man has to have a day job, right?"

"I guess," I dragged out the word, somewhat disbelieving.

"Well I've seen the twins before. They came to my house, some months ago. Clients of my dad's. But at the time he introduced them as Roman and Remy Dulcet."

You ever have a suspicion about something? Someone is lying to you? Your boyfriend or your girlfriend is cheating on you? Something like that? And when you finally have your suspicions confirmed your entire world is rocked to its core, even though you were kind of expecting it?

That's a bit how I felt at that moment. That's when the pieces of the puzzle began to fall into place. It wasn't the Hunters that wanted a war. It was my *brothers*, what the fuck were they up to? Was Alpha seriously so important to them they would jeopardize the entire fucking Pack to get it? I felt sick.

"Remus came up with those names, years ago. Romulus and Remus aren't exactly common or popular names, you know? People would find their names amusing and Romulus always had the worst temper of the two of them. So Remus suggested something a little less unusual so that we could keep Rom's temper down when dealing with people."

"So what does that mean?"

"It means my brothers have conspired with your dad to kill the

Alpha, so one of them could become the new Alpha and drag the entire Pack into a war. If either one of them becomes Alpha, their natures won't let them do anything but destroy the entire Pack."

"What do you mean?"

I groaned and raked my hands back through my hair. I'd never had to explain this to anyone before and I was finding it a lot more difficult than I had expected. "There are two types of wolf-kind. Moon Forged and Blood Born," I explained carefully. "The Moon Forged are wolves that were human first and turned by being bitten by a wolf-kind in their full wolf state. Not the hybrid form you saw earlier."

She considered that for a moment before she nodded once, sharply. "And the Blood Born?" she asked.

"Blood Born are ones that were born from one or more wolf-kind parents. They were never actually human. The Blood Born are also far more mentally unstable as a general rule. Blood Born are responsible for all the old legends of crazed, blood thirsty monsters that you hear of in regards to werewolf stories. The Blood Born are more animalistic. Their rage is harder to control, the wolf is stronger, tougher. At first I started this needing to be Alpha just to stop one of them from destroying the Pack because I thought they wouldn't be able to help themselves. I thought their bloodthirsty nature would propel them into dragging the Pack into chaos. But if they really did work with your dad to kill my father, then this isn't just their animal nature acting up. This is cold blooded murder and there is no way in hell I can let either of them become the new Alpha."

We fell into silence again after that. I don't know what was going on in Chloe's head, but my mind was spinning. If I could only prove that the twins were involved in the plot to kill father. If I could bring evidence of it to the Pack...

"I'm hungry," I said suddenly, startling Chloe out of her own thoughts. "And tired. We need food and we need to sleep."

"What are we going to do about all this William?" she asked. "We have bigger things to worry about than the bottomless pit you call a stomach right at the moment, don't we?"

"Right now, I need to eat," I said, firmly. "The hybrid transformation burns up a lot of calories. If I don't get some food into me I could go feral and you would start to look pretty damn tasty right about then." I sighed at the terrified look on her face. "Look, Chloe. I'm sorry that you've been dragged into this mess. I really am. But do you see now that I'm not the bad guy here? Yes, I kidnapped you, and I'll apologize now for my tactics, but in the long run I saved you from something much worse."

She didn't say anything. I'm sure she had plenty to think about and I couldn't blame her for it. Her entire world had just been flipped upside down for the second time in nearly as many days. But we were running out of time and we really needed to keep moving.

"You turned east when we got on the freeway, didn't you?" I asked and she nodded distractedly. "The twins will more than likely have continued west, expecting us to keep moving toward the coast. If we get some food, and get some rest we should be okay and we can get back on the road tomorrow."

She looked out the window at the barely rising sun. "It's not even day time yet," she said.

"Are you well rested and ready for a day of travel?" I asked and she shook her head.

"I rest my case. Food. Rest. In that order."

"Then you drive." She got out of the car before I could say anything but I slid over as she walked around and climbed back in on the other side. I think she was finally figuring out that I was definitely the lesser of two evils under the circumstances.

Nothing more was said for a while. We filled up, found a McDonalds and loaded up on hash browns and breakfast sandwiches and ate on the drive. I hit the freeway again, heading west toward Seattle and after thirty miles or so pulled off the freeway, taking winding surface streets toward the trees until I could pull off into a wooded area.

The car was easy enough to conceal. I simply broke off large branches from the trees and used them to cover it. It wouldn't hide it from anybody that happened to walk by but from the freeway it wouldn't be visible.

"What are we doing here?" Chloe asked. "I thought you wanted to rest."

"I do. But I don't like the idea of bringing them to any more populated areas, *if* they happen to come back this way so quickly. I don't think they will, but better to be safe than sorry. And here we'll be able to get some rest without them being able to sneak up on us so easily."

I walked over to her and stood next to her. When we stopped for food she'd changed into some better clothes, warmer, thankfully. I can't imagine getting any rest the way I planned if she was still wearing that nightgown.

"Trust me?" I asked and she let out an explosive sigh.

"Do I have much choice?"

She let out a surprised squawk as I suddenly scooped her into my arms. She barely weighed anything, feeling light as a feather and for a moment I worried that she was losing weight. Stress and fear could do that to a person easily enough.

Before she could say anything I bent my knees and leaped. The muscles of my thighs bunched tight, like steel springs then suddenly snapped out as they propelled me, and my attractive cargo, up and into the trees.

She screamed that time and her arms latched around my neck, holding on for dear life as the wind rushed past us and my bare feet landed lightly on a branch high up and as thick as my thigh. Two more jumps had us half way up the tree in a nice crook of branches that would suit my purposes.

I carefully set her down and made myself comfortable back against the trunk, legs drifting to either side of the limb I sat on, there was no way I would fall out. I'd done this, slept like this, a thousand times back home.

"What the hell are we doing up here?" she asked voice pitched loud and high.

I winced, "Good God, please stop screeching like that, it really hurts my ears."

"Answer me William," she snapped, voice high and tight with panic.

"We're going to sleep up here. It'll be harder for the twins to catch our scent at first and up here I can hear for miles, we'll hear them coming long before they get here. Now come here and settle down." She stood awkwardly, holding onto the nearest branches around us with a death grip as she shook and trembled, almost violently, her breath coming rapidly and for a moment I was afraid she might hyperventilate and pass out.

"I can't sleep in a bloody *tree*, William," she cried, "I'll fall!"

"No," I argued. "You won't." I reached up and grabbed her wrist. A quick tug and a bit of a twist to her upper body she fell into place, her back to my front and I got my arms around her. Before she realized what was happening she was sitting, her back against my chest, her head tucked just beneath my chin. I did my very best to ignore the length of her body pressing against me, so warm and supple, so soft.

"I've got you," I whispered and wrapped my arms securely around her, careful to avoid the bruising on her stomach. "Now sleep."

She shook slightly and I felt something damp touch my hand. I breathed deep, the tang of salt touching the back of my tongue. I scented the air again to make sure, but then she shook, and it was unmistakable, she was crying.

"I just want to go home, William," she moaned.

"I know," I whispered again. I couldn't imagine the fear she felt. "But you can't, not right now. It's dangerous and there are still too many questions that haven't been answered. I need you, Chloe Young."

I took her hand, lacing our fingers together and gave it a squeeze. "I need you to save my Pack." I hesitated for a moment. "And I'm not sure that's even possible, not with the twins involved. And I don't know how, but if I can, I'll do my best to save your father. If this is the work of the twins, I'll do what I can. But to do that I have to be the new Alpha."

She said nothing else after that. Simply lay against me, shaking slightly. Eventually the shudders subsided, her tears dried up, and she drifted off into an uneasy sleep.

Not once did she let go of my hand.

Chapter 8
Chloe

"Chloe…" A deep sigh that caused me to rise and fall with it, my eyes snapped open. I sucked in a tremulous breath and held very still, blinking in the late afternoon light that filtered through the branches. Branches, oh God! I stiffened.

"Shh, shh, shh, I've got you," William's arms tightened around me and I closed my eyes.

"Just get me down!" I snapped, I didn't mean to, it's just, I've never been a fan of heights. "Sorry, I'm sorry!" I blurted immediately and he chuckled.

"I'm batting a thousand with you, huh Sugar? Didn't know you were afraid of heights," I felt my chest rise and fall in short, sharp breaths and tried not to panic too much.

"Please, just get us down?" I pleaded, completely failing at putting forward any kind of front of assurance.

"Can you turn? Put your arms around me?" he asked.

Oh great. Getting into this position had been easy, he'd done all the work, now I had to try and turn around and that was gonna be all me, baby! And I didn't want to do it. Mm-mm no way, no how. Oh Jesus!

"Deep breath, Chloe. Breathe, don't panic; just breathe. I've got you," I closed my eyes and tried very hard not to look down.

"Okay, okay, I've got this, I've got this, just promise me no more trees after this, no more heights." William laughed, and I stiffened, I turned, twisting my upper body and smacked him in the chest.

"Look, you Asshole! I don't think it's…" I didn't get to finish, lightning fast he snatched my arms around his neck and crushed my upper body to his, his arm a steel band against my back. He stood in one fluid motion, my feet dangling, lower body twisting around. He smiled a decidedly smart-assed grin at me and caught me up behind the knees with his other arm, lifting me, balanced easily on the wide branch we'd resided on.

"Wasn't so bad, was it?" he asked me and I felt my eyebrows shoot up into my hair line as I felt him start to shift and I suddenly knew what he was going to do.

"William don't!" but it was too late. He leapt and we plummeted and I bit my lips together to keep from shrieking, because I knew he hated that, that it hurt his ears and – *oh holy hell just please don't drop me!* I prayed.

"Open your eyes, Chloe." William's voice was both gentle and chiding at the same time. I clung to him, rigid in his arms, face pressed into the side of his neck. I unclenched my muscle groups one by one and drew back slowly, opening my eyes. We were on the ground.

"I really hate you," I said but I didn't, at least not really. Right now, he'd gotten me back on the *ground*. I really wanted to kiss him for that. The easy smile that made him go from handsome to just plain hot, slipped a little as he tried to decide if I were joking or not. He stood, frozen, me dangling from his arms as he looked me over and the smile faded into nothing.

"Don't suppose I really blame you," he said setting me down carefully.

"I was just giving you a hard time," I muttered, cheeks flaming, as I tugged the sweater down over my dark blue jeans. It was my last pair, he'd thrown a seriously weird mix of clothes into the bag. I don't think he'd really been looking. I had enough bras and underwear for days upon days, he'd thrown in a light and a dark pair of jeans. Two skirts, three dresses... a random selection of shirts, a sweater, and a jacket... I mean, it was a mess.

I looked him over, shirtless, barefoot, I think his jacket was long gone and I shook my head.

"We need to find you some clothes," I eyed his pants and shook my head, "Some clothes that *fit*," I amended.

"I wear 'em big on purpose," he said, frowning. "I can't transform in clothes that fit properly."

"Yeah, well, it makes us stand out. I've seen that fancy credit card of yours. You can afford more clothes if you tear the ones you've got on, so come on. You need to get some serious coin off that card and we need to go."

The smile returned, "On my side now huh?" he asked.

"No, I'm on my side, but for now that seems to be your side too," I shook my head, "I want to call my father, let him know I'm okay." *Even if he doesn't care I want to get some answers of my own.* I thought, but I didn't say that out loud.

"I don't know about that," he said.

"Yeah, well, you don't really get a say in it. You kidnapped me, I'm agreeing to come with you despite everything, so I get this. Okay?"

He nodded, hesitantly, "Okay."

We got into the car after clearing it off and I hugged myself, rubbing my hands together. I was chilled, not cold, but still couldn't wait for it to warm up.

"How can you not be cold?" I asked, eyeing William and his state of undress, which, not going to lie, helped heat my blood some. He looked like some kind of underwear model, a nice physique. The claw marks in his shoulder, which had looked really bad the night before, were scabbed over and looked days old, I was pretty sure in a few hours they would be the pink of shiny new scar. It was impressive, unbelievable, but I went with it. I was pointedly ignoring the fail safes in the back of my brain that kept screaming repeatedly at me about just how fucked up this whole situation was.

"Wolf-kind run hot," he said and I nodded just a little too quickly. He continued on, however, filling the awkward silence that would have ensued with a biology lesson on werewolves, wolf-kind, or whatever. Apparently the amount of calories they expended from their transformations and high body temps is what required him to pack away food like a starving man as he'd been doing since I'd met him. *Since he kidnapped you.*

"So yeah, our average body temperature is like a hundred and three degrees as opposed to a human's ninety-eight. It unfortunately makes it easier for the Hunters to identify us as time goes on."

I quirked an eyebrow at that and he explained.

"Thermal imaging. A wolf-kind's body will show up hotter on thermal cameras than a humans. It makes it harder and harder for us to hide."

I stared out the window for a long minute and sighed. Swallowing hard, I jumped when his hand found mine where it rested between us. He gave it a squeeze and I stared at them, his hand around mine, a gesture meant to comfort. I looked at him and he swept me with a concerned glance, returning his vision to the road, glancing at me, the road, me, the road…

"It's a lot to take in," he said quietly.

"Yeah," I agreed, "So, um, what do we do now?"

"We get me some more clothes, all I have is the dirty set but it should be enough to get into a store if you can get me some boots, those I don't have any extra of."

I frowned at him, "Didn't exactly think this through did you? The whole kidnapping thing." I raised my eyebrows and he smiled, I think my heart did a backflip in my chest. His hand tightened around mine slightly and I was startled to realize he still held it.

"Kidnapping isn't something I've ever done," he admitted.

"What did you do before?" I asked.

He shifted uneasily in his seat, but he answered me, "Usually I just killed whoever, no need for grand plans full of sustainability when all you do is rip someone's throat out," he said quietly.

I faced the window, feeling a little green, "I suppose not," I said quietly and sighed, "Is that what you were planning on doing to me?" I asked, taking back my hand. He let me and I was grateful he didn't push. I felt further chilled despite the warm air pouring from the car's vents. I had a feeling I knew what his answer was going to be… *the debt must be paid…*

"Yes," he said quietly, "But I don't think it will come to that anymore. Not with what you know. As for the others? Before I mean, in my defense they were usually people that'd done very bad things. I'm not an indiscriminate murderer, you know," he said, all of a sudden very defensive. I didn't say anything and after a while he muttered morosely to himself, "Just thought you should know that."

"Why do you care what I think?" I asked softly, sobered beyond belief.

He looked me over, "I just do," he said honestly and it was puzzling.

We drove into the next town in silence, and William found a bank so that he could pull cash funds off his credit card. They would only allow him a certain amount, not nearly enough for what he wanted to do which was get us all the way through the whole trip, but it was enough that we could make some purchases. Clothes, food, another hotel room, gas… enough to get us through the next day, maybe two. So that we could stop, and potentially get more, as we traveled westward, ever onward, tomorrow.

After he'd secured funds, he gave me money to buy him some shoes and turned me loose in front of a discount shoe store. I went in while he sat in the car, watching me nervously. I went to the work boot section and selected the size he'd asked for and paused.

I could run, go out the back, but I knew now, he could track me. With that nose of his, he could literally smell me out. I didn't know what was going to happen, where we were going to end up but… but those twins, those twins with their cold, coal black eyes from the night before had just oozed menace. I believed William, they would kill me or worse, while he was trying to at least keep me alive, to protect me. *For now.* I thought, but still, it was my only chance and better than any I had with his brothers.

I purchased the boots and returned to the car and saw, from the corner of my eye, his shoulders visibly sag in relief as I opened the door and sat in the passenger seat.

"You didn't bolt," he said and his tone held some disbelief.

"Here I am," I said in a dubious tone, pulling the seatbelt across my body.

"Great, yeah, okay," he started the car and we got back on the highway, the afternoon wearing on into evening.

"Clothes, food, hotel?" I asked.

"Yeah," he grunted.

We drove in silence, found a Walmart and dispensed with the

clothes shopping, picking up a pre-paid cellphone while we were at it.

We made the calls from the Walmart's parking lot, William standing outside the car, speaking intently into the line with someone from his family, or Pack, or whatever. I waited impatiently in the passenger seat of the car for him to come back, to let me call my dad.

Finally, he ended his call and got in the car, handing me the cellphone. I stared at his somber face and chewed my bottom lip.

"A little privacy?" I asked quietly.

"I could hear your conversation from across the lot if I wanted to, but if it makes you feel better," he reached for the door handle and I stared at him, incredulous.

"No," I said before he could get out of the car, "I mean, I guess it's fine then..." I looked down at the rectangular glass and plastic brick in my hand and brought the screen to life. I entered my daddy's number and pressed the call button and put the phone to my ear.

"Can I drive?" he asked as it rang and I nodded. He started the car and my dad picked up on the third ring.

"Yes?" my father asked imperiously.

"Daddy?"

"Chloe? Is that you? Where are you?" he asked, voice tinged with the cold hardness that was so familiar.

"I'm okay Dad. It's okay..." I said and I realized I didn't know what to say. I mean my father was an *accountant* for Christ's sake.

"Where are you?" he demanded, "Are you with somebody?"

"Yes! Yes, Daddy I'm with somebody," I looked at William who was searching my face carefully, before turning back to the road. I hated it when my dad was mad at me. He always managed to say just the right thing to inflict maximum damage, you know? One slight remark from my dad and it was like he pulled the loose thread that had me coming totally apart. Maybe calling him really was a bad idea.

"William is taking very good care of me," I assured my dad lamely.

Silence on the other end of the line, dead silence. Oh shit. My father was so quiet, that I pulled the phone away from my ear to check and make sure the call was still connected.

"William Reese?" my father asked and I blinked. William nodded beside me, eyes fixed on the road, and I could tell that he could hear both ends of the conversation. Damn that was freaky.

"How... how do you know William's last name?" I asked my dad, as my whole world began to shift on its axis. *I* didn't even know William's last name. Oh, God... was William right?

"Never mind that, Chloe. Tell me where you are." he said, his tone was angry, but I couldn't tell if it was at me. I didn't want it to be at me. My father had never laid a hand on me growing up, he was worse. Much worse. When I did something wrong he withheld affection. Made me feel like an abject failure. Made certain I knew just how big of a disappointment I was. To say that my dad and I weren't exceptionally close was an understatement, but I hoped. I'd always hoped...

One of my dad's biggest things was honesty. To be an honorable person. You said you were going to do something then you damn well had better do it. If you didn't you weren't worth shit. Truth, honesty, integrity, and obedience. My father demanded all of these things and more out of his only daughter. Set the bar so high it was impossible to reach, then didn't hesitate to make sure I knew that failure wasn't an option.

"Daddy, don't lie to me, please don't lie to me," I closed my eyes. "How did you know William's name?" I asked again and there was another strong silence. *You fucking hypocritical bastard!* I thought. I felt anger, resentment, a lot of things swirl in my breast. *None of this is happening, none of this is real; this can't be happening, my dad...*

"Where are you?" he asked, imperious tone, deathly still and I knew. I just knew... Oh my god. It was true. The whole thing, all of it, it was true. I squeezed my eyes shut tight against the flood of hot tears as the last vestiges of what I'd thought was real crumbled.

"Did you do it?" I asked, "Did you kill William's father? Are you what he says you are?"

William grabbed my hand, his fingers finding the spaces

between mine, and gave it a firm but gentle squeeze. A life line in this whole tumultuous mess of fracturing reality and swirling fantasy. It was ridiculous, the man who'd kidnapped me, who openly admitted he was going to fucking kill me, was suddenly the rock that I could cling to, my shelter from this total shit storm I found myself chillin' in. This was *so fucked up.*

"Chloe…" my father's voice was low with the threat of anger but I just suddenly didn't care. I didn't care anymore. My entire life had been nothing but a bunch of fucking *lies!*

"Answer me, Daddy!" I spat and probably wouldn't have been half so brave if my father had been standing right in front of me.

"You want an answer? Okay fine. I haven't killed anyone," my father said shortly and my shoulders dropped in relief. I sniffed, and William let my hand go so I could wipe at my tears.

"I don't understand any of this," I said, voice tremulous and shaking. I let William retake my hand. My father was quiet for a moment on the other end of the line. Something just didn't feel right, he was being too quiet. Finally he sighed.

"I know Chloe, I know, just tell me where you are and I'll send somebody to come get you," now that was weird. Really weird. It was probably the kindest most understanding thing I'd ever heard come out of his mouth in my direction. That was so not my father. By now I should have expected at least one acerbic remark about stopping my crying.

"I'm fine, I'm really fine. I'm going to take a few days, help William and then I'll call you," I said, decision made.

"No. Absolutely not! You tell me where you are, you tell me right now!" I blinked bewildered by the sudden heat in his voice, the anger. I wasn't doing what he wanted, his manipulation hadn't worked. *This is all real. Everything William's told me is real.* I just knew it deep down, in my gut, everything in my subconscious was just *screaming* at me to wake up!

I looked at William who was giving me side long glances, and I dropped my eyes to our entwined hands. His thumb stroking in a comforting gesture back and forth across my skin and I saw myself at a crossroads, with myself, with my dad, with a lot of things. I took a fortifying breath and did what I knew in my heart was the right thing. I willfully defied my father for the first time since... well since I could remember.

With a bravado I didn't actually feel I braced myself inwardly and said, "Daddy, I'm a grown adult, I..."

"I said no, Chloe!" he cut me off. Just like I was eight years old and I froze, just like I was eight years old and had been caught with my hand in the cookie jar before dinner.

"Now, where are you? Where is that animal taking you?" I gasped. Holy shit. There was no way that was an accident, or a slip of the tongue.

"Daddy?" I asked, not really wanting to believe what I had just heard.

"I'm waiting Chloe." His voice was cold, wintery on the other end of the line. I glanced at William, whose lips were pressed into a grim line so tight they vanished behind the short curtain of his goatee.

"It's true, isn't it?" I asked.

"Chloe..."

"You did, didn't you?"

"Chloe, now I mean it, you tell me–"

"You killed somebody, you killed William's father," I took the gloves off, "You killed their Alpha."

Silence, although this one crackled with an electrified tension.

"They aren't human. I didn't kill anyone. To kill someone they have to be human. Now tell me where you are."

I hung up the phone, numb. I ended the call and rolled down the window, pitching it onto the freeway rushing beneath the tires. I hoped the damned phone would shatter into a million pieces, just like my life, just like everything I had ever believed to be true. So many things about my father made sense now with this new light shining.

Somber brown eyes with deep flecks of amber in them met my own, briefly, before he had to turn his attention back to the road and I found myself clinging to William's hand with the both of mine. At least William was proving to be something solid, at least he was *real*.

He may not have told me what was going on in the beginning, withholding it from me, but at least he had never *outright* lied to me. Don't even get me started on William's lack of being a hypocrite, not like my dad... All this *time*. All those lessons on integrity were just so much bullshit!

"Chloe..." William's voice was as somber as his expression, yet still gentle.

"Just don't ever lie to me William. Please?" I asked abruptly. "Just promise me." I looked at him, fixed him with my gaze that I knew was too wide, a face that I could feel had gone pale, "You haven't so far, and I really need you to promise me this. No matter how bad it gets, no matter what it is, just please don't lie to me. Just tell me like it is, help me understand but no more lies. No more withholding information."

William's face shut down into lines of grim resignation before morphing into sheer determination. He nodded once, a gesture of finality and raised the back of my hand to his lips, brushing them across my skin.

"You've got it," he said and swallowed hard. We drove another sixty miles or so before pulling off and hitting a drive through. He ordered his usual mountain of food and then some and took us further down the road to a roadside motel. I told him to eat and went to go to the front desk to check us in.

"You have to have ID," he called and I returned to the car and dropped back into my seat dejected. I felt stripped of *everything* now. My life and now even my identity. This sucked so fucking hard. I closed my eyes and let my head drop back against the seat. He finished chewing and swallowing and went in to get us a room while I polished off a burger and fries that tasted so much like sawdust but I forced myself to eat them anyway because I needed to. I sucked down some Coke and he returned and took us around the building to our room.

"Take the food up, would you?" he asked and popped the trunk of the car. I nodded and he handed me the key card. I went up with the food and he brought up our things. I was grateful he wanted to finish eating in the room instead of in the front seat of his car.

"You shower first," he said, and with as much food as he still had to go through, I didn't argue. I just gathered my things and let myself into the bathroom. I showered, the temperature near scalding but I didn't care. I was tired. I was a raw, open, and broken. I was wounded. My heart vulnerable and aching. Mostly because I knew I had to let go. That there was going to be no fixing this one when it came to me and my dad. It was just too fucking much on top of everything else.

I went through the motions, shampoo, rinse, condition, wash body, rinse. Stepping out of the shower I dried carefully and slipped on my nightgown, using the hotel's little hair drier to defog the mirror and the brush William had bought for me on my hair until I could see to dry it evenly.

When I stepped out of the bath, William was coming back in through the motel room's door.

"Where did you go?" I asked.

"Moved the car several blocks down, parked behind a bar. Didn't want to advertise we were here." I nodded and he sighed. We looked at each other for a long somber minute.

"Want to talk about it?" he asked and I shook my head. No, I didn't. I wanted to sleep.

"Okay, I'm gonna grab a shower. Try and get some rest."

I nodded and gathered what I'd need to change my Band-Aids while William disappeared into the bathroom. By the time the door opened again, steam gently billowing out, I was tucked in to one side of the too soft, queen sized bed, trying to sleep. It wasn't really working out for me though.

I opened my eyes and watched William trim his goatee and shave the scraggly beard into something neater and more presentable, just generally taking care with his appearance, one of the white hotel towels wrapped around his waist, sitting low on his hips. I'd be lying if I said I didn't admire the view. He had a gorgeous body. Fit and rippling in all the right places. While I understood the functionality of the loose or baggy clothing, I had to admit it was a damned shame. The man would look good in stuff that fit.

I closed my eyes and sighed out, and heard William still for a moment, before the small sounds one made while doing whatever it was he was doing, resumed. I sighed again, and tried valiantly to just go to sleep.

CHAPTER 9

William

I was stalling.

Damn it. I was fucking stalling!

There is a beautiful, strong willed, woman lying in a bed ten feet away from me and I'm dicking around with my fucking goatee! What the hell is wrong with me? I thought angrily with myself. *I haven't felt this nervous since Dad told me I was going to start training with the damn twins!*

There's only so much one can do when your facial hair is as short as mine is though. I shaved my cheeks, jaw, and neck and I ran out of excuses to waste time rather quickly after that. Finally, I ducked around the corner, snatching up a pair of loose basketball shorts, before going back into the small bathroom to shed my towel and pull them on. I might like my jeans oversized and loose but they weren't comfortable to sleep in.

Climbing onto my side of the bed, I sank low into the mattress, creating a depression that Chloe naturally began to slide toward. *Damned cheap hotel mattress.* I griped silently.

"What the hell?" she cried. "How much do you weigh man? Jeez." She struggled to stay toward her side of the bed but no matter what she did, I could tell she wasn't entirely comfortable.

"I'm not exactly light," I muttered, somewhat embarrassed. After a few more minutes of watching her struggle with finding purchase on the shitty sloped mattress, I sighed and slid over until I was in the middle.

"Come here," I said and pulled her toward me. She let out a surprised squawk which caused me to grin and within moments we were finally situated. I lay on my back with her pressed tightly against my side, half sprawled across my chest.

"Are you comfortable?" I asked after a moment and she sighed again, sinking further against me as her muscles relaxed. It was as if her body were molding itself against mine, every inch of her pressed against me and I closed my eyes.

"You really are hot," she murmured quietly and I snorted a laugh, a smirk twitching my lips. "I mean *temperature* wise," she added quickly. "I mean you're hot but... I... you're very warm," she muttered the last quietly, almost miserably and I could feel the heat of her blush coloring her cheeks where her face was pressed against my chest.

"I got it," I chuckled. My right arm was wrapped around her, fingers trailing lightly up and down her back through the satiny material of her nightgown. I was beginning to regret letting her keep that damned thing.

"What are we going to do?" she whispered after another minute. She turned her head, placing her chin on my chest to look up at me. In the dim light her blue eyes shone, wet with unshed tears. Her cheeks still flushed a delicate pink. She was achingly beautiful...

"We'll figure it out as we go," I said. "I'll do everything I can to protect you, Chloe. You understand that, right?"

She was quiet for a moment before she nodded, "I do."

"You don't still hate me, do you?"

She got a coy look on her face at that, "I don't know," she said with a toss of her bright red hair. "You *did* kidnap me, and you *did* make all kinds of threats." The playful tone in her voice died fairly quickly as she spoke her next, and I felt a stabbing sensation in my gut. "And you did kind of turn my world upside down," her voice was soft with hurt and I twisted on the bed, grasping her carefully by the arms. I pulled her up until she was straddling me, her nose inches from mine.

"I can't apologize enough for what I've done to you, or your life. For altering your understanding of the world you live in so drastically, but it was always *there*. The world was always like this, you just didn't know it.

"Your life up until now has been filled with lies. Now it's all out in the open and that might not be considerably better, but at least

it's the truth. At least it's *real*. Understand where I'm coming from?"
I didn't mean to be so intense. I could see a bit of fear in her eyes
and I carefully kept my grip on her arms as light as I possibly could,
mostly because I was afraid of causing anymore bruises on her fair
skin.

"I get it, William, really I do… It's just…" she scoffed, "I can't
get my mind off it. My dad *lied* to me. He's been lying to me my
entire life. He's *murdered* someone, killed them! After mom and…"

She turned her head to the side, away from me and closed her
eyes, forcing back her tears. What she said got to me. She called her
father, a man she had known and loved her entire life, a murderer.
And she couldn't forgive that, could she? She would never forgive
murder, not after what happened to her mom. *And what was I?*
Little better. I'd killed my share of people in my time. I was an
animal, wasn't I? That's what we did.

But her pain, her confusion, it hurt me in ways I couldn't begin
to explain and what I did next had no basis in logic. I just wanted
her to forget. Even if it was just for a time. I wanted to take the pain
away, even for just a little bit. I touched the side of her face lightly
and she turned back to me.

One look from those true blue eyes of hers and I leaned up
without thinking, my body moving before I realized what was
happening. My lips brushed against hers in a touch so feather light
that I don't even think *she* was aware that it'd happened at first.

Her eyes widened, tongue darting out to wet her lips. She stared
at me, for just a moment, eyes so beautiful, so wide, before she
leaned down, just as I had leaned up. Our lips met, and I kept
going, kept sitting up until I was sitting straight with Chloe
straddling my legs. Her tongue darted at my lips, wet and hot and
velvet soft. I pulled her tightly against me and she groaned quietly
into my mouth as our tongues brushed against each other.

I always ran warm but at that moment the blood rushing through
my veins felt like fire. My body burned and the only thing that
occupied my thoughts, my senses, was the woman I held in my
arms.

Her fingers trailed across my back, every touch searing my skin with a line of pleasant heat. I couldn't hold back a groan as she shifted her weight and, I think, quite deliberately, she ground herself against me. I could still smell the peach body wash she enjoyed, but beneath that the heavier scent of her arousal, her desire. Her nipples stood out sharply through the thin material of her nightgown and I licked my lips, wanting nothing more than to ravish her breasts with my hands and mouth.

I was once again fully erect and straining at my clothes, the only barrier between me and her and it was maddening this time, like it had never been before. Still…

"Wait, wait, wait," I hissed and put my hands on her hips, holding her still. She pulled back, a questioning look in her eyes and stared at me as if I had suddenly begun speaking in tongues.

"Are you sure?" I asked.

"What?" she blurted, almost incredulously.

"Are you sure? I mean, you're right, I *did* kidnap you, I *did* threaten you, and I have destroyed your entire view of the world…"

Her expression gentled, "And through all of that you've been the only one to tell me the *truth*. To protect me, *without* lying to me." She smiled and bit her lower lip coyly before she ground herself against me again. I could feel the dampness between her legs begin to seep through my shorts and oh God, just when I thought I couldn't get any harder.

Her voice, when it came was low and husky with seduction, "Unless you want to ruin this, I suggest you shut up and fuck me already."

I smiled, that was all I'd needed to hear. A second later, the room was filled with a sharp tearing sound as I seized the neck of her nightgown in both hands and ripped it clean in half, letting the remnants flutter useless to the bed, leaving her naked and completely exposed on top of me. That first *real* view of her will forever be burned into my memory. The warm flush in her cheeks ran down her neck and across the tops of her breasts, her fair skin giving away what her words couldn't.

From her hips, I slid my hands up her sides, taking my time to enjoy the feel of her smooth skin under my fingers, noting every fine tremble that ran through her body until my hands reached her breasts. I moved past them, cupping her face with both of my hands, before drawing her to me, into another burning kiss. Our breath came fast, mingling together as her lips fought with mine for dominance. I held her tight, kissing my way down her neck, her breasts crushed against my chest as she dug her nails into my shoulders.

When I finally kissed my way to her breasts I made sure to stay away from the stiff peaks of her nipples. I pressed my mouth to her silken flesh, gently cupping her breasts, kissing around the darker color of her nipples until tiny mewling sounds escaped her. Her head was thrown back, eyes closed as she held onto me like a woman clinging to the rocks, lost in a storm swept sea.

When I finally closed my lips around her right nipple and sucked gently at it, she let out a long moan, bordering on a groan, her body shook violently against mine to the degree it almost pulled her breast from my mouth.

"Oh my God," she whimpered, "William that feels incredible."

It's very difficult to smile with your mouth filled with breast, but I managed it and nipped gently at her skin with my teeth, causing her to jump slightly.

"That is the general idea, Sugar," I reminded her and she slapped my shoulder at my smart-assery. A moment later she leaned back and pushed at my chest. There was no way she could *make* me lay down if I didn't want her to, but I went with it and settled back on the mattress as she leaned over me, her breasts hanging down so the tips of her nipples just brushed against my skin... I'd always been a breast man and goddamn that was hot.

She kissed me again, and this time? I let her lead. My hands roamed across her warm skin. Across her back, trailing the length of her thighs and back up to squeeze her ass. My erection was getting painful inside my shorts as the light feel of her nipples continually brushing across my chest, teased me to a fever pitch. Just as I was about to yank the damned things off myself, she threw her leg over me so she was kneeling beside me. She grabbed the waist band of the shorts and I lifted my hips, helping her, as she pulled them down and off my legs. She tossed them to the floor and I suddenly lost all ability to focus on anything other than her hands, on what she was doing to me, as she boldly reached down and grabbed my cock firmly but gently.

The shock that ran through my body was so intense that I simply can't describe it. My hips bucked instinctively, thrusting into her closed fist. The feeling of her fingers wrapped around me, sliding slowly up and down my length from root to tip where she rubbed her thumb gently across my head on each upward stroke... God, it was my turn to release a lust-filled groan that I couldn't have suppressed even if I'd wanted to.

Chloe leaned down and kissed me, swallowing each soft moan, with every stroke of her hand as it passed between my lips, until I felt as if my body were going to explode. Something I definitely did not want, not yet. I growled low in my throat, almost the same growl I use in my hybrid state, and pulled her hand carefully away from my dick.

Before she knew what was happening, I flipped her over on the bed so she was lying on her back. I landed atop her, supporting my weight on my elbows, careful not to crush her. I kissed my way down her body, slowly working my way down, kissing along the inside of her thighs as she sighed and squirmed beneath me. Finally, I placed my mouth directly over the swollen lips of her pussy, scenting her want, her desire, *God she smelled like heaven.*

She sighed and groaned as I ran my tongue along the length of her lips, probing gently at her opening, teasing the tiny bud of nerve endings. *That* had her practically shrieking with every flick of my tongue. I latched my lips around it, sucking softly at her clit and at the same time growled again. The vibrations ran from my throat through my jaw to my lips and directly into that most sensitive place. She cried out so sharply that I winced and almost went to cover my ears but her thighs clamped down tightly on my head, taking care of the problem for me. Her hips bucking against my mouth for several long moments. *Well that was one way to do it.*

When she finally fell limp, I sat up and clambered up the bed to lay next to her, gathering her into my arms. Every inch of her was lightly dewed with sweat, her hair tangled and matted to her damp forehead and neck from her thrashing. Her eyes were softly unfocused and she moaned quietly as she settled in against me. Small tremors, little shivers, still ran through her body periodically and I couldn't help but smile. Admittedly I was somewhat pleased with myself. It'd been a while, but apparently I still had it.

I felt a small hand wrap around my length and my grin fell away as my mouth dropped open. "You didn't honestly think I was going to leave you to your own devices, now did you?" she asked, a salacious little grin tugging at her lips. Damn. Apparently I didn't have room to be as smug as I thought I did.

"I honestly wasn't planning for this," I admitted. "I didn't exactly think to pack any condoms."

"That's alright, I've been on birth control shots for a while now but..." She trailed off and I frowned, finding it difficult to think with the constant stroking rhythm of her hand.

"But, what?" I asked finally, I was the one finding it difficult to focus now.

"Your, um, condition. The, uh, wolf-kind thing?"

"What about it?"

She opened and closed her mouth a couple of times, perhaps looking for a delicate way to put it before she finally sighed explosively and just blurted out, "I'm not going to become one if we have sex without a condom right? It's not like a disease? I only ask because you told me not to bite you; that you had things in your blood I wouldn't like to catch and I don't exactly know how it all works. I mean we haven't really talked about it." She fell silent after her rush of an explanation and her face flamed, almost as brilliantly as her hair.

I blinked, surprised, and my mouth dropped open for a half second before I burst out laughing. Not my best move, I'll admit, but I was just so surprised. When she started to pull away from me, upset by my reaction, I gathered her into my arms and pulled her close, settling her across my chest again, her knees on either side of me.

"I'm sorry, I just really wasn't expecting that, it's a legitimate question though. You're right, you don't know how these things work." I lifted one of her breasts and nipped at her nipple with my teeth in a bid to get her to relax with me again, she held herself so stiff.

"No," I said, running my tongue across her chest to her other breast and giving that nipple equal treatment. "You can't become wolf-kind through sex. It's not an STD. The only way you become a Moon Forged is by being bitten by one of my kind in their full wolf state, not even the hybrid form you saw will pass it."

"So, we're safe?"

I nodded, my face buried in the valley between her breasts and the tension left her body. "I only said what I did because I didn't want you to bite me," I told her honestly.

"Thank God," she groaned, and with that she reached down between us, grabbed my cock with one hand and positioned it at her entrance. A moment later she sank down my length until I was buried inside her to the hilt and every one of my senses seemed to implode, drawing her in further with the action.

I had been wrong before when I thought my body had been filled with fire, when I had thought that the touch of her fingers across my skin had seared my flesh. The wet heat at the center of her burned in ways I can't even begin to describe. I plunged into her and my arms wrapped tightly around her as I threw my head back into the pillow beneath me, eyes sliding closed against my will.

The burning of my skin, the pounding of my blood in my veins, it just grew more intense the more she started to move. Her hips slid up, the muscles in her legs tensing beneath her skin as she slid almost off of me, only to plunge back down until our bodies met with a loud slap. Nothing more was said, we didn't have the breath for it. The room was filled with the wet sound of my length sliding in and out of her over and over. Our moans echoing and weaving around us like a carnal symphony.

She started slowly, but quickly moved faster. I couldn't help moving myself, my hips rising to meet her on each downward thrust, faster and faster until she suddenly stiffened above me, crying out so sweetly, every muscle in her body became granite and the muscles of her core spasmed and gripped me.

I continued to thrust up toward her as her mouth opened in a silent scream which slowly gave way to sound, a gasping moan that seemed to curl up from her toes until it poured from her throat. I sat up, plunged into her one last time and buried my face again between her breasts, kissing. Her fingers tangled themselves in my hair, holding my face against her, nearly smothering me in her soft flesh as I twitched involuntarily inside her, flooding her.

When I finally came to my senses, I turned my head, reluctantly pulling my face from the soft valley or her breasts and drew back so I could look into her eyes. The both of us were breathless, and panted nearly in unison. I pulled at her to bring her closer, not even realizing my hands had been tightly gripping the cheeks of her ass, possibly enough to bruise, holding our bodies tightly together as if never wanting for us to separate.

I collapsed onto my back, tugging her down with me until she lay sprawled across my chest, my length still buried completely inside her, and I let out, probably, the longest most satisfied sigh I had ever exhaled in my life.

We said nothing. No words seemed to be needed. The entire situation felt as fragile as a soap bubble, the merest breath of air might cause it to disintegrate and I didn't want that, not yet. There would be time enough later to discuss, or ignore, as she decided. I wasn't sure, just then, which would be preferable to me.

But I would learn, soon enough, just how much Chloe Young had begun to mean to me. How much she had begun to mean to the wolf, the instinct that resided buried deep inside me.

Within minutes we were both fast asleep, Chloe using my body as her own personal bed as she lay across me, her weight a comforting thing in the dim light of the motel room. Before I dozed off I managed to think that that hadn't been *exactly* how I had wanted to take Chloe's mind off her troubles, but in the end, it was definitely the best choice and I was glad we'd made it.

Chapter 10
Chloe

Warm and solid beneath me, I came back to myself listening to the steady cadence of William's heart and breath. I sucked in a deep one myself to clear the cobwebs from my mind and listened to the bass rumble of the man I'd slept with the night before give an appreciative hum.

"Hmm, welcome back," he said, a slight smile tinging his voice. I pushed off of him, sitting up so I could look into his lovely brown eyes. His lips curved up into a warm, heart stopping smile and he gave a luxurious stretch. I bit my lips together and wondered to myself if last night were a onetime thing or not and was startled to realize that I really hoped it wasn't. Well wasn't *that* confusing?

"What's wrong?" he asked and sat up, concern radiating off of him.

I felt my shoulders drop, and took a deep breath and asked, "Kiss me?"

I wanted to see what he would do, see if he was still interested maybe? I don't know. Whatever I had been concerned about, whatever uncertainty I'd had, evaporated in an instant when William's expression gentled and he reached for me. His calloused hands were so sweet, as he cupped my face, and he leaned in to kiss me. His lips moved over mine so carefully and my hands smoothed over the hard plane of his chest, over his shoulders and the sides of his neck so I could bury my fingers in his hair, holding it back from our faces as we kissed.

I lay back down, drawing him with me and he came to me, willingly, nudging my legs apart with his knee. I sighed in relief and he knelt above me, kissing, licking along my tongue, nipping my bottom lip as his hands wandered appreciatively, warm and alive over every inch of me he could reach. Smoothing along my skin, making me squirm with want of a deeper, more meaningful touch.

William broke our kiss, both of us breathless from it, and reared up from me, eyes hooded with desire. Drunk on lust he rubbed the head of himself against me, looking for entrance and I couldn't help but be flippant, "Not going to ask me if I'm sure this time?" my voice was soft, playful and coy and he smiled, a wicked grin full of very white teeth.

"I'm wolf-kind, Sugar. I've already marked you, and besides that," I gasped as he eased his way inside me, he brought his lips to mine, bowing over me. Holding himself aloft to keep from crushing me, he finished what he was going to say, "I can smell how much you want me," he breathed and stroked himself deep into my body and back out.

I moaned and writhed underneath him, and he settled over the top of me, caging me in a protective embrace. He found his rhythm, his mouth seeking out mine, kissing me, his cock stroking in and out of my body slowly. While the sex of the night before had been fiery, wild, and untamed, this, right now, was sweeter somehow. Softer, kinder. I stroked the sole of one foot up his calf and twined my arms around his shoulders, raising my hips to meet his slow and deliberate thrusting.

He broke his mouth from mine and gasped out my name, "Oh, Chloe..." and I felt my heart give a strong and steady throb. It sounded so beautiful, the way he said it and I didn't know what to do with that, so I didn't do anything but accept it for the gift that it was.

I pulled his mouth back to mine and twined my legs around his lean hips, begging silently for more. For whatever he was willing to give up of himself. William broke our kiss and pulled one of my hands off from around his neck. He continued to stroke in and out of me, placing a reverent kiss in the center of my palm, nipping the inside of my wrist and I couldn't help but arch beneath him.

His pace quickened, he'd found that place inside me and now, now he drove me mad with pleasure. I closed my eyes, my body coiling tight and I felt his fingertips trail down my body, lingering between my breasts for a moment.

William reared up so that his hand may continue its descent. I was close, I was so close, moaning breathless, passionately begging with my body, with my eyes, for him to tip me over that edge. He smiled down at me and slicked his thumb through my wetness, gently teasing my clit. The sensation of him inside me, of that light teasing touch, it was too much but at the same time, it was perfect, just enough. I clapped a hand over my mouth to stifle my scream as I came. I shivered and jumped and William soothed me with his voice but didn't let up, drawing my orgasm out into the ether. Until I lay limp and spent beneath him.

He bent over me once more and kissed me languorously, until I whimpered with satisfaction into his mouth. He drew back and smiled down at me and whispered, "My turn, hold on to me, Sugar."

I wound my arms around his shoulders and held to him as he renewed his thrusting, and didn't stop until he attained his satisfaction. God. I never wanted him to stop! We lay in a tangle of limbs for the longest time, catching our breaths before finally showering together silently.

There was no need to speak, we simply moved around and against each other in this comfortable quiet, dressing and packing up. We stopped and ate before continuing on towards the west coast.

"Can you tell me what's happening?" I asked when we'd finished eating. I was balling up wrappers back into the bag the food had come in while William piloted his car down the freeway.

"What's happening in regards to what, precisely?" he asked, glancing at me out of the corner of his eye.

"With your whole situation, you know? I mean, I'm sorry to bring it up, but your dad was murdered and it sounds like he was important… what's happening with that? What does it all mean?"

"Without an Alpha the Pack is as close to chaos as it's ever been," he said. "The Arbiter will be holding things together until an Alpha is agreed on, but the longer that takes, the higher the chances for trouble, that someone could go rogue and expose us." He shifted, making himself comfortable.

"Okay, so you guys, what? Vote someone in or something? Like a Presidential election?" I shrugged. I really wanted to understand.

"Packs are small for a reason. When they get too large the question of leadership becomes muddled. My Pack has close to two hundred and fifty members, that's monumentally huge, it complicates things."

I waited for him to gather his thoughts patiently, finally, he continued with, "The only way to keep members from going off on their own or perhaps attempt to take trouble directly to the Hunters is with strong leadership. If too many decide to leave that makes us vulnerable. It leaves our territory vulnerable."

"So that's what an Alpha does? Maintains your territory?" William winced, and changed lanes over into the fast lane.

"The Alpha protects the Pack. Makes the decisions that keeps the Pack strong. It was Father's decision to relocate the Pack to Seattle and since then, the entire state of Washington has become our territory, no other Pack would dare hunt on our land without our permission."

I considered what he was saying, "So, you guys hold some kind of election then? Nominate and vote on a new leader? A new Alpha?"

"Not exactly. Wolf-kind are instinctive. Basically, we trust our guts. Candidates are presented to the Pack and the one, that the Pack as a whole feels is a strong and capable leader, will get the opportunity to prove themselves as Alpha."

I stared at him, incredulous, "You know that sounds really stupid right?" I put on a mocking tone, "Oh you seem like a really nice guy, you should run our country!"

William laughed, "Isn't that how you elect your president every four years?" he asked and I blushed.

"Yeah," I said sullenly. He laughed again, harder this time.

He shrugged after his laughter died down. "It's not a perfect system but it's what we've done for centuries."

"Centuries?" I echoed, I guess I hadn't really thought about how long werewolves, I mean wolf-kind, had been around.

"Mm-hmm. If the Pack thinks one of the twins a better candidate they'll accept his leadership over any other. It's kind of like mass hysteria or a psychic link, it's hard to explain. Basically if the vast majority of the clan feels strongly that a certain person should be Alpha, then the entire Pack will accept that person as Alpha. At that point the only option would be to challenge for leadership, meaning a fight."

"Wow," I sighed and sagged back into my seat, "To the death, or just until there is a winner?" I asked softly, worried. William was silent for a while before he spoke again.

"Among wolf-kind, you haven't won if your enemy is still breathing."

I shivered and hoped that William didn't see it, I threaded my fingers through his and sighed. "It sounds like a brutal way of life," I said softly.

"It can be," he said, carefully neutral. He brought the back of my hand to his lips and brushed it with a kiss. He shrugged, "But there's nothing like it. Your senses are so *powerful*. I remember when I was a kid my mother would cook lasagna for dinner every other week. I could always smell it down the block. I'll never forget that smell. The day after I was turned and woke up? My new senses made me feel like I had been deaf, blind and unable to taste or smell my entire life up to that point. Suddenly, everything was like that lasagna that I could smell from two blocks away.

"And you're stronger and faster than you ever were. Pain isn't as bad, you heal faster. There are so many benefits that it's hard to imagine my life without it, my life before."

"So you're one of the other ones then? Not Moon Forged but Blood Born or whatever?" I stumbled over the unfamiliar terms and hoped I got them right. He'd confused me with the lasagna story.

William smiled, "No, I'm Moon Forged. I was born human then bitten and became wolf-kind."

I sighed out, a harsh exhalation of breath and quailing inside asked the hard question… "And what about the Hunters? My father? Who are they?" *You know, other than racist, prejudiced killers on par with the lynch mobs of the KKK or the fucking Nazi's?* I thought to myself bitterly.

He shrugged. "No wolf-kind knows. As long as our history extends there have always been Hunters. They were the Knights Templar for a while. There's an ongoing theory that the reason the Pope of the time ordered the Knights murdered in that massacre was that some of them had become Wolf-kind, endangering their entire organization," he pondered. "The Spanish Inquisition wasn't a good time for our people either, but we've never really been able to get very close to them to find out more."

"Wait, so you don't know how they originated? You don't know why they started hunting you in the first place?"

He shrugged again, "Their origins have never been clear, or high on our list of priorities. But the one thing that *has* always been a constant? They're part of an organization. A focused group with their only goal being the eradication of my species. Maybe at one time they were run by the Catholic Church, maybe some government another time. Who knows? But it has always been a unified force, all part of one larger group. Survival has taken precedence over digging into the Hunter's history though, and it's just getting harder."

"Why?" I asked, genuinely curious. William smiled and kissed the back of my hand again, I think he was slightly entertained by all the questions, which I would have been too had I been in his place, however, there was just something so damned tragic and sad about *everything* that had brought us to this point that I couldn't see the humor in much of anything right now.

"Why is it getting harder?" he asked and I nodded.

"Advancements in technology and weaponry, mostly. Like the myths say, silver is fairly toxic to my kind. So it makes a good material to coat weapons meant to fight us and they keep finding new ways to use it. As society moves on, it gets harder to create false identities. More information than ever is online and in the governments' hands. It's getting harder and harder to stay on the fringes of society."

I turned my attention thoughtfully out the window and relished how William's thumb stroked gently back and forth across the back of my hand. I worried my bottom lip between my teeth and thought long and hard about everything he'd told me. Uneasy with some of the revelations, I decided to pick a different topic that was no less important to me.

I had a lot to think about and I felt like I had barely even scratched the surface.

Chapter 11

William

"You talked about when you were a kid, your senses being sharp and all of that, how old were you? I mean, when were you… turned?" She'd been silent for a long time and her voice nearly startled me, I'd become so lulled by the road, by the miles passing beneath the tires.

I thought about it for a moment before I was able to answer. "Well, let's see, I was twenty-four or twenty-five, I don't remember the exact month so it's hard to say for sure."

"And how old are you now?" she asked curiously.

I really had to think about that one. "Umm… twenty-five in 1966 but I was born in '41 so… Seventy-three? Give or take a few months? I should probably find out about that one of these– Ow!" I yelled as she suddenly punched me in the shoulder. "What was that for?"

"Dirty old man," she said with a bit of a grin.

"What?"

"You should have told me before you fucked me that you were old enough to be my grandfather."

"Well I'm sorry! It didn't exactly come up!" I winked at her. "But, correct me if I'm wrong, I believe you were the one that said, and I quote, 'shut up and fuck me'."

"No one likes a smart-ass William," she muttered but she was smiling.

Things went a lot easier after that, with Chloe as my partner instead of an unwilling captive. She drove and I slept, I drove and she slept. When we finally crossed the border into Washington State I breathed a huge sigh of relief. Pack law dictated that the twins couldn't attack me inside our Pack's territory. As long as we were inside the state they couldn't touch me without tipping their hand to the Pack. We kept driving, and all too soon we were cresting

94

Snoqualmie pass in the Cascade Mountain Range. I couldn't help the sigh that escaped me as, after another half an hour and we'd crossed the I-90 floating bridge and gone through the long tunnel and my city came into view. Chloe gave me a sidelong look.

"Good to be home?" she asked and I could hear a touch of sorrow in her tone.

I took her hand again, brushing my lips across her knuckles. "You'll get home, Chloe. I promise."

She sighed and shrugged but didn't pull her hand away at least. "I'm not sure I really have a home to go back to at this point. I don't think I could look my dad in the eye, knowing now how he's been lying to me my entire life. That he's been killing people."

I didn't know what I could say to that so I simply squeezed her hand.

"We'll be at my place in a couple of hours, why don't you try to get some sleep?"

She nodded and pulled her feet up, curling into a ball on the seat. Minutes later I heard her breath settle into a deep even rhythm as sleep claimed her. She was exhausted. I could tell, even though she tried to hide it. The entire trip had been taking a lot out of her. The stress of learning the truth about her family on top of being kidnapped would be enough to stress anyone out, add the whole discovering an entire hidden race? I felt she'd held up fairly well. Still, I would be happy to get home where I could get her comfortable and get her some *real* rest. Food, sleep in a comfortable bed, a real shower. All of it sounded good to me.

My house was located on the Northern Olympic Peninsula, just outside of Port Townsend. Probably one of the most beautiful, historical port towns within a thousand miles.

"Where are we?"

I glanced over at Chloe. Her eyes were open and alert but she hadn't moved otherwise. She'd slept on the drive through Seattle to Edmonds and all the way through boarding and disembarking the Ferry to Kingston. It was another hour or so drive from there to Port Townsend and another fifteen to twenty minutes to my place. She'd slept through it all. She really was exhausted.

"Almost home," I said. We made small talk, returning to discussing music for a while and I learned even more about Chloe Young than even my extensive research into her had revealed. And the more I learned, the more I liked.

An hour later I leaned forward and peered through the window. "Here we are," I said as I made a left turn onto a small dirt and gravel track. An old mailbox on a wooden post at the head of the track bore the name 'Reese' in faded white letters. Chloe sat up, staring out the window as the car bounced its way over the rough terrain until we came out in a clear space between the trees.

Tall evergreens separated my home from the road, giving a degree of privacy and making the whole house feel like it was far off the beaten track. After parking and shutting off the engine I climbed out of the car and stretched, shoulders and back popping loudly as I reached as high into the air as I could.

Across the car I heard a low whistle and turned to see Chloe standing on the other side, staring up at my house. "Nice," she said, appreciatively and shut her door.

"Thank you," I grinned at her. "I put a lot of work into the place. Come on, lemme give you the ten cent tour." I walked around the car, took her hand and led her up to the house. From the outside the place looked like a two story log cabin. Larger than most, but still, a log style cabin. The far left side of the house had a round tower that ran three floors high with a series of ornate, stained glass windows at regular intervals on the first two floors. The roof of the tower was a round dome of dark wood panels. I couldn't wait to show her that. It was my favorite part of the place.

"Wizard's tower?" she asked looking up at it with a small smirk and I grinned at her.

"Even better," I said but refused to elaborate as I led her up to the front door. A dozen large, flat, river stones created a path leading up to the door and I stooped and dug my fingers into the dirt by the last one before the porch, lifting the heavy rock up to reveal a key hidden underneath.

After I put the rock back and straightened up I noticed Chloe giving me an amused smile.

"What? No one other than wolf-kind would even think to look under there and anyone else wouldn't even be able to lift the damn thing." Okay, so I might have been a bit defensive but I wasn't used to bringing normal people around my house.

She laughed and I growled and jumped for her. Grabbing her around the waist I threw her over my shoulder carefully and marched up the steps to the door.

"Put me down, William!" she shrieked, laughing.

"Nope! You mock my hiding place, I get to have a little fun with you," I reached up and gave her gorgeous ass a little slap. "Now hold still or you're going to fall."

I got the door open and set her down in the front entrance. The door shut behind us plunging the room into darkness and I heard Chloe let out a startled gasp next to me.

"Crap, sorry Chloe. I forgot your eyesight isn't as good as mine, hang on just a second." I darted across the room, skirting around the large structure in the center and on the far side found the switches I was looking for. Flicking all four of them into the 'on' position brought up the lights. Long fluorescent tubes buzzed to life, giving a soft white glow that illuminated the large space.

Chloe gasped again and I moved back to her to find her staring, shocked, at the contents of the room. A pneumatic hammer stood near her with a welding helmet hanging from it. Oxyacetylene tanks stood in a rack against the wall, just beside the door. Numerous other hand and power tools dotted the room. Each neatly, precisely put away in specific places on peg boards, racks, and tables.

In the very center of the room stood the structure I had moved around on my way to and from the light switches. It looked like the trunk of a tree, an old, gnarled, oak or something. If trees came with odd, straight angles and were made out of chunks of metal welded together. Roots spread from the base of the tree, giving it a realistic look as well as adding support for the structural integrity. On one of the large tables in the cavernous room that took up the entire first floor of my home, there lay, what would eventually be, the canopy of the tree itself. I hadn't put it all together yet because my ceiling wasn't tall enough. The piece would have to go together on-site where it was to be erected.

"What in the hell is that?" she asked, cute little nose wrinkling.

"It's a tree," I said with a smirk and she absently back handed my shoulder again.

"I see that," she chided. "What's it doing here?"

"I haven't finished making it yet."

Her eyes widened in astonishment, "You *made* this?"

I nodded, a proud smile on my face as I looked at her looking at the tree. "Yeah. That's what I do, I'm a sculptor. Some of my pieces have sold for as much as low six figures. This one was commissioned by a wealthy local client. He wants it to stand on a section of his private property. I'm hoping to have it ready and delivered to him by the end of the month."

"You're a sculptor?" she asked, a mixture of awe and confusion filling her tone.

"Yeah. What? You didn't think I had that fancy black credit card for nothing, did you? I've gotta pay the bills and fifty plus years since I was bitten, is plenty of time to perfect a skill. I like working with metal, I like art, just seemed like a logical transition."

I took her hand, shaking her out of her shock and she turned to look at me, her eyes glittering strangely. The half-finished tree couldn't have brought on tears, could it?

"Are you okay?" I asked and cupped her cheek with one hand, rubbing my thumb against her skin.

"I'm fine." She gave me an unconvincing, watery smile, but I let it go. I wasn't sure it was the right time to push her really. She'd been through enough and there was still a lot left to go.

"Come on, let me show you upstairs." She followed at my gentle tug of her hand, moving along calmly. To the far right from my front door, a simple staircase led from my work room to the second floor, where I lived. The second floor was as different to the ground floor as night was to day. Instead of the cold concrete floor below, the floors upstairs were a mixture of polished hard wood and plush carpet. The front entryway upstairs had thick, dark red carpet and brown wood paneling on the walls and ceiling with a large skylight directly overhead letting in the last vestiges of sunlight as night began to come on.

A long hallway split the upper floor in two as it ran the length of the house. At the far end of the hall was a large living room, comfortably, if sparsely furnished with the same red carpet running the entire length. A well-appointed kitchen stood directly opposite the stairs with a full bathroom next to it. A study broke the left hand wall half way between the stairs and the living room and on the right was the door to a guest room with an adjoining bath.

I explained all of this to Chloe as I showed her around. At the words 'adjoining bath' she let out a small groan and I grinned. She had complained a few times about the poor quality of the showers at the motels we'd stopped at, and I agreed entirely. Plus we hadn't stopped in the last two days except for food, gas, and restroom breaks.

I pulled open a hidden cabinet door, built to blend into the wall in the main hallway, and pulled out a thick red towel and handed it to her. She arched an eyebrow at it but took it from me anyway.

"What?" I asked, confused by her reaction.

"You sure do like red don't you?" she asked and I blinked a couple of times, my mind not quite catching up to the comment for a moment.

I started laughing when it finally clicked though. "Honestly, I just grabbed the first towel off the top," I told her and she shrugged.

"Not a big deal, I just found it interesting." She glanced around, a brief look of confusion crossing her face before she spoke up again. "You said this was a guest room?" she asked, indicating the door next to us and I nodded. "Well, where's your room?" she asked hesitantly, almost timid.

"Did you want to see?" I asked and she nodded.

"You still haven't explained that tower either."

"Bring your towel." I took her hand again and led her back to the living room. To the right of the TV was a simple dark wooden door which opened into dimly lit space. I led her inside, closing the door behind us and held her hand as I reached out in the dark and flipped a single switch.

The shocked gasp that escaped her was one of the most satisfying sounds I had ever heard. I designed the place because I enjoyed it, but sharing it with others was an absolutely wonderful feeling.

We stood on a second floor balcony that ran the entirety of the inside of the tower wall. The center was an open space looking down onto the first floor, were several plush couches and armchairs sat in a haphazard arrangement across beautifully detailed, hand-woven carpets from cultures all over the world. The walls were lined, floor to ceiling on both floors with shelves and each shelf was stuffed nearly to over flowing with books.

"It's a library?" she asked, eyes wide and her towel hanging almost forgotten in her hands. "You have a *library* in your house?"

"I like to read," I said and pulled a book from the shelf nearest to me. An early edition of *Jane Eyre*, and held it out to her. "There's a lot to be learned from books. There's a lot that has been shared by people wiser and greater than us. Honor and integrity. Books tell us a lot about ourselves and about the world we live in and the way others view the same things that we see and take for granted. It's nice to know how they see things differently depending on their own thoughts and experiences. I like other perspectives."

She seemed at a loss for words when I finished talking and I shrugged, suddenly feeling self-conscious. I put *Jane Eyre* back on the shelf and led her to the left along the balcony. Half way along the wall the balcony ended in a wrought iron spiral staircase that led up to the third floor.

"What's up there?" she asked, trying to see up through the gaps in the staircase.

"That's my bedroom."

She arched an eyebrow at me. "You live at the top of a tower?" she asked, almost disbelieving.

"Hey, it isn't reserved for Disney Princesses. Besides," I said with a wink. "This isn't that kind of tower," I gestured up the stairs. "After you."

She took the steps ahead of me, her footsteps echoing slightly on the metal stairs until she disappeared up through the ceiling and stepped out onto the floor above. I turned on the lights as I joined her and watched as she took a few steps out into the room and spun in a slow circle, eyes trailing around the circular space.

"Go shower," I said and pointed at the door across the room that led to the master bath. "I'll explain what's so special about this room later. You've got your stuff right?" She patted the bag she'd brought in with her and nodded before she disappeared into the bathroom. I stared at the closed door for a moment before I turned and started back down the stairs.

Chloe Young was in *my bedroom.*

Two days since that night and subsequent morning of amazing sex and now, here we were in my home. My bed not far away. I was going to get her into that bed soon enough, I promised myself.

While she showered I went through the house, making sure everything was as I'd left it. I had been away for almost two weeks altogether with driving to New York then driving back. My cleaning service was definitely worth every dollar I paid them though. Everything was immaculately clean and my fridge was even freshly stocked with food.

My stomach rumbled and I sighed, for once I was annoyed with my body's insistence on packing away ridiculous amounts of calories. I pulled open the fridge and pulled out a few ingredients. Chicken breast, bell peppers, an onion, and a half a dozen links of Italian sausage, and got to work.

By the time Chloe came back into the main part of the house from the Library, I was putting the finishing touches on a simple meal. Spaghetti smothered in sauce with diced chicken and Italian sausage.

"So you're an artist, a scholar, and a cook, huh?" Chloe asked as she slid into a seat at the small table I kept in the kitchen. God, I loved her scent. Sweet, like sun-ripe peaches, and I didn't know what was worse, her in that nightgown or what she was in right now. Just one of my shirts. I smiled and set a plate in front of her along with a can of coke from my fridge.

"I dabble," I said and handed her a fork.

"Eat Sugar, I'm going to jump in the shower."

She mumbled something around a mouthful of pasta and waved

her fork at me in a shooing motion, which just made me laugh as I made my way down the hall and up the stairs.

I've known plenty of people that like to spend their time bathing. They luxuriate in the hot water for like an hour or more. I've never been that type of person. But I couldn't help taking a few extra minutes just to stand beneath a scalding spray of water, letting the jets beat down on my back and shoulders. A level of tension that I hadn't even been aware I'd possessed melted away under the heated water and my muscles felt loosened and limber when I finally stepped out. The bathroom floor was grey ceramic tile with thick rugs strewn across it to ward of the natural chill of the floor material.

I left deep footprints in the plush red rugs as I walked out into the bedroom, still dripping, in search of the towel I had forgotten to grab when I went in to shower.

I found Chloe waiting for me, an appraising little smile on her lips, a towel in hand. My lips quirked up into a smirk and I held my arms out to my sides.

"Well?" I asked.

"Well, what?"

"Are you going to give me the towel? Or should I just drip dry?"

She seemed to consider it for a moment, her eyes constantly moving across my body. "Well I wouldn't want the towel to ruin the view," she said with her trademark little smart assed smirk that I was pretty much growing to adore. I growled and stepped quickly across the room toward her. She tried to back pedal but I had a definite advantage. I was faster, and I knew the layout of the room. She didn't.

The backs of her legs hit the edge of my queen sized bed and she let out a surprised yelp as she tumbled backward, landing heavily on the soft mattress, laughing. I yanked the towel from her hands as she tried to crab walk away from me. I dove onto the bed, trapping her beneath me, one knee between her thighs, holding her legs open, the other planted next to her hip.

"Now what are you going to do, Sugar?" I whispered, our faces inches apart and she leaned up and kissed me as her hands stroked my skin. Water dripped from my hair as I returned the kiss, plunging my tongue into her mouth. I groaned into her as I felt her hands roaming lower until she wrapped them around my cock, stroking me, quickly, to full hardness.

I'm not entirely sure how she ended up naked. The loose tee shirt she had thrown on after her shower was bundled on the floor and I let my hands and mouth wander across her body. I counted each rib beneath her skin with my fingers and my lips as she writhed and moaned beneath me. She was too thin.

"Please," she whimpered as I teased her entrance with my fingers.

I turned and slid up the bed until I was sitting with my back to the headboard and motioned for her to join me. She crawled over, breasts swaying hypnotically with each motion and went to straddle me, but I turned her so her back was to my chest and settled her against me. My hands slid up her stomach to cup her breasts and she arched her back, moaning softly as she bent her head back to kiss me again. *Oh yeah, just like that…* I thought.

Reaching down, I guided myself into her, first rubbing my head along the length of her lips then slowly sliding into her until I was buried to the hilt. The firm flesh of her ass was pressed tight against my abdomen and I returned my hands to her lush breasts.

We rocked together, gently, slowly, building an agonizing amount of pressure over time. I splayed one hand across her abdomen, feeling the taught muscles moving beneath her skin as I thrust into her, one breast gripped tightly in my other hand as I kissed and bit gently at her exposed neck.

Our moans grew louder, faster and I finally slid my hand from her stomach to gently rub that bundle of nerves at the top of her sex that served no purpose other than to bring pleasure to the woman I was reasonably sure I was falling in love with. Because I wasn't fucking her, not this time. I wasn't sure that I ever had, from our first time until now.

As I slid my finger across her clit lightly, she bucked hard against me and her moan cut off in a strained grunt. Her muscles clamped down tightly around me and I thrust almost frantically into her for a few more moments until I came too, slamming hard into her and holding still as I released myself inside her.

At the same moment I clamped my teeth into her skin, just where the sensual curve of her shoulder met the delicate slope of her neck. She moaned even louder, crying out, her pussy echoing the sentiment of her cry by fluttering and pulsing around me again. I was dizzy, almost light headed before we finally regained our senses. Her body relaxed completely against me, as weak as a newborn kitten and I carefully withdrew my teeth from her flesh and inspected the area.

I hadn't broken her skin, thankfully, but there were deep teeth marks left behind that stood out sharply against the pale expanse of her neck.

"Sorry for biting you," I murmured quietly into her flaming hair, breathing deep her smell, like peaches and fucking sunlight. A few heartbeats later she gave a quiet, sensual and satisfied moan in response.

"It's alright," she drawled, "I kind of liked it, made things more intense."

"It isn't, really," I hated to say it, I really did. Considering the circumstances, any chance she had to enjoy something pleasurable should be taken to its fullest. I really didn't want to inject any stress into her already tumultuous life, but I felt I owed her an explanation, at the very least. To be honest with her, completely honest. As much as it might lay bare feelings that I wasn't even positive I really had yet. I sighed inwardly, instinct, when it came to my people, was a powerful thing, and I couldn't argue with the evidence, I mean I *could* but it wouldn't change anything.

"What do you mean?" Her tone was sharp and she tensed, nervous energy suddenly flooding into her as her hand flew to touch the place I had bitten. She pulled her hand away, looking at her fingers before she swiped at the place again.

"I didn't break the skin," I assured her, "Don't worry." I lifted her gently and moved her so we were sitting beside each other.

"This isn't necessarily something bad. But it is something I should explain since you're still new to the whole wolf-kind thing.

Let's get dressed and head back to the kitchen. I think we could both use a drink after the last few days don't you?"

Her eyes held concern, but she nodded silently and scrambled off the bed to get dressed. She was trusting me, and I appreciated it.

I followed, pulling on a pair of jeans that she had selected that actually fit well enough that I didn't need my belt. They hung low on my hips but were in no danger of falling off so I shrugged and led the way back to the kitchen.

"Red or white?" I asked as I pulled a couple of bottles of wine and some glasses out.

"White." She had taken her seat at the table again, arms crossed protectively over her and I could almost see worry radiating off of her like a cloud. I could smell it, actually, her anxiety perfuming the air with a sharp, almost bitter, tang.

"Chloe? Look at me?" I pleaded and she reluctantly met my eyes. "You aren't hurt. You aren't in danger of becoming like me, if that's what you're worried about." I pulled the cork from the bottle and poured her a generous glass which I set in front of her. Her shoulders dropped and she looked so torn. I poured myself a glass and turned, my back against the counter and my arms crossed over my chest, glass dangling from my fingers.

"One thing you have to understand about wolf-kind is that it's almost like dealing with a split personality."

She arched an eyebrow at me in the middle of taking a sip of her wine. She swallowed and set the glass down. "So you're saying that you're crazy?" she asked, cautiously and I sighed and shook my head.

"No, nothing like that. Nothing quite that simple. I'm human, right?" She arched an eyebrow again and pursed her lips thoughtfully, I could see the struggle on her face, the hurt, the fear that she would hurt *me*; it made me smile. I made the concession for her, "Okay, human-*ish*. My point is that I have thoughts... feelings and desires as a man. I like art, I like food and cooking. I enjoy music and reading and I have hobbies.

"But I'm also part animal," I said soberly, "And animals operate largely on instinct. It's something passed down from generation to generation. Each animal instinctively knows things without having to be told or shown how to do them. Birds, for example. Birds know to fly south for the winter and bears, bears know when it's time to hibernate. Wolves know things too. The wolf inside me, the wolf that is a part of me, knows things about the world around me and the people that I meet that I, as a man, don't consciously know or even understand."

"Okay, so you've got a hyperactive sixth sense."

"So to speak, yes." I took a deep breath and then a large gulp of my wine. "One of those things the wolf looks for in people, is potential for a mate, that's what the bite is about."

She looked even more confused. "So, what? You bite every girl you sleep with?"

I shook my head, my still damp hair flopping into my eyes until I brushed it irritably away. "No, that's not what I mean. Sex is one thing. I'm human, humans have sex. It's one of the things we greatly enjoy as a species. And humans also get jealous, and territorial, like wolves do. Especially about their boyfriend or their girlfriend."

"So what are you trying to get at?"

I sighed again and ran my hands through my hair. There was nothing for it but to say it flat out. "The wolf in me recognizes something in you. Strength, character, will, *something* and he feels that you would make a good mate for me. That's what the bite is. If I break the skin, if I leave a scar, that's the equivalent of asking for your hand, hell, of taking you to Vegas and sealing the deal. It marks you, telling others of my kind that you're my mate. And wolves mate for life."

Chapter 12
Chloe

I opened my mouth and closed it, opened it again, drew breath to speak then closed it again. William held my gaze across the short expanse between us as he leaned against the counter. His deep brown eyes with their gorgeous amber sparks were dim with almost sorrow. I bit my lips together and looked away because I couldn't stand to see that look in his eyes. Here he was, telling me the truth, knowing how overwhelming it would be, how frightening, but telling it anyways. Because I'd begged him to never lie to me, no matter how bad it got.

Holy. Shit.

"I... I don't really know what to say to that," I told him and when I looked, his head was turned, eyes trained intently at the top of the steps leading down to his work shop.

"Shhh," he set down his wine glass.

"Wow, okay, I'm sorry you just told me some really heavy shit, I'm just trying to process..."

"Chloe it's not you, now hush! Someone is coming," he said. I straightened and moved to stand up but he waved me back down into my seat.

"Is it the twins?" I asked fearfully. I *really* didn't want to deal with those assholes again.

"William?" a deep voice beckoned from downstairs. William's shoulders dropped, the tension easing out of the muscles in his back.

"Yeah, we're up here Markus!" William called down the stairs.

A man, who appeared to be in his mid-forties, military style haircut going gray at the temples, appeared at the top of the stairs. He wore a green flannel shirt, white crewneck tee peeking out at the collar, tucked into dark blue jeans. A brown belt with a leather-man tool case on it, along with a matching pair of laced up work boots completed his look.

He filled out his clothing nicely, for his age, with plenty of muscle, and he looked me over just as I was looking over him when a feminine voice piped up behind him, "It smells like sex up here."

"Oh, that's just fucking great," I muttered and felt my face take off flaming to match my damned hair. How could they smell it with the bedroom so damn far away and behind a closed door? William laughed which just pissed me off more. I gave him a tight-lipped smile and flipped him off, that just made him laugh harder.

The military man raised an eyebrow at our exchange and stepped aside to let four others come up the stairs.

"You sleeping with the enemy now, Son?" he asked William, but he was clearly sizing me up. There was no hostility in his tone, he just struck me as one of those kind of guys who spoke what was on his mind and fuck whoever got offended. That it was their problem and not his. I suddenly felt way underdressed in just William's tee under the man's scrutiny but I would be damned if I would let this guy's sizing me up get the better of me. I ignored him and turned my attention to the rest of the crew that'd followed him up the stairs.

There were two women and two more men. One woman looked like a librarian of all things. Prim, pressed slacks, and a floral blouse with a light blue cardigan sweater over it. She even had on the little old lady slip on shoes to complete the look. She wasn't old, maybe early fifties with short, graying hair styled in a cute pixie cut. She wore gold earrings and a gold crucifix necklace, a wedding set on her left hand. Everything about her screamed 'good Christian woman' right down to the disapproving glare she had fixed on me.

"What?" I asked her softly taken aback a little by her intense stare. Where the other guy was curious, she was downright hostile. She growled at me, like a full on growl that would come out of a dog, well, wolf. Like human vocal chords shouldn't be capable of making that sound.

Military man Markus and William stood their ground, unphased by the display. But the others? They all shifted on their feet, nervousness flickering in their eyes, across their faces, like lightning over the city. I stared at her, taking my cue from William and didn't let the display phase me. I'd be lying if I said it didn't though. My heart picked up pace and my mouth went a little dry.

"Sharon!" Military man barked, "Calm your shit, woman."

The librarian lady's growling ceased as if by a flick of a switch. It just stopped, gone, and the uneasy silence that rushed in to take its place was damned uncomfortable. I got to my feet, slowly and William held out his hand to me. I took it and he towed me in front of him and put his arms around me.

I got the distinct feeling from the surprised and incredulous looks on their faces that he was calmly staring them down over my head. The librarian lady, Sharon, scoffed, making a rude, disgusted sound and looked away from us and I sighed inwardly.

"Nice to meet you too," I murmured and William's hold on me tightened.

"Chloe," he said calmly, an edge of warning to his voice, but I was done. I had nothing else I could say. It struck me then. Came down on me like a ton of bricks, and fuck what these people thought of it but tears sprang to my eyes. I forced them down. Didn't let them spill over but... Shit.

I very highly doubted I would ever be able to go home. My father, like his daughter, wasn't exactly the forgiving sort. But, neither were these people. Even if I did find that I maybe was starting to fall in love with William, this, *this* is what we would get. Disgusted looks. Rude noises and people turning away.

"It's not my fault my dad's been running around my whole life acting like some racist hillbilly piece of shit," I said quietly and I shrugged gently out of William's embrace. Five sets of curious eyes and one sorrowful one followed me as I stepped up to the Military Man, Markus. I stuck out my hand.

"Chloe, Chloe Young," I introduced myself.

"Markus," he said, taking my hand in his much larger, much warmer one. "Markus Lance, I'm Arbiter of the Pacific North West Pack," he said.

"I'm a... I mean, I *was* a law student. Now I guess I'm just a Hunter's daughter." I sighed, "Sorry," I added for Sharon's benefit.

Her brow crushed down in confusion as she looked me over. She wasn't giving an inch, but it wasn't like I knew her story, so who was I to judge? I was just going to leave all that up to her. I didn't have the energy.

I shook the hands of the rest behind Markus. There was Brent, who looked like he was seventeen and belonged behind the counter of a record store. Then there was Dave, who was wearing a mechanic's grease stained shirt. He looked to be in his late twenties with his deep brown hair under a baseball cap. Finally there was Nora. Nora was a Goth girl and Brent's fraternal twin sister. I raised an eyebrow at William at that and he just smiled like a sphinx.

"It's nice to meet you all," I said after all the introductions had been made. Well, except for Sharon, but I wasn't about to say that out loud. I went back to William who placed his hands on my shoulders, kneading between them gently which did nothing to dissipate my nerves.

"Really William? A *Hunter?*" Sharon asked after a protracted silence. The others with her turned and the looks weren't all entirely friendly.

"A Hunter's *daughter*," William snapped. "Who had no idea what her father really was or what he did."

"How about we all just have a sit and let William explain? How does that sound?" Markus said and it was probably the most reasonable suggestion made thus far, except for it wasn't exactly a suggestion. Not the way he said it. Nope, no and no. Though he spoke the words the tone he used made me want to snap to attention and be the first person with their ass planted in a seat, listening attentively.

I let William guide me to the large living room with a couch and some recliners, easily able to seat a dozen comfortably. He dropped down onto one end of the couch and pulled me into his lap. I went gratefully, folding myself against him. He wrapped one arm around my waist, the other he settled across the tops of my thighs, palming the outside of my right one, squeezing gently, a reassuring touch. I soaked in his warmth and resisted the urge to kiss him.

I felt calmer, when he held me like this. It felt like, in such a short time, William had become my only constant, my only shelter while the whole world went topsy-turvy around me. He spoke and the people around us listened. Expressions went from curious, to somber, to outraged, to grim.

"She's The Hangman's *daughter*. Do you honestly expect anyone to believe her?" Sharon asked disgusted after he finished explaining how I got my dad to cop to killing their Alpha. I perked up slightly when she called him the Hangman. What was that about? Now obviously wasn't the time to ask but I made a mental note to grill William about it later.

"Do *you*?" I asked her, meeting her light hazel eyes with my own.

She huffed out a sigh, "Yes," she growled as if it was the most painful thing she had ever been forced to admit. "I don't smell any lie coming off of you. I always knew that Romulus and Remus were power hungry, but *patricide*? I never thought they would go that far."

"Trouble is proving it. Chloe's word isn't going to be enough." Markus rubbed his chin thoughtfully, "There's a lot of support for Romulus becoming Alpha, Boy. He's strong, he has his brother for Beta and Lucinda–" Nora scoffed and turned her head to the side, staring out the window into the dark.

"That power hungry cunt," she said bitterly.

Okay. No love lost there, obviously. Sharon looked Nora over and nodded her agreement with the assessment.

"That may be, but I don't see any other female Pack member challenging her for Alpha Bitch," Markus remarked dryly. William pulled me down to him, placing his lips against my temple, he closed his eyes and breathed me in for a moment, pressing a kiss to the side of my head before letting me straighten again.

Everyone present stared at him with gross fascination which made me blush hotly. I mean, they were *really* staring, like we'd just done a new and interesting trick.

"Pack meets tomorrow. Unofficial like, the full moon ain't until two weeks from now. Best shot you have at swaying them for the Full Moon Council is then. After that it's up to the Pack as a whole."

"I don't like this," I whispered and searched William's face.

"Don't have to like it, Darlin'. This is just how it is," Markus remarked. I nodded silently. I mean, what could I say? This was William's world, and while I'd been forced to leave mine behind, there was no telling where my future was going to lie, not now. I certainly didn't have a place here.

"Any idea who else might still be in my camp?" William was asking, but my eyes were skating across the mistrustful looks that were being cast in my direction.

Markus was in the middle of speaking when I suddenly got to my feet and William let me, slightly surprised by my leaving his embrace. "Excuse me please," I said politely, "I have a lot to think about." I left them to their wolf-kind political machinations and slipped through the door and into the Library.

I didn't know where else to go. Behind me I heard Nora hissing quietly, probably to Brent, "William doesn't let anyone in there."

"Don't exaggerate," William chided her and their voices faded to a muted background noise as I climbed the stairs to the tower. "No wonder he's in such good shape," I muttered. "These stairs'll kill yah if you don't get stronger."

I climbed up on the bed and hugged a pillow to my chest and stared off into space. From the foot of the bed, half way between me and the far wall stood a large telescope pointing up at the blank, windowless ceiling. I looked around for a moment but I didn't see any windows of a size that would make a telescope useful up here when my eye landed on a length of chain hanging from the ceiling. It was a pull system. The chain ran around a wheel set into the floor and up to the ceiling above. A tug on one side of the chain revealed nothing so I pulled on the other and gasped as a crack appeared in the roof. I pulled again, and kept pulling, hand over hand as the roof slid back almost silently on a hidden track until it was a wide opened door, revealing the night sky in all its brilliance. The true purpose of the tower finally becoming clear.

It was an observatory.

With the roof opened up, the air coming in was a bit chilled so I sat on the edge of the bed and wrapped myself in a blanket, unwilling to close off the view yet. I thought about a lot of things. My dad, William, his Pack, my life up to this point, and what would happen after tomorrow... still, what hit me hardest, I mean literally right between the eyes was the fact that the only thing left out of all that damn thinking to make me tear up, to make me want to sob like a little girl, was the thought of leaving William.

My tears did spill over then, hot and salty slick down my face and though I didn't make a sound, William was there, kneeling by the bed, his warm gaze so full of tenderness pinning mine in place. Cool moonlight washed over us, drenching everything in a liquid silver radiance. He sighed and raked his hands through his hair, holding it back from his face, to the back of his neck. He bowed his head, pulling on his neck with his hands to ease the tension there as he huffed out a frustrated sigh. I reached out and cupped the side of his face with my hand and he looked up.

"Just make me forget for a little while... I'm so tired and I don't want to think about anything but you. Fuck those people. Fuck your brothers, and my father, and this whole screwed up mess, just for a couple of hours," I said and sniffed.

William closed his eyes and pressed his palm to the back of my hand. He turned his head, pressing his lips into my palm, breathing me in and nodded as if he had made some kind of decision. He pressed a kiss to my palm again, once, twice, and drew back to look at me.

"Okay, Sugar. I can do that," he said, voice gentle yet low and intense. He stood and discarded his jeans, the moonlight causing deep shadows to play across the lines of his body. I set the pillow aside and he gripped the hem of his tee, whisking it off over my head, leaving us both completely naked.

"Lay on your stomach," he commanded softly and I was so tired, I didn't argue. I lay on my stomach and William straddled the backs of my thighs. He pressed his palms into my back and applied gentle pressure until the bones popped quietly into place and the muscles gave a delicious little stretch that had me sighing out, groaning in relief. The heat of his body against mine and the cool breeze blowing across our flesh created a sensational counterpoint that put my body into a relaxed and floating state of euphoria.

"I'm so sorry, Chloe..."

"I don't want to talk about it, William," I said and winced at how sharp it sounded, "Please, it will be there tomorrow. I just want this, right here and now, with you. Just you, just me, no more visitors or guests. Can I please just have that?" I asked and I hated how I sounded like I was begging.

"They're gone, Sugar," he bent over me and planted a gentle kiss to the back of my shoulder, "It's just you and me."

I closed my eyes and relaxed under the heat of his body against mine, protected, safe in his embrace. I was mentally and emotionally exhausted and I knew it. William did too I think. He massaged my back until I was limp and almost drowsing beneath him before he nudged my legs apart with one knee.

I went to push myself up, but a gentle palm between my shoulder blades pressed me back to the mattress. He leaned over the top of me and sought my entrance with the head of his cock. I was more than ready to have him inside me. I ached for it, I wanted nothing more than to be as close to him as possible. I was well aware that these stolen moments were growing fewer and that I may not be able to stay with him or him with me. The future was such a convoluted mess of secret organizations, political dealings and an utter cluster fuck of race wars... God! I resolutely shoved those thoughts from my mind as William slid into me, making me groan, my hips raising off the bed ever so slightly to meet his gentle thrust. And there it was. With William inside me we were very nearly as physically close as it was possible for two people to be. And I needed that. I needed to feel close to him to feel filled by him.

His palms found the backs of my hands, his fingers laced between mine and he held them to the mattress and let his hips do all the work.

"William!" His name spilled from my lips, an impassioned plea for him to never let me go and he moaned, a tortured indecisive sound. I cried out, "Oh!" as he rode over that sensitive place inside me, his thrusting causing just the right amount of friction against that sensitive bundle of nerves against the covers.

My body grew weighted with that sense of impending orgasm and I squeezed my pussy tight, down around him. William gasped and bit the back of my shoulder sending a jolting little thrill through my body.

"Oh God! Oh Yes!" I gasped desperately. I wanted him to. I could deal with forever tomorrow, but I wanted him to so badly. He growled, a passion filled, yet frustrated sound and I bit my bottom lip.

"Please? Oh God, please William!" He bit down harder and I screamed as the wave of orgasm swamped me, pulling me under, rolling me so completely that up became down, left became right, and night became day, as wild starbursts of white hot light went off behind my tightly shut eyelids.

I lay panting on my stomach, William a warm weight pressing me into the covers. He groaned and rolled off to the side of me, slipping from my body. I pushed myself into a sitting position slowly, my left shoulder where it curved up into my neck giving an angry throb. I looked at William who was looking at me, deathly pale. Panic in his eyes, a dot of crimson on his bottom lip. I touched my shoulder and neck and looked at my fingertips which were stained with a bit more of my blood.

"Oh shit, oh Chloe…" he looked so afraid and I didn't want him to be, I wanted him to know that I accepted this. I understood, I looked at William who looked at me with an expression that was half drunk and half dazed. I scooted across the bed closer to him, and reached for him, capturing his face between my hands.

I kissed him then and sweet copper pennies exploded across my tongue. Beneath that, the pure masculine taste of William. He froze for a moment then crushed me to him as I kissed my hearts blood from his lips and drank his insecurities. I loved him. It was terrifying and things were so uncertain and I quailed when it came to saying the words aloud and so I let my body do the talking. It could speak for me when I feared my voice would only betray me. I was so afraid, afraid for William, for myself, and for what all of this would mean and I didn't want him to think I feared him. Because I didn't. Because I couldn't. Because there, bathed in moonlight and held in his embrace I knew that I loved him, and I didn't even know how it'd happened.

CHAPTER 13

William

I'm sure my eyes were ridiculously wide. They certainly felt like it. My heart was pounding so hard and so fast in my chest that I couldn't get my breath. I felt like I was having a heart attack. *Could I even have a heart attack? Was that even possible for one of us? A stroke perhaps?*

Then she kissed me, and some of the terror fled from my body. There was a fervent desire in her kiss. A passion that hadn't been as prominent before. She was always passionate, but that kiss just seemed different, stronger, more sure than any before it.

We made love again and after, she fell asleep, tangled in my arms with her head resting comfortably on my chest, the blankets drawn over us to ward off the chill. I had tried to get up to close the ceiling but she had refused, watching the stars from her place on my chest until her eyes had grown too heavy and she'd fallen asleep. I'd found sleep to be a far more elusive thing. Wolf-kind mating with a person still human wasn't *unheard of*. It just wasn't exceptionally common. But still, it *did* happen. The problem was, I honestly hadn't paid that much attention when the Betas went over the lessons on the mating bite. I needed to talk to someone. I was going to lose my mind if I didn't, and so I carefully extracted myself from beneath Chloe.

Dressing silently by the light of the moon, I quietly closed the ceiling to make sure she would be warm enough, before I headed for the stairs and padded down them as silently as I could. I really needed to make a call and I didn't want to wake her. I slipped through the house, bare feet silent on the carpet leading to the stairs by the kitchen that led down to my first floor workshop. I stepped into a pair of my steel toed work boots at the bottom of the steps before I stepped out onto the concrete floor. With a flip of a switch the lights came on, glinting cold and bright off of various bits of metal. I pulled my cell phone from my pocket and hit a single speed dial number. The phone rang and I bounced nervously on my toes while I waited.

"Come on, come on, come on, you cantankerous old bastard. Answer your fucking phone. Please."

"I picked up five seconds ago, Pup. Cantankerous?"

I couldn't help but grin. "I noticed you don't question 'old' or 'bastard'."

"Can't question what's true," he laughed. "It is two in the morning though, Son. What's the problem?"

"I need to talk to you, Markus."

"I gathered as much, thought that was why we were on the horn."

"No, not on the phone. In person."

He sighed, not exactly upset but I could tell he had other things on his mind.

"All right. Head on over and–"

"No," I cut him off. "Sorry, Markus. Could you come here? I don't trust the twins or any of their supporters, I don't want to leave Chloe alone if I can help it."

There was silence for a few moments and I fidgeted anxiously, shifting my weight from foot to foot. Back and forth, back and forth, back and forth. Markus always had a way of making me feel like a little kid being sent to the principal's office at school and his weighted silence on the other end of the line was no exception here. I couldn't fault him for it. It was just in his nature.

"I'll bring the beer," he said finally.

"I have the troubles," I said, tone weighted with guilt, heavy with regret.

"See you in fifteen, Pup."

I hung up and went about straightening up my work shop. It was already neat and orderly with a damned near military precision, but the whole place needed dusting. My cleaning service might have done an excellent job with my living space upstairs but they were under very strict orders not to touch my workshop, so for the last two weeks it had simply been collecting dust while I was gone on my cross country kidnapping expedition.

True to his word, fifteen minutes, almost precisely, after he hung up I heard the crunch of gravel under tires outside and the telltale glow of headlights under the crack in the front door. I pulled the door open before he could knock and beckoned for the old wolf to come in.

"Thanks Markus," I muttered and he nodded once before he pulled a Coors from the case he held in one hand and held it out. I took the beer and he set the case down on the work table nearest the door, giving my tree an appraising look.

"Another week?" he asked with a jerk of his head toward the monstrosity.

"'Bout that, if I get a chance to just sit and work without all the chaos."

"Can't count on that, Son, you'd better be prepared to work when you can around everything else, structure things so you've got the most opportunity possibly. Did you never pay attention to anything I taught you?" his words were reprimanding but his tone was gentle. Markus had been there my entire life since becoming wolf-kind. He was as close to an uncle as I had after my family died and now Father…

"What's got you so anxious, Son?" he asked. "I ain't seen you so nervous since you asked Nora out twenty or thirty years ago."

I winced at the memory. "Yeah, I don't really remember asking her out. I was pretty drunk. But I do remember her kicking the ever loving shit out of me for my efforts."

Markus cracked open a beer and chugged down half of it in a single go before he set it down and grinned at me.

"Yeah, we had a few bets going on how many of your bones she was going to break," he said with a laugh and I glared at him. "Anyways, quit stalling, Boy. What'd you drag me out here for?"

I looked at the still unopened beer in my hands, turning it slowly round and round in my fingers. 'The Silver Bullet' it read on the side. Ironic. I cracked the can open, shaking a bit of foam off of my fingers and looked directly at Markus.

"Is the wolf ever wrong?" I asked. He arched an eyebrow at me and considered that for a moment while I chugged down some of my beer.

"Wrong how? About what?"

"About a mate?"

Both eyebrows went up this time, climbing toward his hairline in record time until he had the most gob-smacked expression on his face that I think I'd ever seen on him.

"You didn't?" he almost whispered. I didn't say anything, just stared down at the can clasped tightly between my hands.

He blew out a breath and leaned back against the table, grabbing another beer out of the case both for me and for himself even though neither of us had finished our first can yet.

We chugged back the last of our beers and cracked open the second can as he crossed his arms over his chest and scowled at the floor in fierce contemplation. I drank my beer and waited as patiently as possible for him to finish his thought.

"Ever hear, 'the heart wants what the heart wants', Boy?" Markus shook his head. "Our hearts are wild, our hearts are our wolf. You can't argue with them, you can't reason with them, and you usually shouldn't try, they really *do* know best."

I sagged with a sense of relief that was painfully short lived as he took another long swig of his beer and continued talking.

"That being said, just because the wolf wants a certain woman, doesn't mean that it's going to work out. That's why we're so careful about choosing a mate. And if she's wolf-kind, well that just makes it easier."

"How do you mean?"

"The problem with marking a human is they don't have the wolf to tell them if they find you a suitable mate. Yeah, your wolf recognizes that she would make a fine mate for *you*, but what if her wolf, theoretically, doesn't feel that *you* would be a good mate for *her*?"

I was getting confused, I'll admit. "But she doesn't have a wolf..."

"Exactly my point. Would you let her stay that way? Would you want her to? Would she? If she doesn't become wolf-kind now then you're in for a world of hurt, Son. Wolves mate for life, you know that. If she stays human you'll outlive her by a fair stretch. Eventually she'll start to look like your mom, then your grand-mom, then she'll die of old age and you'll look like you're in your thirties at best.

"And since she *doesn't* have a wolf, we don't know how she thinks of you in the end. If she were to mark you too, that would be ideal, but she doesn't have a wolf, no mark from her would be taken seriously at this point." He chugged back some more of his beer. "And did you even stop to consider the *political* ramifications right now?"

"Political… what?" my head was spinning. I really wished I had paid more attention when this was explained to me years ago.

Markus tossed aside his empty can and came over to put his hands on my shoulders. "William, look at me." I met his eyes, fearfully I must admit. "You're angling to become the new *Alpha*. Personally, I think it's a brilliant idea, especially over either of those brothers of yers. But what do you think this decision, this action will mean to the rest of the Pack?"

I felt a stab of anger at that. "And what, if any opinion, does the Pack think they have about my private life?"

"There's your problem, Boy. You want to be Alpha, and I agree that over the twins you're a *much* better choice, but you seem to think that you can be Alpha of the largest Pack around and still live your life the way you have been. You'll be responsible for *hundreds* of wolf-kind. Protecting our territory. Negotiating with the Alphas of other Packs." He jabbed his finger into my chest. "And if the Pack feels that you marking a human, a *Hunter's daughter especially*, is a hasty or stupid decision? Do you honestly think they'll see you as Alpha material under those circumstances?"

Oh.

"Shit," I muttered and Markus snorted out a laugh.

"Yeah, you stepped in it Sonny Jim, and it might not be an easy fix. I like your little girlie. She's got some fire in her and I can see what you like about her…" A low growl erupted from my throat before I even thought about it and he stepped back, hands held out in a warding gesture. "Hey, don't get me wrong. She's a beautiful and interesting girl but she ain't *my* type. And that's what I'm talking about. You can't have reactions like that over something as simple as someone paying your mate a compliment. You've got to learn to pick and choose your battles, Boy." I stopped growling, feeling a touch contrite for my reaction. It was definitely overkill and uncalled for. I would have to watch that, and *carefully* in the future.

"You're gonna have to prepare her, William."

"I'm not exactly sure how."

"Does she know what the mark means?"

"I explained it to her, briefly. We were talking about it just when you guys showed up here earlier."

He nodded and tossed me another beer.

"Alright," he said as he cracked open his third. "We've got a lot to discuss. First and foremost. Don't worry about if she loves you, or if the mark would be reciprocated for now. Even if it's driving you crazy, you act like it's the furthest thing from your mind, especially in front of the Pack. Pack members like Sharon won't get it. Nora might be willing to give you the benefit of the doubt, but it's hard to say, so better not chance it." He took a swig and pointed at me around the can he still held. "And you can't bring up becoming wolf-kind to her, you get me? You don't say word one to her about that."

"But–"

"Not word one. You promise me, Son. I'm speaking as Arbiter now, if that adds any weight. Trust me, you do *not* want to throw that kind of pressure on her right now."

"I promised her, and myself, that I would never lie to her."

"This is a different situation, Kid. You keep this from her and maybe she'll be mad at you later. You don't, and she feels pressure to become wolf-kind when it's not a fit for her, she learns to resent you, maybe even hate you later. Do you really want that, seeing as the deed is already done? To be mated to someone who hates you? Ain't no such thing as a divorce in our world, you know that." He set his half empty can down on my table and straightened up.

"Look. Think about it. Don't make any more rash decisions, alright? Go upstairs, get some sleep, and we'll talk more tomorrow. Got it?" I nodded, feeling miserable. I had dug myself a hole here and I didn't see any way out of it. Markus hugged me and I returned the gesture.

"Thanks Markus."

"Don't sweat it, Kid." He gestured to the cardboard case on my work table. "And you can keep the beer. Save it for later though, eh? Clear head tomorrow."

I nodded and saw him out, locking the door behind him and arming the security system. A part of me wanted to just leave the empty cans and the half empty case of beer to be dealt with tomorrow but I couldn't do it. The cans were collected, washed, and placed into recycling. I took the beer upstairs and tucked it onto a bottom shelf in my fridge.

Once that was done, I dragged myself to my bedroom. The nervous energy I had felt before gone. My arms and legs felt heavy, something I couldn't blame on only three cans of beer. It was like the crash after a rush of adrenaline. I had a *sort of* answer to the troubling questions that had been keeping me awake earlier, but I didn't really feel any better.

In fact, I think I felt worse. Guilty, in particular. Markus was right though. I couldn't remind her about how differently we would age. I couldn't bring anything like it up to her or I would be influencing her and her possible decisions and that wouldn't be fair to her or to myself in the long run. It still sucked rancid buffalo testicles, but I understood.

I sighed and dragged myself into my room to find Chloe still sound asleep in my bed where I'd left her. She had rolled onto her side beneath the blanket facing away from the door and I winced slightly, seeing the dark mark on her shoulder left by my teeth. The wound had scabbed over already, which wasn't too surprising. Wolf-kind made it, so it would heal faster than a normal bite would.

I pulled my chair over, a leather wing back that I had picked up years ago in an antique store, and sat in it near the bed. I wanted to lay down. I wanted to gather her into my arms and close my eyes and just sleep surrounded by Chloe and her smell of sun ripened peaches. But I couldn't. My body was dead tired but my brain wouldn't stop spinning. Chloe. Romulus. Remus. Mathias. Markus. The Pack. There were so many things that counted on me, so many things I needed to deal with to secure being the Alpha. And any one thing going wrong could spell disaster for all of it.

And what about the Hunters? Come to think of it, Mathias wouldn't take this lying down. He was probably chomping at the bit to get his daughter back and here she was, marked as a wolf-kind's mate. That was sure to give the man a coronary. I couldn't help but worry that it added another dimension of danger for Chloe. Hell, I knew it added more to the pile for *me*.

"Oh crap," I whispered as a sudden thought struck me. *I'm married. I'm married and my father-in-law killed my adoptive father in a conspiracy with my adopted twin brothers... This is so fucked. I* sighed and raked my fingers back through my hair. *My whole damned life is fucked up.* I groaned and Chloe stirred quietly in her sleep but quickly settled back down. My whole life was fucked up and I'd fucked hers right along with it. Selfish bastard that I am, I'd wanted her, I'd taken her and now look what I'd done to her...

I slumped in my chair and sulked for a while. I'm not afraid to admit it. I was sulking. I was in a shitty situation, partially of my own creation. But I needed to suck it up at the meeting tomorrow and pull out all the stops to win back some of the Pack, it was imperative. *More than just my immediate friends would be there and I really needed to garner some more support from the rest of the–*

I hadn't realized how tired I had really been. To fall asleep mid thought like that. When I woke I was slightly confused and a low groan slipped past my lips. My head lolled back against the chair and without realizing it my hands moved, landing on a bare pair of shoulders, swept by silky soft hair.

"God I really must have been tired," I moaned and Chloe hummed a quiet laugh, sending the most amazing vibrations through my hard cock as her mouth slid slowly up and down my length. I felt a rough spot on her skin beneath the fingers of my right hand and gently traced it, feeling the knife of guilt, of anxiety, twist in my gut a bit more.

I opened my eyes and tilted my head forward, looking down at the much healed bite mark on her shoulder, feeling once again that stab as I realized that Markus was right. I couldn't tell her anything, not right now. Not until my position was secure.

My eyes slid to hers and most of these thoughts fled my mind entirely. I could feel the head of my dick push past the back of her throat and she swallowed me almost to the root before slowly backing off. Throughout it she never broke eye contact with me and I couldn't help but feel a startling warmth and affection in her clear blue eyes. She was so fucking beautiful it slayed me.

There was a quiet popping sound as she pulled my head from her mouth and ran her tongue along the underside of my cock. I moaned again, fingers tightening slightly on her shoulders.

"Not that I'm complaining," I gasped. "But what prompted this?"

"Just something I've wanted to do," she said in between small licks of my head. "So when I woke up and saw you sitting here, instead of lying there with me, I just had to take the opportunity as it was presented." With that she slid me back into her mouth and winked. She took me in completely again, moaning slightly as she swallowed me.

Her head bobbed slowly up and down, lips and tongue building an incredible pressure along every inch of me until I was fighting back the urge to hold her head still with my hands and shove my cock down her throat. I took my hands off her shoulders, gripping the arms of my chair tightly, so tightly the wood creaked and groaned beneath my grip.

She hadn't managed to pull my sweats down very far, just enough to get her mouth on me, but I lifted my hips and she yanked my pants the rest of the way to the floor leaving them bunched at my ankles. Her breasts rubbed against my legs, soft and heavy and it drove me almost as much to distraction as her lips and tongue.

"Oh God, Chloe you have no idea how good that feels," I groaned, my voice strained. Every muscle in my body was coiled tight, trembling as she pulled back and sucked hard at my head for a moment. She wrapped her hand around me, slowly stroking my length in a firm grip that had my hips bucking instinctively against her hand.

She took her mouth off of me long enough to say, "That's the general idea, Sugar," throwing my words from our first time in my face and I couldn't help but laugh which turned to a moan, my mouth dropping open and my head falling back against the chair again.

"You need to lay on the bed, right now," I hissed, desperate to plunge into her and she shook her head. Quite the trick with more than half my length in her mouth.

She backed off, "Not a chance," and plunged me back into her hot waiting mouth to continue her assault.

I squeezed the chair arms even tighter and a loud splintering crack echoed under my right hand. "Why?" I grunted and she licked my head again before she grinned up at me.

"Because I want to make *you* feel good right now. And it's kind of fun seeing you like this," she added with a grin.

"Oh my god, you're an evil, *evil* woman."

"And you love it," she said with a smile that lit her up from the inside out. Before I could say anything else, she pursed her lips and pushed my head past them into her hot mouth. The pressure and heat forced another loud moan from me and I looked down, holding her eyes as she slowly bobbed her head up and down. With one hand she cupped my balls, massaging them gently as the other gripped my shaft beneath her lips, moving slowly, in time with her mouth.

She started slowly, her hand and mouth taking several seconds to travel my length back and forth. It didn't take her long to speed up considerably and the chair continued to suffer the abuse of my grip as my fingers tightened more and more with every passing second.

Within a few minutes I was well past the point of no return. "I'm going to come," I warned her breathlessly, but instead of pulling back she seemed to redouble her efforts. My breath burned in my throat, I couldn't keep my eyes open anymore as they slid closed completely against my will and I let out a loud, animalistic moan as that wave of pressure finally crested and spilled over.

She stopped moving, holding my head between her lips as I came, each twitch sending another shot into her warm mouth which she swallowed almost greedily and with a loud crack the right arm of my chair ripped completely off in my hand.

When I was finally able to catch my breath I dropped the useless chunk of wood and looked down at her sitting before me, licking her lips with a rather smug, rather pleased, expression on her face. Taking her hands I pulled her to her feet. I stood, and scooped her into my arms, twining her legs around my hips.

"You," I growled in a low tone, "are entirely more than I deserve!" I tossed her onto the bed and she let out a high squeal and laughed as she hit the mattress. Before she could attempt to escape I kicked my sweats away and followed her up onto the bed. Using my elbows to support my weight I settled above her and kissed her as gently as I could. She responded in kind, raising her leg to rub against my side as our lips and tongues gently caressed.

I shifted my weight and slowly guided myself into her after several minutes of kissing her and feeling her naked body against mine brought me back to a full, nearly painful, erection. As I slid home she moaned quietly and her eyes drifted shut. I kissed along her throat, enjoying the same flush on her neck and chest that I saw that very first night, her fair skin admirably showing her arousal, as if my nose hadn't already told me the same.

I wanted to say it.

With every slow thrust into her the words trembled in my mind.

I love you.

Three simple words with infinite reach and meaning under normal circumstances. Given our situation though, those three words meant far more than most would *ever* understand. I held them back though. Whispering in her ear how beautiful she was to me, how amazing she felt against me, around me... Our bodies fit perfectly together, her small frame melding against my larger build as her hips began to move to meet mine with every thrust. Her legs wrapped around my hips, heels digging into my ass, as if trying to pull me ever deeper inside her and I fucking loved it.

When her orgasm hit, she cried out, her voice echoing loudly throughout my home and I joined her, growling in deep satisfaction, low in my chest as I emptied myself a second time inside her.

"Is it because you're wolf-kind?" she asked some time later. I was lying on my back in the bed, one hand behind my head while my other arm was wrapped around her as she pressed herself against my side.

"What? I mean, is what because I'm wolf-kind?" I asked, a little drowsy.

"Is sex with you so completely incredible because you're wolf-kind? Like is that a normal thing for your people?"

I chuckled quietly. "I couldn't say, wolf-kind don't tend to openly discuss the finer points of our physical relationships any more than normal humans do."

"So it's just you then?" I turned my head and kissed her hair, just above her forehead.

"Or it's just you. You must bring out the best in me."

She snorted out a laugh and sat up. I immediately felt a sense of loss as she moved away from me, but shoved it away to admire her body as she reached into the air with her fingers laced together and stretched as far as she could. Not for the first time I worried she was too thin.

"Okay," I groaned. "You need to put some clothes on or I might not be able to control myself around you." She gave me a smug smile and arched a single brow questioningly at me.

"I'm hungry and I'm sure you have questions. Let's get some food in us and sate that curiosity of yours as best we can, shall we?" I suggested.

She laughed but moved to comply, dressing again in one of my tee shirts. She almost disappeared in the thing she was so tiny, but I thought it looked so hot on her.

I pushed the thought aside though and pulled on a pair of sweats myself and led the way back to the kitchen. A glance at the clock told me it was nearly noon so I threw together a light stir fry while she sat at the table and watched, a small smile curving her lips.

"What?" I asked as I set a plate in front of her.

She laughed again and waved one hand in a dismissive gesture. "It's nothing," she said. "It's just interesting seeing you in your natural environment." She laughed again at the confused look I gave her but I shrugged it off and served myself a plate.

She stuck her tongue out at me and asked, "Don't you watch Animal Planet?" I smiled and shook my head, "National Geographic?" she asked innocently. I laughed, ignoring her playful jibes.

"So," I said as I sat down across from her. "Questions?"

She thought about it for a moment, eating quietly with no trace of the humor she'd been so filled with just moments before and I felt a pang at the thought that I had helped bring her down from her joyful mood.

"Okay, first of all, I've got to ask. Why weren't you in bed with me this morning?" she fixed me with a worried and somber gaze, insecurity wrapping her like a cloak. I knelt by her chair and sighed.

"You're fine," I told her, "I couldn't sleep. I didn't want to wake you with all my fidgeting, so I got up and puttered around downstairs, when I came back you were sleeping so peaceful I just wanted to sit and watch you for a minute. I just fell asleep." I cupped her face, fingers curving around to the back of her neck and drew her down so I could kiss her forehead. Her eyes drifted shut and she nodded faintly against my lips.

She looked at me and I smiled, feeling like a total tool for lying to her, for breaking my promise. I got up and returned to my seat and we ate for a few minutes in silence.

"Okay, so how does this wolf-kind thing work?" she asked.

Not a vague question at all. I swallowed the food in my mouth and gave her a look. "How so?"

"Well, to start with, where does it come from? How do you guys change? What started it? Was it like a curse or something or..." She trailed off with a helpless shrug and I nodded, finally getting her question.

"You mean origins? How did the species start?"

She nodded, I frowned, and thought about that for a minute. Honestly that was a difficult question.

"There isn't much that's known, really. I mean with proof to back it up at least. There are myths and legends about people that could change into animals in almost every culture. In Greek mythology there was a story about a man who invited the Gods to dinner but he served them human flesh and Zeus cursed him for it. His name was Lycaon, or something like that. So theoretically he would have been the first werewolf.

"Stories exist everywhere, but they're mostly just that, stories. Every story, every myth, has a little truth in it though, at least according to common understanding. The little I know, however, describes things more spiritually."

"Spiritually?"

"Yep, spiritually," I said with a nod. "As the story goes our ability to change into the wolf is because of a link to a wolf spirit. Like a guardian. I don't get it. I didn't much study it. It's almost like a religious belief system to some wolf-kind, but I never cared much one way or the other why. We can, the biology is what it is and knowing why won't make any difference in it." I shrugged, feeling somewhat lacking in my explanation but not knowing what else I could really tell her.

"If you really want to learn more you could ask Markus about it. He's the resident expert amongst the people I know on the subject of our origins as wolf-kind. He's kind of a history buff."

"I think I'll do that. He's going to be at this meeting tonight, right?"

"Yeah, as Arbiter he's required to attend any gathering such as this. Even informal ones where conversation will include matters that would affect the Pack as a whole."

She raised another eyebrow at me. "And yes, people do, at times, lie about what a gathering is for so he doesn't attend every single such meeting," I admitted, "But in our case we're trying to keep things as transparent and above board as we possibly can. It wouldn't do for an Alpha candidate to be seen behaving in an underhanded manner."

"Think that's stopped either of the twins?"

"Touché."

As I was cleaning up the dishes there was a loud pounding on the door downstairs and Chloe jumped in her seat.

"It's just Markus," I reassured her. "We need to talk before we head to the meeting."

"I'll go grab a shower and get dressed then."

I nodded, distracted a bit, as she slipped across the living room, through the door that would lead back up to my bedroom. Footsteps on the stairs leading down to my workshop told me who was there. I distinctly recognized Markus' heavy step followed by Nora and Sharon. I didn't immediately recognize the fourth until they crested the top of the stairs and came out into the kitchen.

"Tell me again why it was that you insisted on setting up your house so your guests had to climb a flight of stairs to get to the living area?"

"Losing strength in your old age?" I asked Nora's twin. Brent laughed as he flipped me off. "It was keep the workspace downstairs or be concerned about getting my sculptures out of the building without cutting a hole in the roof or floor."

He shrugged and pulled the half gone case of beer from that early morning talk with Markus out of the fridge, he may look seventeen, but we all knew better. He tossed a can to everyone except Sharon who turned up her nose at it and they all cracked them open.

Markus was in the middle of telling me who we expected to see at that night's meeting when Sharon suddenly let out a shrill shriek that had my ears ringing and caused Nora to drop her beer entirely in favor of wrapping her arms around her head in a vain effort to block out the sound.

We all looked to Sharon, took in the gob-smacked, horrified expression on her face and the direction her raised arm was pointing and turned to look at what had caused such an uncontrolled reaction from the normally reserved woman.

Chloe had just rounded the corner into the kitchen, she was wearing a spaghetti strapped baby doll camisole over a pair of snug fitting jeans, a hooded sweatshirt dangling from her fingers. The bite on her shoulder stood out sharply against her skin. Still healing faster than it should have by human standards. It was a dark scab that looked a day or two old on the smooth pale canvas of her skin and easily visible, even to those without supernaturally enhanced senses.

"Have you completely lost your fucking mind?" Sharon cried. I turned to her, a frown beginning to crease my brow. Just as I completed the turn, her hand struck. The slap landed solidly against my left cheek, so hard that I was thrown to the side and staggered to keep my feet under me.

"Hey!" Chloe barked but we ignored her for the time being.

"You're looking to gain position as the Alpha of this Pack and you would go and claim a fucking *Hunter's bitch* as your mate? Seriously? On the eve of the most *important* Pack meeting to get you there?" She pulled her arm back to slap me again and as she let fly a hand flashed into view and grabbed her upper arm, hooking her back like a performer on a vaudeville stage so hard, that she almost came off her feet entirely.

She growled, the inhuman growl that tells someone when a wolf-kind is really annoyed and turned, her teeth bared in a vicious snarl to find herself face to chest with Markus.

"You know exactly where you can shove that kind of bullshit Sharon. What happened to you is no excuse to take your anger out on a girl that hasn't done nothing to deserve it. So if you can't keep that in mind, then you are more than welcome to take your ass somewhere else. This Pack doesn't need people like you in it if yer gonna harbor that kind of attitude. That's a Hunter's attitude, a different Pack's attitude... not this one's."

I blinked as Markus concluded his speech and I realized that Chloe was standing next to me, her mouth pursed into a grim flat line, hands balled into fists at her side. Her back was straight, shoulders back, proudly baring the mark on her skin for everyone to see. It definitely gave me a strong sense of pride for a moment before I had to fight back the overwhelming sense of guilt that still lurked behind everything else.

"You have no idea how much trouble this is going to cause! You're a fool William Reese. And I for one, don't want a fool leading this Pack!" Sharon snarled. She glared at me for a moment before she yanked her arm out of Markus' grip and stalked her way back down the stairs. Nora glanced up from where she was in the process of cleaning up the beer she had dropped and stuck her tongue out at the matronly woman's retreating back.

"That's not going to go over well," Markus muttered quietly, even though he knew damned well that everyone in the room would be able to hear him.

"She's got a lot of pull," I agreed. "But we can't worry too much about her. There are a lot of other, more important things, to worry about. She's angry and bitter and I get it, I won't take it personally. But if she tries that again I *will* drop her, I don't care if she *is* one of our Betas."

I could almost see Chloe's ears perk up at that and I turned my head slightly toward her. "Yes, there are Pack Betas as well, male and female. I'll explain their positions in the Pack structure a little later."

She nodded and I turned my attention back to Markus. He was giving me a considering look and finally nodded, "Can't drop her 'til yer Alpha boy," he reminded me.

"I don't think she'll do much," Nora spoke up to fill the ensuing uneasy silence. She tossed the last of the paper towels into the small trash can I kept under the sink and pushed the door shut with her knee, before she turned and leaned against the counter with her arms crossed beneath her breasts. "Sharon's bark is far worse than her bite, no pun intended. She's surprised and upset."

"And it's none of her damned business who I choose as a mate," I muttered darkly.

"It is when you remember what she went through." Brent reminded us.

"What happened to her?" Chloe asked hesitantly, but curious enough for that to override her caution. We all exchanged looks and in the end they all ended up staring at me.

"It's not my story to tell, Chloe," I said gently, "It really isn't. So if you really want details you'll have to ask Sharon yourself. She's one of the oldest members of the Pack, age wise, not as in actual membership. She's been around the block a number of times. But of all the wolf-kind that I've met, she has, by far, the strongest hatred for Hunters…"

Most of the time the Hunters just hunt to kill us. But occasionally they decide that they need to study us and every now and again one of us will be taken captive. Sharon was held for six months by men that saw her at best as an animal, and at worst as a monster as they pulled 'scientific' experiments on her. Science experiments on level with the type of shit Joseph Mengele pulled during the holocaust. It really wasn't my story to tell. It was Sharon's own personal hell.

Markus sighed, "Don't think too badly of her," he urged Chloe, "She's had a hard time of things and it's just going to be difficult for her to accept you with our boy here."

I glanced at my watch. The meeting was supposed to start at five. It would be dark right about that time as well. "Come on, guys. We've gotta get moving or we're going to be late. It'll be dark soon."

I ran upstairs and changed while the others waited. When I returned, we filed down the stairs and out the front door as one. As far as meeting spaces went, there wasn't anything spectacular about this one. The Olympic National Forest had plenty of space away from prying eyes and ears. Our meeting space was a large clearing that held nearly fifty members of the local Pack comfortably. It was about a mile and a half hike in off of one of the popular trailheads.

On the drive, Markus gave us a rundown of how the night's event was supposed to go. It wasn't a meeting of my supporters as we had originally thought. Because we had been so transparent in the meeting's time, it had turned into a formal nomination of candidates for Alpha.

More than a majority, closer to seventy-five percent of the Pack, had to feel that a certain candidate was a better choice for Alpha over another. If enough of the Pack felt it, it would be communicated throughout the entire Pack. Almost like a psychic link amongst the members but more of a non-verbal language specific to wolf-kind.

"So this is your big chance to impress basically?" Chloe asked as we parked and climbed out of Markus' Jeep.

"More or less. The Alpha won't be *officially* announced until the next Full Moon but tonight will give us a very good idea of who that is going to be," I explained.

"Things sure do move fast in your world."

"Which is odd considering we live so long, eh?" I gave her a wink and led her across the parking lot to the mouth of the trailhead. It was packed with cars and my nerves started to jangle.

A mile and a half in, just off one of the trails, we reached the large clearing. Almost perfectly round, it'd been lined with torches. Two large bonfires burned in pits within the clearing, and it was filled with people that smelled strongly of wolf to my nose. I know that to Chloe it was just filled with people, many of whom were dressed in jeans and shirts even as the evening temperatures continued to drop.

"So is the entire Pack here?" Chloe asked. I was proud of her. She didn't bother to whisper, my girl was too smart for that. She crossed her arms, rubbing them slightly through the light sweatshirt she had dug out of the bag I had packed back in New York. It had only been a handful of days, but it felt as if considerably more time had passed considering everything that had happened and the long road that was still ahead of us.

"Cold?" I asked her and she shrugged.

"Maybe a little. I'm mostly just nervous about the…" she trailed off and looked around at the assembled members of the Pack. She gave me a meaningful look and I nodded.

"Try not to worry about it. We're here to meet people, so let's get to it."

She was amazing. I led Chloe from one group of people to another and every person she met she introduced herself as the Daughter of Mathias Young. Reactions ranged from shock, to curiosity, to fear, or hatred and she handled each with aplomb.

"I never knew anything about what my father has been doing, and I don't agree with it in the slightest," she was saying a few hours later. "I met Romulus and Remus though, about six to eight months ago in my father's home. They were introduced to me as Roman and Remy Dulcet, as clients of my father's accounting business."

"Names that Remus made up years ago," I pointed out for the twentieth time.

"And for good reason."

I wish I had been paying closer attention. I wish I had considered what Markus had been saying in the Jeep. This meeting was to meet the candidates for Alpha. Rom had made it pretty clear that he and Remus wanted a shot, so of course they would be here as well.

Without thinking my arm went around Chloe's waist, pulling her against me. She stiffened and let out a slight squeak as Remus rounded from behind us.

"Yeah," I said, turning to face my brother. "You wouldn't want Romulus' unstable temper to cause trouble out amongst humans. He's a danger that would just draw the Hunters' attention to us."

"Like you haven't? Kidnapping the daughter of The Hangman? Mathias Young is by far one of the most ruthless members of an already ruthless organization that have spent centuries attempting to hunt our entire species to extinction!" He raised one hand, shoving one accusing finger into my face in a perfectly dramatic display. "You're more of a danger to our Pack than anyone else and *least* fit to be the new Alpha."

"So if anyone should be the Alpha it should be you, is that right Remus?" I asked. He grinned and shook his head.

"Not me," he said. He turned to his right and pulled Romulus over to stand beside him. "Romulus. He's the strongest and he loves this Pack and its members with more passion than anyone I have ever seen–"

"And he helped orchestrate the murder of your last Alpha!" Chloe interrupted him and Romulus let out a harsh growl for a moment before he could stop himself. "I'm just a human, and worse, the daughter of a Hunter. But you all know that already. I've been saying it all night. I've admitted where I came from and that I don't know all the details around here. I don't know your laws and your culture, but it seems to me that *patricide* is probably something that would be frowned on in any culture, don't you think?" she arched one golden-red brow and stared my brother down.

"You don't know what you're talking about you little bitch!" Romulus growled and he reached out and grabbed hold of the front of her sweatshirt.

I saw his hand moving and in the same instant I responded. My arm cocked back and shot forward. His fingers closed on her zipper, just as my knuckles slammed into the side of his jaw with as much force as I could muster with being off balance like I was. All around us chaos erupted as people started yelling. Grasping hands reached for us and beneath all that a loud ripping sound echoed in my ear and I saw the manic grin that lit up Rom's bloodied face as his eyes locked on the bite, now a newly healed scar, on Chloe's' shoulder.

Damn it!

"STOP IT!" Markus bellowed and everyone froze. Silence fell over the clearing. Rom pushed himself to his feet and spat a mouthful of blood to the side before he straightened up and glared at me.

"You're going to get yourself into more trouble than you can deal with one of these days, Little Cub," he sneered at me. "You don't deserve to be the Alpha!" With that he turned and stalked away into the night outside the reach of the firelight.

The positive vibe that I had been getting from the crowd vanished rather quickly. And the smug grin that Remus gave me didn't make me feel any better about the situation.

"Something's not right here," I muttered to no one in particular ten minutes later. The meeting was beginning to break up, people starting to gather their belongings to leave.

"What is it, Son?" Markus asked.

"Rom left too easy, and Remus is still here, he looks smug too."

"So?" Markus glanced over at Remus standing a few yards away with his hands shoved in his jeans pockets. "What's that matter?"

"Have you ever seen the one of the twins without the other being nearby?" I asked. "Ever?"

Markus frowned as he considered that. "Rom is still around here somewhere. But why?"

"That's what I can't figure out. He already did enough damage pointing out that I brought a hunter's daughter– NO!" I had turned as I spoke, unconsciously looking for Chloe in the crowd and when I spotted her the entire purpose behind Remus and Romulus' lingering presence fell into place for me.

Off to my right, about twenty feet away Remus stood, watching me, an openly curious look on his face. Forty feet away, directly across the clearing from me stood Chloe next to Nora. The two were talking amiably enough and behind them, running silently on four feet came Rom in his wolf form. Not his Hybrid. I rushed forward but there was no way I would make it in time.

He leaped into the air and a low, thunderous growl echoed across the clearing. He body checked Nora in midair, sending her flying before he planted all four paws into Chloe's back and knocked her onto her stomach, his teeth flashed once, gleaming in the torchlight.

"Romulus no!" Remus shouted and Chloe screamed my name, panicked.

"*William!*" Rom's head darted forward and then reared back, his teeth stained with a splash of crimson.

The agonized scream that tore its way out of Chloe's throat reached in through my ears, past the human portion of my brain, grabbed my wolf and pulled, *hard*. I barely remember what happened next. A red film of pure rage coated my vision and the next clear memory I have was of lying in the dirt with my arms held and a heavy weight across my back.

"No, Kid, you can't do anything right now," Markus was shouting insistently in my ear. Someone was screaming over and over, a masculine counterpoint to Chloe's high shrieks and cries of pain. Took me a moment to realize it was me.

"Calm down Pup, you don't want to do this right now," Remus said. He was on my right, my arm held in a complicated hold that I couldn't pull free of. He sounded almost as stunned as the rest of the wolves standing around openmouthed.

"I'm going to kill you both, you motherfucker!" I roared in his face. He didn't even blink, taking my anger calmly.

"And you probably have every right to, but you're not going to do anything. Not right now."

Rom stood across from us, back in human form. He'd acquired a pair of pants from somewhere, thankfully. At his feet Chloe lay in a crumpled heap, sobbing, screaming from the pain. The initial bite hurt like a motherfucker. Like your blood had been replaced with acid from the sight of the wound, spreading throughout your whole body. Not everyone survived a bite to become wolf-kind...

"Chloe!" I screamed while the Pack stood around us, some of them muttered quietly, angrily, but I couldn't tell with who, Romulus or me.

Blood had already begun to pool beneath her from the deep lacerations in the shoulder opposite my bite mark. She bit down on her cries and whimpered, tears streamed down her face as her blue eyes met mine across the pine and leaf litter. The pain in those eyes, that had just hours before sparkled with her smile, fuck, it tore at me.

"Chloe!" I screamed again and struggled anew against the hold they had on me. I just managed to shake Markus loose enough that I got my arm free, twisted and punched Remus as hard as I could throwing him back and away from me. I heaved off whoever had been on my back and lurched to my feet, sprinting across the grass toward the vertical dead man I had my eyes set on. Rom simply grinned as a weight slammed into me and I was driven face first into the dirt again. Chloe screamed, her voice high and tight with fear and enough to make everyone wince at the sound.

"Shut up!" Rom yelled. He spun and one foot lashed out catching Chloe squarely in the face and sending her sprawling in the dirt, almost close enough for me to reach her.

A hand came down into my view, grabbing Chloe's sweatshirt and ripping it the rest of the way off her body, exposing the healed scar on her shoulder.

"So! Baby Brother chooses a mate," Rom said mockingly, with a heavy sneer. "And not only that, but he chooses a Hunter's bitch, I mean, bad enough to be human but one of *theirs?*" He threw back his head and laughed uproariously as the muttering spread through the crowd even louder and faster.

"I'm going to fucking kill you!" I swore and he looked down at me, disdain clear on his face.

"You can't touch her right now. I've bitten her. She's Moon Forged, and by Pack law, my progeny. She's *mine* now." He picked her unconscious body up and threw her casually over his shoulder as I started fighting against my new captors.

"I'll kill you!" I screamed.

Without a word he turned and walked away, Remus joining him with one last backward look at me, the expression on his face dispassionate but also, spooked somehow.

"Do you hear me, Romulus?" I screamed my throat raw. "Do you hear me? I'm going to fucking kill you, you motherfucker!"

* * *

A couple of hours later Markus was shaking his head at me as we stood in my shop.

"It's not good, Boy," he uttered. I could have guessed that but I grunted quietly to tell Markus I was listening.

"I'm serious!"

"I get it. Start talking and give me something I can work with. Give me some fucking options, Man, because I'll tell you, I'm really not in the fucking mood, Markus."

He grabbed me by the shoulders and pulled me away from the tree sculpture.

"A little under three hours ago you were beaten by Romulus."

"And thank you for twisting the knife," I snapped and threw down the rag in my hand.

"I'm not twisting the knife, Boy! I'm trying to explain the lay of the political land to you. Jesus! So instead of sulking like the goddamned Cub Rom is forever calling you, you might want to get your head out of your ass and try listening to me.

"Now Romulus beat you. Not physically, he outsmarted you this time around. The Pack doesn't feel very secure with the idea of you as our Alpha if you couldn't even protect your mate from your own damn brother. You should have known better than anyone what he's capable of."

I lowered my head and he stood there, pushing me up against the side of the tree.

"Look at me," he snapped. "The Pack has already decided that Rom should be the new Alpha, it's over, unless you exercise your singular right in this situation. It's your last option and it might be your only chance to get your woman back so I suggest you take it! Even if I think it's a damned fool idea." He shook his head, "I ain't blind, William. I saw the way you looked at her before you called me in a panic, you were already mated. Didn't need no bite to seal the deal."

I said nothing and after a minute he sighed and let me go. I took up the rag I had dropped and turned back to the tree, wiping away the dust that had accumulated on the surface where I needed to attach another branch for the canopy support. When I said nothing, Markus sighed again and turned away.

"Markus?" I said when he reached the door and pulled it open.

"What is it, Son?"

"I need to tell the Arbiter something."

He hesitated for a second. "Well, I *am* the Arbiter."

"I know."

"What did you need to say then?"

"I need the Arbiter to tell Romulus that I, William Reese, am issuing a formal challenge of combat for the position of Alpha of the Pacific North West Pack which holds the Washington Territory."

There was a heavy silence for a moment, and when he spoke again I could almost hear the pride in his voice through the fear.

"The challenge will commence on the next full moon, as dictated by tradition," he uttered.

"Conditions of the challenge?" I asked, to be clear.

"Winner of the challenge will become the new Alpha, barring another challenge from someone else."

"And the loser?" I just needed to hear him say it.

"The loser won't have much to worry about. You know as well as I do that to wolf-kind you haven't won a challenge if your opponent is still breathing."

Chapter 14
Chloe

I winced, and raised my hand to my face which itched. Something flaked, under my nose, over my mouth and I squeezed my eyes shut, opening them onto an unfamiliar bedroom done in grays and blacks. I pulled my hand away from my face and winced at the flakes of dried blood there.

I felt hot. Like feverish, and I was scared. I couldn't remember... oh. Oh, no!

I closed my eyes and hot tears gathered beneath my eyelids, seeping from between my lashes. I could hear *everything* and it was unnerving as hell. I could hear the water in the pipes, the thrum of electricity along the wires in the walls... I could hear the twins arguing out in the main room but when I tried to focus on what they were saying it was too late.

"Shh! She's awake," one of them said and I bolted into action. I pulled myself across the bed to the opposite side, away from the door and wedged myself into the corner between the nightstand and wall on that side.

I wasn't any kind of match for the two of them, but if they wanted to get fresh, then fuck, I would make them work for it! The door opened. I couldn't tell them apart but if I had to guess, I would place Rem as the one through the door first. His expression dour. Romulus followed, a nasty grin on his face. Rem put his back to the wall and crossed his arms over his chest, scowling at his brother who crouched down in front of me, arms resting on his knees.

"Looks like you made it, Little Pup," he smiled and it wasn't nice. He reached out to touch me and I snarled, snapping at him. I clapped a hand over my mouth at the inhuman sound and fresh tears leaked. I felt such an incredible amount of anger, coiled in my chest, swirling... no, *circling*. I could almost visualize it now. A wolf, padding in circles in my mind's eye. Wary, cornered, she looked at me with sympathy in her white-blue eyes, her coat a lovely cream, frosted reddish at the tips.

"Oh my God," I moaned from behind my hands and Romulus *laughed*. He fucking *laughed* like it was the funniest goddamned thing on Earth and that anger surged again, but I had started out human and I wasn't willing to let that humanity go just yet and so what I did next was a very human thing to do.

I spit in his face. I spit in his face and I had to smirk because I got him good! He didn't like that, he didn't like it at all because I heard Remus shout at his brother, "No Rom, don't!" just before Romulus' fist crashed into my face. Bone crunched, pain shot through me at a phenomenal rate and my head snapped back into the wall behind me and everything went dark again.

* * *

The *second* time I woke in the bedroom, I was back on the bed and I was worse off than I'd started the first time. The first time I'd woken up, I had been in my own clothes. The ones I had left William's house in, even if they had been pretty crusted with dirt and my blood. This time I wore nothing but a slinky black satin nightgown that left little to the imagination.

I sat up sharply, movement off my right side startling me. A growl escaped me and I bit my lips together and waited for my pounding heart rate to slow. It was a mirror. Just a mirror. I blinked at my reflection, hardly recognizing myself. I mean, I looked like me but it was like I had been nearly blind my whole life and now the veil had been lifted off my eyes. I swung my legs over the edge of the bed and stared into the mirrored, closet doors.

The thin, spaghetti straps of the nightgown left my upper chest and body bare, the sweetheart neckline plunging low. I swallowed hard. The material clung to my body, accentuating what curves I did have, tumbling so long it hid the tops of my feet. I guess I could be grateful for that. I brushed fingertips over my shoulder where Romulus had bitten me.

Oh God, I had never been through anything like it before. The bite had burned like acid but it hadn't stopped at just the site of the wound, no, that acid had spilled through my blood, traveled through every vein and vessel, burning me hollow from the inside out. I couldn't stop my screaming, I'd wanted to, I knew it was probably hurting William to hear it but I couldn't. No matter how hard I had tried. I couldn't keep myself from making a sound.

I closed my eyes and sniffed, tears leaking free and felt a mixture of so many things. I was afraid, but that was minor in comparison to the quiet desolation creeping out from my center.

There was no bite mark, no scar; no hint of where Romulus had bitten me, and for that I felt such gratitude. I closed my eyes and let my tears fall, hot and salty, tightening my skin where they trailed down my cheeks and brushed the mark left behind by William.

I felt a sharp, fractured ache deep in the center of my being at having been parted from him. I opened my eyes and studied the delicate ring of scars that his very human teeth had set into my shoulder where it met my neck.

The slightly raised scar tissue was paler than the rest of my skin and I felt my brows draw in. I leaned closer to the glass, my mouth opening in a tiny 'o' of surprise. It shimmered, the scar did, as I turned, twisting my body this way and that in the dim light of the room. A faint, pearlescent, blue sheen shimmered across its surface. *Like moonstone*, the thought came unbidden, instinctually, and I swallowed hard.

The door to the bedroom swung inward and Remus stepped through with a tray in his hands. I took a deep breath and halted. *I knew it was Remus and not Romulus by smell*, I was jolted to realize. Oh, God this was crazy.

"Where's William?" I asked and my voice startled me. It sounded like me but didn't. The nuances and tones richer somehow. I closed my eyes. All of my senses were pretty much on overdrive and it was *not* fun.

"You need to eat," he said sternly.

"I'm not hungry."

"Chloe…" he said, and arched one of his dark brows, "You need

145

to eat," he said calmly and set the tray on the foot of the bed.

"I told you, I'm not hungry…" which was only partially a lie. I was hungry, just the thought of food made me feel sick to my stomach. *God, I missed William.*

He laughed softly, but there was nothing happy about it, "So it *does* go both ways, interesting."

"What goes both ways?" I asked.

"Come and eat and I will tell you."

I smoothed my damp palms along the satin of the nightgown nervously and Remus scoffed, "Don't worry. I tended to you, not my brother. Your virtue is safe," he mocked. I ignored him.

"How about you tell me what you were talking about just then and then maybe I'll eat something?"

"Do you enjoy being difficult just for the sake of being difficult?" he asked with a frown.

"Yes," I replied honestly. His eyes widened and he suppressed a smile. He raked a hand through his spikey, short dark hair.

"You were here for three days before you woke up the first time. Rom knocked you out and you've been out over a day more. Surely our little brother filled you in on the ridiculous calorie intake required by wolf-kind?" I nodded and he looked pointedly at the covered tray, whisking off the lid.

Steak and chicken breast cut into neat, bite sized pieces rested on a plate along with some Asparagus and a roll. It was quite a bit of food, but not totally overwhelming. I perched on the end of the bed and put the napkin in my lap, frowning at the ensemble. The tray held silverware, and when I say silverware I mean the real deal, except it wasn't silver it was *gold*.

"Where's William?" I asked again after taking a bite and Remus gave me a half charmed smile. He sank into a chair by the dresser, hiking back the sleeves of his black thermal over his forearms.

"At home, working on one of his sculptures I'd imagine." He took a seat in a chair beside the dresser and leaned back in it, hooking his thumbs through the front belt loops of his dark jeans.

"Has he tried to…?"

"No," and his mouth crushed down into a thin line, "Eat some more." I stopped defiantly, the steak turning to so much ash in my mouth.

"Why?"

"Don't worry about that for now."

"You're kidding me right? What's he done?" I demanded.

"What's who done?"

"Your asshole brother! What's he done to William?" I demanded. Remus laughed outright at that.

"Nothing, he hasn't done anything. William has challenged Romulus for Alpha," I felt my face shut down and Remus looked on, bemused, "Eat, Chloe."

I pushed the tray away from myself and stood, going to the window. I pulled the drape aside and looked down into a bustling intersection. People dressed for a night on the town. All of the buildings were old and stone.

"Where are we?" I demanded. It was nothing like the woods we'd left behind, no this was decidedly an urban area.

"Seattle, that's Pioneer Square. The historic district. You're in the loft I share with my brother."

"Where is he?"

"Not home."

"Good."

A long silence ensued as we stalemated for the time being. I stared down at all of the people wandering through the intersection, slipping in and out of the clubs and bars and all I wanted was to see William. To feel his arms around me, his lips on mine. I closed my eyes and could almost feel the echo of his kiss.

A harsh sigh behind me made me turn, my fingers were pressed unbidden to my lips.

"It goes both ways," he explained to me, "William claimed you as his mate but even without the benefit of a wolf of your own, you claimed my little brother too. Remarkable." Remus had stood from his place on the chair and now, he stuffed his hands in his pockets. He turned his back on me with another heavy sigh and went for the door.

"Eat, Chloe..." he said, and leaving the tray behind, went out into the rest of the loft. Leaving the door swinging wide. I returned to staring out the window.

William had challenged Romulus for Alpha. A challenge like that only ended with one of them dead, from what I had gleaned about Pack politics. I wasn't sure how I felt about that. I was reasonably confident that William would be able to take him. I had faith, at least. I believed in him. But, he'd challenged for Alpha. Did he challenge to get me back? Did he challenge to get me away from Romulus? Was it possible to do such a thing?

I had felt a deep hurt when Remus said that about William. Like being Alpha was more important to William than I was. But I didn't know. I didn't understand how this all worked, I couldn't just assume that he didn't care about me. My mind continued to spin in ever more dizzying circles of logic until I had driven myself to a state of paranoia.

Sometime later Romulus returned and though my gaze remained fixed on the nightlife below, I could hear them talk about me. It wasn't as if they could or would hide it.

"She's pining, Brother," Remus said.

"So?"

"So, you need to talk to her. Fulfill your obligation to her as her sire. Jesus Romulus! What were you thinking turning her like that?"

"What? Seriously? You're just pissed because for once I outsmarted you." I didn't have to turn, I didn't have to go to the door of the room and look to know that Romulus had a malevolent smirk on his face, I could hear it plain as day.

Remus scoffed and there was a sharp slap as I imagined he threw up his hands and let them fall back against his denim clad thighs.

"That's the trouble with you, you *don't* think. You *never* think beyond the immediate Romulus. You never look at the big picture! Do you have any idea what you've done?" Remus shouted.

"You keep asking me that! Fuck, man! Yes! I know exactly what I've done. I took Alpha from our little brother, like taking candy from a fucking baby! What's more, I took his bitch right out from under him too, and the cherry on top? I pissed all up in those fucking Hunter's Cheerios by turning Mathias fucking Young's daughter into one of *us!* Do you not see how much we've scored here?" Romulus sounded downright glib and it blew my mind. I chewed my bottom lip and felt a solid echo of unease that wasn't just my own.

Remus made a sound of disgust and stalked off, "Try to get her to eat something," he snarled at Romulus and a door slammed. I swallowed hard, suddenly very afraid of being left alone with the obviously crazier twin.

"Chloe?" Romulus called and I swallowed the bitter tang of fear.

"Yes?" I asked half-heartedly.

"Lucinda's coming over. Fucking eat something and stay in there," he called out.

"Okay," I called back and glanced down at the plate of food that had grown cold at the foot of the bed. I turned back out the window and jumped when Romulus' reflected hulking frame filled the doorway to the bedroom I was standing in. My heart leapt into my throat as I met his dark eyes in the night shrouded window glass. He trailed his eyes up and down the back of my body, letting his gaze linger a touch too long on my ass.

"Okay what?" he asked.

"O-okay, Sir?" I tried, and he laughed.

"No, bitch. I'm your daddy now," he said and I felt bile surge into my throat as my stomach churned. I looked over my shoulder at him and stuttered a spastic nod.

"Say it," he demanded, a cruel edge to his smile.

"Okay, Daddy," I eked out, and I wanted to throw up.

"Fucking right," he muttered and stepped out of the room, shutting the door firmly behind him. I let my fingertips trace the bite left by William and I closed my eyes, taking some comfort in the scar as the only thing I had to remind me of him.

I love you, William. I thought into the ether, and rested my forehead against the cool window glass. "I'm sorry I never told you," I whispered.

CHAPTER 15

William

"He can't just mope around, he's got to do something."

"What is there for him to do? The challenge was issued and Rom has accepted even though he has no choice in the matter. He can't turn down a challenge from William at this point, not without losing face and possibly his position as Alpha."

"But he *isn't* the Alpha yet! William could still beat him."

"Nora, that's what the challenge is about. If he defeats Rom in the challenge then he'll be the new Alpha."

"And his brother will be dead. And if he loses? Did you consider that when you suggested this lunatic idea to him, Markus? Because Romulus is older, stronger, tougher, generally harder to hurt and to kill and odds are that William *is* going to *lose!*"

"You do realize that he can hear you?" Markus asked calmly and I heard Sharon growl at him.

"He should hear me. He should be listening to me. And so should you! Has your old age finally caught up to you?" she demanded, and her voice raised, "You're going to die, William! Do you hear me? You're going to fucking die and then where will the rest of us be?" She kept talking but the rest of it was suddenly muffled and I could hear the sound of feet scuffing over the carpet in the hall, down the stairs and out the front door where her voice resumed screaming but far more muffled.

I was lying in my bed, so recently had it been occupied by Chloe that I swore I could almost feel her residual warmth on the bed beside me, but it was just my imagination. My fingers were linked together, hands behind my head and I stared listlessly up at the ceiling. My room had stopped smelling of sunlight and peaches a day or two ago, but if I closed my eyes and breathed in real slow and real deep…

"She isn't entirely wrong, you know," Markus said as he stood at the top step leading into my room. I had been a bit irate when I went upstairs the morning after the meeting. When Markus left I spent the rest of the night working on the tree in my shop and when I went upstairs I'd closed the door to the library so hard that the frame splintered and the door itself was left hanging from one hinge. When it had come time to leave I had simply ripped the door the rest of the way loose and tossed it aside where it still lay against the wall at the base of the spiral staircase.

"Thank you for the vote of confidence," I muttered, the first words I had spoken in days actually. How long had I been laying there anyway? It didn't matter. Nothing mattered without her.

"The man I saw four days ago I had some confidence in. I believed he could take Romulus and win the challenge. But you? You're not that man anymore."

"Same skin, same me," I muttered and Markus sighed explosively.

"Look at yourself, Pup!" he snapped. "When was the last time you took a glance in a mirror? When was the last time you cleaned anything or picked up around here? Your place is turning into a dump and for a kid that I knew to be full on obsessive compulsive about keeping his place neat and tidy, that's a pretty dramatic change for you."

"What's the point?" She wasn't here... I couldn't protect her. She was gone, although if she'd died I am sure Rom would have rubbed my nose in it by now. Markus let out an explosive sigh and tried again.

"Try looking at it from this perspective," he said in a resigned tone. "If you lose, you die, and at least you didn't leave a mess for someone else to pick up. But if you win, do you really want to bring Chloe back here for her to see how much of a wreck you were? Do you want the rest of the Pack to know that you fell apart? Even if you win the challenge they still might not accept you if you can't even hold yourself together for two god damned weeks!"

His voice got louder as he went until the last few words were bellowed at full volume. "Right now I'm not sure *I* even want you as

Alpha. Not unless you can pull your shit together. This is your only chance to save Chloe and the entire Pack right along with her. There are hundreds of people counting on you right now so you'd better pull your head out of your ass and stop your goddamned pining or a lot of people are going to get hurt."

He was right.

They both were, he and Sharon.

I was going to die if I didn't pull myself together, but I just didn't have the motivation. I needed to find it though. As much as I hated to admit it, I needed to get my ass out of bed and go about my business. Handle my shit. Lying around and doing nothing wasn't helping my girl. Shit. Wasn't Chloe all the motivation I needed? I was suddenly starving.

"Come on, old dog," I grumbled and pushed myself up to a sitting position. "I think we need to talk."

He gave me a wary look and nodded but said nothing, perhaps afraid that if he spoke he would pop the bubble of motivation I had managed to scrape up from somewhere. And if that popped, who knew when I would get up again.

"I don't understand what I'm feeling here," I said. I led the way out of my room and to the kitchen. Beer cans littered the counter, food wrappers and pieces of trash were scattered across the floor. I arched an eyebrow at Markus and he grinned and shrugged apologetically.

"Brent and Nora decided to finish off that beer from the other day last night."

"And they couldn't be bothered to clean up after themselves?" I asked, somewhat irritated.

"Why? You were already turning the place into a disaster area compared to your usual."

He was right. I never would have allowed my place to get so messy under normal circumstances. It had been commented on numerous times by friends and family so it seemed like a good place to start.

"Talk to me," I told Markus while I started gathering the cans and the trash.

"Your pining, it's not good or healthy, Boy. I've seen wolf-kind die from it. Wasting away to nothing from a loss of a mate, but hell! Chloe ain't *dead*, you can't do anything about where she's at now but come the Challenge? That's your chance! Your *only* chance to get her away from that animal. You moping around here ain't gonna get you through that challenge."

I sighed and pinched the bridge of my nose between thumb and forefinger. "The Challenge. What exactly am I looking at? How does it work? Father had shit locked down, I've never seen one and it's never been talked about really."

Markus pulled out a chair and sat at the table, his hands clasped together in front of him. "The Challenge takes place in front of the entire Pack. Every member must be present, and that'll include your Mate," he fixed me with a hard look, "So you had better hold your shit together for that. You can't lose it again."

"I won't."

"It's not good for people to see you this way."

"I won't," I said again.

"Seriously, Boy–"

"I said I won't! How many times do you need me to repeat it?" I snapped and glared at him. He just arched an eyebrow at me and I sighed and slumped against the counter by the sink. I scrubbed my face with my hands and stared at the ceiling a minute before letting out a pent up breath.

"Alright," I said. "Point taken."

"Good."

I started cleaning again. "How does the challenge itself actually go?"

"There are three stages. Simple enough in the long run but not as easy as it sounds."

"Such as?"

"The fight is broken into rounds. Two, five minute long rounds. Round one, you fight in your human form, hand to hand, no weapons." I nodded to indicate I had heard him as I started wiping down the counters with some cleaner and a rag. "Round two, you go to hybrid form and keep fighting. Round three, full wolf. It's a cycle of hand, claw, and tooth."

"You said two rounds," I interrupted him.

"I said two, five minute rounds. The third isn't five minutes."

"Winner is decided by death?"

"Those are the rules."

"So the third round is as long as it takes for..." I trailed off and glanced up to see Markus nodding, a grim expression etched across his grizzled features.

"The round continues until someone breathes their last." He leaned forward, looking intently at me. "Do you really understand how difficult that's going to be, Boy?"

"How do you mean? I did pay attention during some of my lessons with the Betas, Markus. I know how hard it is to kill one of our kind. Silver would make this simpler but it's not allowed, not by Pack Law."

"Right, and since silver is the easiest way to kill us then you need to find a harder way. Meaning snapping his neck or crushing his skull, ripping his heart out completely. Those'll all do it. But if you get to the third round, you *know* he'll have the advantage at that point. He'll have weight and strength over you and you won't have opposable thumbs to help you fight anymore. You'll only have your teeth. If he gets ahold of you first it'll be over."

Markus lapsed into silence and I kept cleaning until there was nothing left to do but start dirtying things again. Cleaning and cooking and working helped me think, it helped me focus and helped me to quit dwelling on my own misery. It directed me to focus on the important things. *Chloe...*

An hour passed in silence until I set a plate of food in front of Markus and sat down across from him.

"So how do I beat him?"

Markus picked up his fork and gave me another of his piercing looks before he spoke.

"You forget that this man was once your brother. You forget that you have spent decades with him. You forget *that* above anything else and simply see him for what he is. A mad dog. One that stole your father from you, who stole your mate from you, and stole Alpha from you too. When you face him in the circle you forget everything except those facts and the hatred they should bring."

"And then?"

He took a large bite of his steak and used a roll to mop up some of the juice that escaped when he cut into the meat.

"Then? You kill him."

I gave the old dog an incredulous stare for a moment before I noticed the smirk dancing around his lips and I threw a dinner roll at his head.

"Very funny, Captain Obvious. If you're not going to be helpful then you can just get out, and leave your plate there, I'll eat your share, no worries." I said it all with a relieved smile on my face so Markus new I wasn't truly annoyed with him. He threw back his head and laughed.

"That's what I was looking for," he said. "Sorry, Boy. I just needed to be certain that you were still in there."

"Well I am, Markus. I'm not going to fall apart again. I know what I have to do, just needed a little help figuring out some direction. Now a little help figuring out the *how* would be appreciated."

We had ten days left. Ten days of waiting until the night of the Challenge. As Markus and I discussed combat strategy and tactics long into the night, I could only hope that Chloe would still be alive for me to save. Because whatever I'd told Markus was a lie. I didn't give a damn about the Pack or being Alpha anymore. Not if I had to do it without Chloe Young at my side. If she wasn't alright Romulus and Remus were both going to die, and then I was leaving. The Pack could fend for itself for all I gave a fuck. I just wanted *her...*

Chapter 16
Chloe

I only left the room to use the bathroom, the rest of the time I stood at the window, or slept. I barely ate and finally, on the second day I was awake, Remus cornered me. I slipped from the room to cross the hall to the bathroom when he looked up from the cutting board he was at in the kitchen.

The loft was a big, open expanse and the kitchen was almost free floating in the center of it all. He pinned me where I stood, half way between my appointed room and the bathroom door with his dark gaze and set down his knife with a scrape and a clack. I turned my eyes to the floor and moved toward the bathroom when his voice stopped me.

"Chloe, come here."

I swallowed, "I just need to use the bathroom," I said.

"Fine, but come here when you're done."

I used the facilities and slipped back out into the big expanse of room that was divided only by furniture and slipped up to the kitchen island. I'd learned quickly not to defy Rom. Remus, however, I had a little more leeway with. Romulus was fucking crazy. Remus was a lot calmer and the much more reasonable of the two.

"What is it?" I asked.

"Drink this," he said and set some kind of a protein shake in front of me. I stared at it, hard, for a long minute.

"Chloe," he said and the gentleness of his tone brought my eyes up to his. He radiated concern and I bit the inside of my cheek.

"I'm not hungry," I repeated softly for the thousandth time.

"I know, Sugar. But your body can't take it. Not like it used to."

My breath caught and my eyes welled at the term of endearment and I missed William with this awful ache of raw emotion. I closed my eyes and swayed on my feet and Remus was suddenly there, pressing the glass into my hand. I drank the whole thing.

"How's it taste?" he'd asked me.

"Like chocolate, why?"

He'd nodded as if that had confirmed something for him and he'd let me go back to my appointed room, my gilded cage, without answering me.

That had been three days ago. I'd had one of the chocolate shake things at least once a day since then, sometimes more. They were easier to get down than food, and if I drank them he didn't bug me nearly as much about eating, so there was that.

I pressed my hand to the window glass and watched the rain trickle down the pane. I stared at the rain slicked pavement two stories below and watched it turn from a wash of green light to red as the stoplight changed. The streets were nearly deserted this time of night, it being the middle of the week.

"Where is she? I want to see my new pet." I frowned at the unfamiliar woman's voice and my shoulders dropped when I heard Romulus' deep laugh.

"Chloe!" he called from the living area, "Get out here; let Lucinda have a look at you."

I closed my eyes and wondered, briefly, if Remus were going to be out there to cushion the interaction I had with his brother.

I was in luck, sort of. Remus was at the kitchen island, cooking something. He was eying his brother darkly and when he turned his gaze to the woman standing beside Romulus, his expression grew even darker. I looked her over even as she did the same to me.

She was tall and model thin, her long dark hair falling artfully in waves down her back. She wore a skintight, black tube dress with a lace overlay making up the upper chest and long sleeves. The dress ended mid-thigh and her legs, encased in sheer black stockings, were tipped in a pair of very expensive red bottoms. She stalked towards me and around me, her hands clasped together in front of her like a gleeful child.

"She's so tiny!" she exclaimed and I turned to keep her in my sight. I did *not* want this bitch at my back.

"Fun sized and foldable, might even fit in your purse," I muttered sarcastically and she stopped, eying me sideways out of her grey eyes. Her hand flashed out and caught me in the mouth. I let my head fly with the slap and it seriously rang my bell. I saw stars.

"Bad dog!" she snarled and stalked back over to Romulus. She made this whining noise and hung off him. Romulus put an arm around her waist and kissed her, some of her dark burgundy lipstick smearing against his mouth.

"Little puppies should be seen and not heard," he said arching a brow, "Apologize, Pup."

"I'm sorry," I grated.

"I'm sorry what?" Romulus demanded and I choked on the bitterness that formed with the words.

"I'm sorry, Daddy." Goddamn it Rom was a sick freak!

"You're going to be so much fun to dress for the Challenge!" the woman cried in a sing song voice and I caught Remus leaning forward sharply out of the corner of my eye. He had both fists planted firmly on the countertop.

"She's not a doll, Lucinda," he said.

"She's whatever the fuck I say she is," Romulus said.

They started to argue and I managed to slip back into my room. The brothers shouted, Lucinda whined and the whole thing culminated in slamming doors and a ringing silence. I waited, breath held for several moments and when the silence persisted I let it out and my knees went out right along with it. I sank to the carpet by the window and leaned my forehead against the windowsill.

I'm going to die like this, I thought, and it was much closer to the truth than I would have liked. Romulus returned, and he was angry. He yanked me up by the hair, a hand at my throat and slammed me against the brick that made up the outside wall beside my window. I grasped his wrist with the both of my hands and tried to pull breath.

"You listen to me! You naughty little girl," Romulus spoke through gritted teeth, our noses almost touching. I clawed at his wrist and tried valiantly to draw air but I couldn't, the pressure on my throat kept building until I thought my eyes were going to pop out of my head.

"Lucinda is the Alpha Bitch of this Pack and you will treat her with the love and respect that position deserves, do you understand me?"

My eyes grew wide and I began to panic. I couldn't breathe! I couldn't draw breath to answer! His hand tightened on my throat even more and starbursts of light started going off at the edges of my vision.

"Romulus!" Remus shouted, "Romulus stop! Stop it, Brother! You're going to kill her, you're going to kill your own progeny!" Remus had both his arms wrapped around the one that Rom was using to choke the life out of me. I stared into Rom's dark eyes and saw no pity there. No one was home, he was empty inside, as soulless as they came. I couldn't hear what Remus was shouting anymore, everything blurred together and was going hazy. Sight, sound, even touch... I was going numb. Romulus' hand convulsed on my throat once before he opened it and dropped me.

I drew in a savage choking breath into my oxygen starved lungs and coughed. The twins had some kind of exchange and Romulus stormed out. I stayed on hands and knees and relearned what it was to breathe when a shadow fell over the top of me. I jerked and flinched and Remus knelt down beside me. He grasped me by the shoulders and sat me up.

"Chloe, are you okay?"

"What do you care?" I rasped as if I were gargling gravel and he let me go, sitting back on his haunches. A trickle of blood seeped out of his nose and he sniffed, wiping it with the back of his hand. He looked at it as if he had never seen his own blood before and his expression settled into one of tired resignation.

"Get some sleep," he ordered, but there was no heat to his words. He stood and marched for the door, snapping off the overhead light as he went by. I stayed on my floor by the window for a long time, rubbing my throat, staring at nothing as despair swallowed me whole. I suddenly didn't mind dying. It would be preferable to a life lived with Romulus.

I woke to Remus barging into the room. I sat up startled on the bed and he held a hand out to me.

"Come on, let's go. There's only two nights left until the Challenge and Rom is going to be out all day, we need to move," he said. I stood up and rubbed my eyes.

"Where are we going?" I asked and was surprised that my throat didn't hurt. I looked in the mirrors on the closet doors and was startled to see nothing. No bruising, not even so much as a red mark on my pale skin.

"You're healed, you're wolf-kind now. Now come on, let's *go*," he urged. I came around the bed and followed him, my curiosity winning out. We got to the front door of the loft and he looked me up and down.

"Fuck," he muttered and tugged on the sleeves of his great big biker jacket, shrugging out of it he put it around my shoulders.

"Put your arms in the sleeves," he ordered and I obeyed. I went out the door and followed him down the steps, padding along the wood then cement until we stopped at the bottom and he opened the door into a parking garage. He hit the button on a key fob and the lights flashed on a black Range Rover down the line.

"Get in," he commanded.

"Where are we going?" I asked and shut the passenger door.

"Field trip. Shut the fuck up, you ask too many goddamned questions."

I shut the fuck up. I didn't know where we were going but it involved a major freeway and then a wait for a ferry across the water. I huddled in the too-big leather jacket grateful for its warmth. He drove, his disposition agitated but I didn't care.

I started to care when the highway he turned onto started to tickle my memory. I sat up completely from my miserable slouch, suddenly caring a whole lot when he turned down the driveway.

He let out a curse when he slowed the vehicle and I opened the door without letting it come to a complete stop. I was too excited. I jumped out onto the gravel drive and ran towards the house.

"*William!*" I screamed and like magic, he appeared in the portal of his front door.

CHAPTER 17
William

Time is a funny thing. When you're waiting for something or anticipating something the minutes, hours, and days seem to drag on interminably. Everything just feels like it takes forever, as if time has slowed to a crawl but only you're aware of this strange distortion of time, of the seeming temporal shift, until whatever you're anticipating, or dreading, comes closer.

Then, all of a sudden the nearly infinite seeming amount of time that you had stretching out ahead of you like an impossibly long road has been reduced, sliver by sliver, to almost nothing and you feel as if it is hurtling toward you with meteoric speed and the inevitability starts to close in.

There were only two nights left until I would face one of my adopted brothers in the circle. Two nights until my world would center around one thought. To kill, or be killed. Not a pleasant concept, let me tell you. Especially as I had once looked up to Rom and Rem. They had taught me a lot when Father first bit me, after the accident... They helped me adjust to my new life, they helped me to mourn the loss of the parents that had raised me until I was twenty-four. They helped teach me to fight and how to survive in the wilderness, away from the city. Hell, Rem even bought me my first welder which got me started on the path to being independently wealthy as a sculptor... and now I was going to try to kill one of them. It was soul crushing.

I looked up from the tree, nearly completed as I'd had little else to do but work on it. Everything else was just eating, sleeping, or bathing otherwise. Life had lost all its color without Chloe. I'd fallen that hard for her.

I was just about to spark the welder to life when I heard the sound of a car turn down the gravel drive leading down to my house. The engine sounded vaguely familiar, large, like an SUV, and as it slowed I heard a door open before the vehicle could come to a stop and a muffled curse in a voice I recognized all too well.

I set the welder aside and threw my helmet down. I was already moving toward the door when I heard her screaming my name and I practically threw myself the remaining distance, ripping the door open so hard I very nearly tore it from its hinges. There she was, ankle length nightgown snapping around her legs and Rem's heavy biker jacket swallowing her whole, giving her a sense of modesty with how skimpy the gown was up top. I was barely able to take it all in, scarcely able to believe what I was seeing as she ran across the drive. The gravel must have been digging painfully into her feet but she either didn't notice or she didn't care. Either way I ran to meet her, opening my arms and gathered her to my chest as she crashed into me, cradling her with one arm across her shoulders and the other along her lower back, crushing her to me. It felt so *good* to have her back again.

She felt warmer than ever and for a moment I worried she was sick, until I remembered how Rom had bitten her; that image of her fear and pain having been burned into my mind's eye forever. She was wolf-kind now. She was one of my people and we could be together without the Pack throwing a tantrum over her being human. We could... she was being taken from my arms.

I snarled, a low rumbling sound that would have frozen most creatures in a sense of abject terror but Remus simply kept pulling until Chloe was yanked from my grip with a broken cry of protest. He set her on her feet next to him after backing up a few paces.

"William," he said in an even tone. There was something in his eyes. Remus had always been the more emotive of the twins. He *felt* where Romulus didn't. Many people liked to say 'the lights are on but nobody's home' when it came to describing a crazy person. When it came to Romulus, I preferred to say 'the wheel was spinning but the hamster is dead' because that man was a corpse inside. A deadened heart incapable of feeling anything that didn't further his own desires and ambitions. By comparison Remus was, by leaps and bounds, more human.

Still, I needed to be suspicious. Needed to be on my guard. This wasn't a social call. Remus' specialty was manipulation. I needed to remember that.

"Remus. To what do I owe this unexpected pleasure?" My voice was tight and my fingers curled and flexed, wanting nothing more than to reach for Chloe again. She didn't struggle in Remus' hold. She obviously knew she would never break free if he didn't want her to, so she stood, a pleading look on her face, in her eyes, as she looked up at him.

"She isn't yours anymore, you know that, right?" he asked and I frowned, teeth baring themselves in a snarl before I could stop myself and force my lips into a thin line behind my goatee.

"You would come to my home, with my mate, and insult me? Are you trying to get your brother hurt worse before I kill him? Because you know as well as I do, Remus, that Romulus needs to be put down. He is a danger to us all and shouldn't be Alpha."

"I just had a moment and thought you might like to know that your mate is *dying*," he gave me a meaningful look. I stared blankly at him then looked to Chloe. She looked painfully thin, worn, and tired.

"She's been pining for you," he snarled and jerked at her arm thrusting her a half step towards me for a better look. "She won't eat, and Rom has no intention of teaching her anything about the change. He hasn't told her shit. If she survives her first full moon, it will be a miracle! Not to mention the most agonizing experience of her life," he added with a vicious grin and a cold look in his eyes that I couldn't help but find suspicious. My instincts were telling me something wasn't right here, but my brain and my heart were so busy screaming at me to take her, to grab her and hold her and never let her go that I couldn't put two and two together. He suddenly shoved her the rest of the way toward me and she stumbled before she caught herself.

"Go," he said. "Give your mate a last kiss. One or both of you will die in two nights. Him beneath my Brother's claws, and you by your own stupidity. Or maybe Lucinda will kill you after Rom is officially the Alpha."

We ignored him. Chloe flew into my arms and I held her close, breathing in her scent as if it was the only thing keeping me alive. She no longer smelled of peaches, but she still smelled bright, like sunlight and clean air, like Chloe, and that was even better. I drew back enough to look into her clear blue eyes, smoothing some of her copper hair from her face. It was clean, but not as bright. She was losing nutrients and I glanced at Rem who was scowling at her back. Things snapped into place for me.

"Listen to Remus," I whispered into her ear. "He's trying to help here, I'm not sure why but he knows you won't trust or listen to him. Well I'm telling you Chloe, to *please* trust Remus. I need you," I looked into her pained and worried blue eyes, "And I need you to eat something, Sugar. You have to keep up your strength. Listen carefully, anything Remus says around you might be useful so pay attention, even if you don't understand it."

She nodded and pressed a kiss to my lips. I kissed her back carefully. She felt so thin, so fragile in my arms. Even more fragile than she had when she'd been human. The kiss was short lived. Too soon Remus was pulling her away, shoving her back into the car. She stared at me through the window, tears staining her cheeks and my hands clenched themselves into fists at my sides. She was still Rom's progeny. It was still before her first change. I couldn't keep her with me without violating Pack Law, so I had no choice but to let them go.

Before he got into the car Remus paused and looked at me over the hood of the Range Rover.

"Romulus is insane," he said, "Even I can see it. But he's the more powerful." He stared a moment longer and I saw it in his eyes, clear as day. *Be careful, Little Brother.* With that he pulled open the door to his Rover, jumped in, and backed around so he could drive back the way they'd come. He turned the vehicle, threw it in gear and started up the drive back to the road with Chloe twisted in her seat, staring out the back at me.

I continued to stare up the drive long after they had gone, silently thanking Remus. I had a better chance against Romulus now. I had a renewed resolve to end him. He wasn't teaching her *anything.* Nothing at all! She hadn't been listening to Rem, so he'd brought her to me. To try and talk some sense into my beautiful, brave, and entirely too stubborn, girl. I raked a hand back through my hair, holding it back from my face. Both hands on top of my head, resisting the urge to scream my frustration and anger. I needed to hold on to every damned bit of it.

Two days… just two more days! It couldn't come fucking fast enough.

Chapter 18

Chloe

We rode in silence and I stared out the window. I'd been so speechless, hadn't wanted to let him go. I had clung to every word, every touch and glance as if it would be my last and in being so enthralled with just being near William I had completely forgotten to say 'I love you'. Damn.

"Why did you take me to him?" I asked and turned to look at Remus. His jaw tightened along with his grip on the steering wheel and he remained resolutely silent.

I scoffed. "Whatever," I muttered and sighed. My stomach burned with hunger and I bit my lower lip.

"Can we stop and get something to eat, please?" I asked grudgingly a few minutes later and he turned to look at me, studying my face.

"Absolutely," he said, relief evident in his voice.

"I love him," I said abruptly, staring out the passenger side window as he pulled into a McDonald's drive through. The ferry terminal was just ahead, waiting to whisk us back across the water, further away from the man I was just *so desperate* to be with.

"I love him and I'm scared that I'll never see him again, that I'll lose him." I turned to stare back at Remus who was as stoic and shuttered as I had ever seen him. He was stopped in front of the metal box where we would place our order.

"Welcome to McDonald's may I take your order?"

I stared at him and he stared at me and a long silence ensued.

"Hello? I said, welcome to McDonald's may I take your order?"

Remus spoke but he was looking at me the entire time. He placed an order that would have made William proud and I smiled a little ruefully. God I missed him. The now familiar ache of longing settling back in. Our reprieve had been too short.

"Don't do that Chloe," Remus said gently and I looked at him curiously, "Just eat, stay strong, William's going to depend on it."

"Why are you doing this?" I asked again.

"Why can't you just accept that I am and go with it?" he shot back.

Touché.

The moment Rem pulled the food through the window and the smell hit my nose, I was *dying*. I mean absolutely starving. The hungriest I had ever been. I think I caught him quirking a hint of a smile but I couldn't be sure and I didn't really care. I was too busy ripping into the first cardboard carton containing a burger.

I ate like a dude. No. Seriously. Just like a dude. I went through two burgers, a twenty count of chicken nuggets with sweet and sour sauce and had sucked down about half of my extra-large Coke while we waited in line for the ferry to dock and disembark. Remus just sat there quietly and kept handing me food.

For the first time since I'd been taken I felt like my brain was firing on all cylinders. Like I could *think* rather than just feel and I could almost picture my wolf chasing her own tail in glee over it.

"Is this normal?" I asked, before sucking down more Coke.

"Is what normal?"

"Getting there, had to wash it down. Is it normal to feel and think like I'm me but have like these clashing feelings or whatever at the same time?" He nodded, like an 'ah-ha' and fixed me with a look.

"For some Moon Forged, in the beginning, the wolf side of them is almost a separate entity. Like you are you, but another being has taken up residence in your head. At least, that's how I've heard it described.

"They say after the first change that eases up. Once you start to work with your wolf side, and you integrate better, you can't feel the separation. It becomes more natural." He fixed me with a somber look.

"You're defiant," he stated and I snorted a laugh.

"What was your first clue?" I asked and took a huge bite out of a McChicken sandwich.

"You need to watch it around Romulus and Lucinda, Chloe. I know it's your personality to not go down without a fight but you need to understand," he shifted uncomfortably and started the Range Rover; it was our turn to board. He had my attention though. William had told me to listen to Remus, had told me to trust him. While I didn't, I trusted William and I had to admit Remus had done quite a bit to try and keep me alive if not exactly comfortable over the last week and a half or so.

"I'm listening," I said softly when he hadn't continued.

"Your first shift doesn't have to hurt," he said quietly, "Rom…" he sighed as if pained, "Rom is like a little boy pulling the wings off a fly when it comes to you. He's a bully, he's not telling you what you need to know to get through your first shift alive. He expects your writhing on the sidelines will distract William from his purpose and he's not wrong… It will."

He pulled the Range Rover onto the ferry and shifted it into park, turning in his seat to look at me.

"Are you going to tell me what to do?"

"Are you going to listen?"

"Yes."

He frowned at me, "Because my brother told you to?"

I swallowed hard and nodded, "Yes."

"Why?" he asked and he looked genuinely confused.

"Because I trust him."

Remus made an incredulous noise, "He kidnapped you around three weeks ago and dragged you all the way across the country! I don't get it, I really don't." He linked his hands together behind his head and pulled his chin to his chest, likely to ease the tension in his upper back and shoulders and I felt a pang of sympathy for him.

"He kidnapped me, threatened to do a lot of things, rape me, hurt me…" I agreed.

"So how can you love him?"

I looked him in the eye, "Because he never lied to me, he never hid anything from me, and he told me the truth. Even when I tried to run away and I hurt myself, he took care of me. And when you guys showed up? He put himself between me and you and protected me... Kind of like you're doing now," I frowned, "Why is that?"

Remus looked at me mystified. Speechless. I'd caught him off guard, I think. He shifted in his seat and turned to look out his window, though there was nothing to look at but the other cars and the white and green wall of the ferry on his side. He propped his elbow on the windowsill of his car door and covered his mouth with his hand in a decidedly thoughtful gesture. I resumed eating quietly.

Sometime later, as we were docking on the other side of the water, he sighed out. I looked over expectantly and he didn't disappoint.

"When you change, your natural human instinct is going to be to fight it. Only the strong survive their first change, and I'm not talking physically strong, I'm talking mentally. You need to let it happen. I don't know how to explain this *exactly*, I mean, I'm Blood Born, not Moon Forged. The change has always been like second nature to me." He started the Range Rover again and waited for the ferry boat attendant to wave us on.

"So it's going to hurt, like what though?"

"Can't really tell you, never really cared to pay attention to the Moon Forged before."

I sighed, "Okay, so expect pain, but don't fight it."

"Look, it's been said that if you can keep the fear in check, if you can just let it happen and you don't force the change to rush, or try to keep it back, the change can actually be quite nice. Freeing. Some have even described it as pleasurable." He had the grace to look embarrassed and I couldn't resist.

"Pleasurable?" I prodded and he shifted in his seat.

"Orgasmic, okay?"

I laughed and he frowned again, "What?"

"I figured that was what you meant, I just wanted to make you say it." He frowned harder and I laughed, I mean really laughed, *hard* for the first time since... since the morning of the meeting when I'd been in bed with William. After we'd made love.

"You'll see him again," he said, "Just two more nights."

"Yeah, but it might be to say goodbye."

"It might," he agreed and I turned to look at his stoic expression that he wore like a mask. He glanced in my direction.

"I thought you liked honesty," he said gently, "You said you loved William because he didn't lie. He didn't hide things."

"You want me to like you?" I asked.

He shrugged. "Couldn't care less if you like me or hate my guts," he said. "But I do want you to listen to me."

"I'm listening," I said which was funny, because that was the last thing we said to each other the entire ride back to the loft he shared with his psychotic twin. We pulled into the garage and I followed him up the stairs.

"When we get inside, give me my coat and your nightgown and get in the shower. I'll find something else for you to wear," he said intently.

"Why?" I frowned and jerked back when he leaned in and sniffed, he raised his eyebrows at me and I felt like the stupid puppy that Rom was forever calling me.

"Oh, right."

He unlocked the front door and I shrugged out of the jacket and handed it back to him. I went straight for the bathroom and started the shower, handing him the slick satin gown from behind the door.

"Wash well, Chloe," he intoned and I paused, just before stepping into the shower and closed my eyes. I pressed my hands to my face and breathed deep and slow.

Beneath the food I had eaten, he was still there. That masculine clear smell of the outdoors mixed with the rugged tang of burning metal. I could still smell William on my skin and I didn't want to let it go. But Remus was right. If I could still smell it then Rom could and the evil twin would blow a motherfucking gasket. I shuddered at the thought and got under the spray, washing myself down twice, then a third time for good measure.

When I got out, as I wrapped in the towels from the bar, the door opened. I looked up and quailed inside when I saw Romulus scowling down at me.

"Here, Lucinda wants you in this when she comes over tonight. She's got outfits for you to try." He thrust another fall of black satin with more lace at me and I took it. I waited.

"Got something to say?" he asked.

"Um, thank you, Daddy." I murmured and he nodded with satisfaction.

"You're learning," he said and stood there, "Well, put it on!" he said with a malicious look. He crossed his arms and it was awkward, ungainly with how big they were.

I shook, and felt my face flame with embarrassment as I slipped the gown over my head and tried to keep the towel in place. I wasn't overly modest, but he made me want to be with the way his gaze roamed over me. He grunted and snatched the towel from around my body and I let the gown fall. Tears sprang to my eyes. I knew he'd caught a glimpse of my body, but it was only that. A glimpse. I hadn't given him the satisfaction of a protracted peepshow.

I followed him out into the main room and got to spend the rest of my night playing dress up with Lucinda in these absolutely trash-tastic hooker clothes. She fluttered and cooed and clapped her hands like a ninny while Romulus cooed right back. Even though it was obvious he was getting off on my discomfort more than on anything that she put me in.

By the time I was dismissed I was exhausted and I was hungry again. I gave a longing glance towards the kitchen and returned to my gilded cage.

Two of the chocolate protein shakes were waiting for me on the dresser. I drank them both. I had followed the path of least resistance tonight. Kept myself safe, and whole, all the while hatred and anger were burning me up from the inside out. I went to my place by the window and I stared out for a time.

William, you had better fucking kill that S.O.B. I thought to myself. Not only because Rom was a seriously sick puppy – no pun intended. But also, because I really didn't want to live another minute without my mate.

I sighed and turned in. What else could I do?

Chapter 19

William

The day of the Challenge dawned silently, as dawns have a tendency to do. There was no fanfare or brass band striking up a chorus as the sky was first stained a steel grey, then slowly turned to orange before bright yellow sunlight spilled over the horizon.

I had barely slept, of course. This was worse than Christmas morning, the day before surgery, or waiting for the jury to come back with a verdict in your trial, I was unable to rest for even a moment. My life was going to be decided in several different ways before I sought my bed that evening. I would either be dead, and without worries or concern anymore, or I would be the Alpha of the largest Pack in the entirety of North America. I would have hundreds of people counting on me for leadership, strength and guidance. And I had better have Chloe with me as well, or there would be hell to pay.

"Did you sleep at all, Pup?" Markus asked.

I didn't turn from the tall window in my bedroom, my eyes still fixed on the slowly rising sun. I had heard Markus pull up outside, the distinctive rumble of his Jeep ingrained in my memory. I would recognize that vehicle anywhere. The door downstairs had opened and he had walked purposefully up the stairs until he stood where he was now in the doorway.

"Didn't feel like it... couldn't." He gave a tired sigh and I spoke up again in my defense. "I tried, honestly. I just couldn't." I'd lain there with the smell of her still fresh in my mind and I just couldn't sleep. Every time I tried to close my eyes I would find myself staring up at the ceiling with no idea when or how I opened them again.

"And I'm sure that Rom slept like a baby and will be well rested and ready for tonight."

"He may think so but I've made a practice of working with little to no sleep. It won't affect me much."

"You're walking a razors edge here, Kid. The slightest dulling of your edge could get you killed. Even an hour's sleep could mean the difference."

"Are you going to sedate me to get me to rest?"

"I was thinking I could just get you drunk," he said and I could hear the grin in his voice which made me turn and stare at him, one eyebrow arched high in surprise.

"Seriously? And you think being hungover will make the fight any better for me?"

"No, not seriously, ya dumb ass." He raked his hands back through his short cut hair. Well, more like rubbing his hands over his hair more than through it. He sighed again, his arms dropping back to his sides, his palms slapping his jean covered thighs with a loud snap.

"Look, you need to try to get *some* rest. For Chloe's sake if nothing else. Lay down and try, even for just an hour."

I gave him a wary look. I couldn't deny the logic to his advice, but logic and emotion very rarely go hand in hand, and at that point? I was exceedingly emotional. I wanted nothing more than to go right over to Rom and Rem's apartment in the city and rip my brother's throat out with my teeth. At the moment I wasn't entirely certain which brother I most wanted to destroy. I was half afraid that Remus was playing me, playing Chloe, but something about the way... My instincts were solid, my wolf was *sure* that my brother's intentions were above board but I'd seen it out of him before, the down and dirty manipulative side of him. I couldn't be sure of Remus' intentions. Nobody could.

Markus was still giving me an expectant look, waiting for my answer and finally I sighed and walked over to the bed. "I'll try," I muttered. "But only for an hour, if I can't get down by then, then I'm getting up and doing some work."

"Almost finished the sculpture?" he asked and I nodded as I flopped face down on the bed.

"I've just got to add a bit of tarnish to it, make the whole thing look old and weathered." My body felt heavy and I heaved out a deep sigh before I vaguely heard Markus retreating and consciousness fled me entirely...

* * *

"He was exhausted even if he didn't want to admit it. He hasn't slept in at least two days, minimum, but I wouldn't be surprised if he spent half the night every night in that shop working on the tree, did you look at it when you came in?" Markus was saying as I opened my eyes an indeterminate amount of time later. I had passed out, holy crap, how tired had I really been?

"Yeah, it's amazing."

"That's not the point, Kid," Markus snapped and I heard Brent chuckling and Nora whined slightly. I could just picture her ducking her head in deference to the higher ranking Arbiter.

"That wasn't cool," I said with a halfhearted glare at Markus a minute later when I walked into the kitchen. A glance at the clock on my nightstand when I had been climbing out of bed told me it was already past noon and I had slept for a good six hours.

"Hey, I didn't do a thing but talk you into laying down for five seconds. You passed out all on your own."

"And would one of you have woken me in time for the Challenge if I hadn't woken on my own?" I couldn't help but ask. I knew none of them really wanted to see me fight Romulus. If I won or if I lost I was going to lose something no matter what. This wasn't a situation where a victory would feel much like one. I wasn't at all looking forward to that.

I *was* determined to see it through though, that made anyone who tried to get in my way a liability. A liability that I couldn't, and *wouldn't*, afford.

"Of course we were going to wake you," Brent said with a derisive snort. "Why do you think we didn't bother to keep our voices down? If that hadn't woken you up we were gonna come get you within the next hour or so."

"Why so late?"

"Why are you in such a hurry?" Nora shot back.

"I would rather not be late to an event like this. It's considerably better to arrive early."

"Actually it is best to arrive neither late nor early, but on time. If you're late it doesn't look good, and if you're early it makes you look afraid, or anxious, neither of which look good either."

"Have you picked out my clothes for me, Dad?" I couldn't help but snap and I immediately felt a pang in my chest and I closed my eyes taking a long breath through my nose and expelling it out of my mouth. "Sorry, Markus. That was uncalled for."

"No worries, Pup. You're under a lot of stress right now."

"And the Alpha is always under a lot of stress. I can't afford to be biting the heads off of my friends and family when I'm stressed if I want to be an effective Alpha. Father built this Pack but we've been floundering for years, just sort of keeping our heads above water and the Pack has a great deal of potential to actually become a serious force in this state."

"What do you intend to do?" Markus asked, curious now that I had given him a hint into my thoughts about the Pack. I knew it could be more. I knew it could be better. And I obviously had an idea of how to go about it. But I wouldn't be getting into that yet. If I didn't become the Alpha it wouldn't matter.

We killed a few hours. I cooked again and we all ate in the living room until it was finally time to leave. They filed out of the shop ahead of me and I turned, giving my workspace a last look before I turned off the light and stepped out into the gathering dark, closing the door firmly behind me.

The drive from my house to the Olympic National Forest wasn't particularly long. Fifteen, twenty minutes at most. Part of the reason I had chosen that area to live in in the first place.

On that night though, I kind of wished it had taken a bit longer. The majority of the Pack had already arrived when we got there, much deeper in the forest this time than the previous meeting two weeks ago. It was the night of the full moon and once it rose, those of us that were still young would undergo the transformation into our wolves, most without any control. It took a few years before one was able to resist the monthly change and I wondered briefly if Remus had been able to get through to Chloe in regards to her first transformation.

I pushed the thought aside and climbed out of Markus' Jeep. I didn't have time to worry about that. I needed to keep my head in the game or Romulus was going to remove it from my shoulders.

"Romulus should be here any minute," Markus muttered so quietly that even with the enhanced hearing of our kind I was barely able to hear him standing right next to me. Absolutely no one else would have been able to hear him speak and I nodded slightly to show that I had heard, my eyes raking through the crowd, searching constantly for a familiar shock of red hair. "You know he's going to do something to try to piss you off, throw you off balance. Don't let it get to you, whatever it is."

I nodded again but I didn't trust myself to speak. Romulus had just made his entrance and Markus was right, he really was pulling out all the stops. He'd succeeded in making me blindly furious too.

Rom strolled calmly into the large clearing, the she-bitch, Lucinda, hanging on his arm like the simpering cunt that she was. In his right fist he held the end of a heavy length of stainless steel chain. The other end was clipped to Chloe as he led her in like a dog. The chain was hooked to a leather collar, an extremely *high* leather collar. It covered her entire neck and forced her to hold her chin high to prevent it from digging into her flesh. The center of the collar was fixed with a solid metal ring to which Romulus' had attached the chain leash.

Her eyes were tight with anger, her cheeks blushed with her humiliation. Lucinda had very obviously dressed her for the occasion. Her dress had a low cut, strapless, sequined bodice that adequately covered her breasts but from just below her breasts to her waist it was a sheer, transparent lace. The skirt hung on the ground in the back but was cut so high in front that it did little to hide the fact that she wasn't wearing any panties beneath it. Her feet were strapped into a delicate looking pair of extremely high heels which made her stumble, partially because she couldn't look down with the collar holding her head high, but also because the heels sank into the soft forest loam.

To sum it up, she looked like an extremely high priced hooker dragged behind Rom like she was on display, up for bid. I felt my blood, which was feverish to begin with, absolutely start to boil in my veins. A hand on my shoulder was all that kept me from throwing myself at Romulus right then and there. He knew it too, the bastard, because a moment later Rom grinned at me and gestured to my mate with one hand.

"How do you like the easy access dress I put your bitch in, little brother?" he asked and I heard a smattering of shocked gasps and some uneasy mutterings run through the assembled Pack members like a wildfire. *Yeah all you motherfuckers wanted him so bad. Now you get to see what you're dealing with and you ain't so sure,* I thought grimly. I said nothing, simply glared at him and fought the urge to bare my teeth and growl. I needed to be cool. I needed to contain my shit. I needed to prove I could do this. That I was worthier than him, but I wanted to fucking kill his ass so goddamn bad it made me itch from head to toe.

"Such behavior is hardly becoming of an Alpha," Markus pointed out to the crowd, fixing Rom with a calm but withering look. Another round of mutters spread through the crowd. I could already see support dwindling for Romulus, but it was going to be too late if I couldn't beat him. Still, it was his own desire to push the envelope and attempt to humiliate me that was doing it to him, undercutting his support. He was destroying himself and by extension would destroy the Pack our father had worked so hard to build.

In the crowd I saw more than a few members that I knew to be mated pairs, looking at Chloe with sympathy before looking back to Romulus with open disgust on their faces. Yeah, he was going to destroy this Pack over my dead body. Which it was likely that it would and could come to that. I stared at my mate, her blue eyes so full of trust and belief in me over the whore red lipstick Lucinda had painted on her. I felt my determination redouble. I wasn't going to leave my woman like this, in Rom's hands.

"Are the combatants ready?" Markus asked and stepped away from me, raising his voice slightly to ensure that he was heard throughout the clearing.

As quickly as that, the Pack's attention was diverted from my mate, from her humiliation and it was back to Rom and I and the circle. Romulus handed the end of Chloe's leash to Lucinda who jerked hard at it, almost pulling Chloe off her feet as she led her to the side where a set of stands had been erected for the Pack. One set of bleachers stood at either end of the clearing with a large circle in the center outlined by a ring of charred grass. A fast burning accelerant had been poured there and ignited to create the thirty foot wide circle that we would fight in.

I removed my coat, boots, and pants and handed them to a Pack girl who gave me an appreciative look up and down once before she winked, laughed and turned away. One of Rom's supporters. I made a note of it; if I survived this I could do something about a few of them.

Clothes would only be a hindrance in this fight, so there really wasn't a need for them. I turned and walked across the grass, the slight wind playing across my body, and ignored the hundreds of pairs of eyes that followed me. I'd been wolf-kind long enough that it didn't bother me to be nude in front of them all. Ten feet away, Romulus came to a stop facing me, similarly naked, and raised his fists in a simple boxing stance.

More muttering ran through the crowd. Individual words were impossible to make out but I could guess the gist of it. At half a foot taller than me and twice my bulk, Romulus was an impressive looking specimen. His chest, shoulders and arms were massive, almost grotesquely over developed. Every muscle looked to be carved from stone beneath his skin. I wasn't a ninety pound weakling myself, but I knew I didn't stack up visually in comparison to my brother. I would be relying on speed and skill more than strength to win this fight. It felt like the wolf-kind equivalent of David versus Goliath.

"The Challenge Circle has been called for this night," Markus started. Tradition needed to be observed. "Through a majority acceptance by the Pack, Romulus Reese has been named Alpha of the Pacific Northwest Pack. William Reese has issued a formal challenge for Alpha and Romulus has accepted. The Challenge fight will proceed according to the law of the Pack!

"There will be no outside interference of any kind. The battle will consist of three rounds. In the first, the combatants shall fight each other in human form. In the second, they will fight in their Hybrid form. And in the third, they will fight as Wolves. Each of the first two rounds will last for five minutes, at the end of which we move immediately to the next round. The third round will last until one of the two breathes their last."

The entire Pack raised their voice at that in one long howl that seemed to rip the night apart. The torchlight wavered and Romulus and I never once took our eyes from each other. We were simply waiting for the signal. As I watched him, Romulus grinned slowly, his smile growing wider and wider until he was showing an unnatural number of teeth in a caricature of humor. His eyes were wide and wild and he licked his lips. He was already enjoying this and was looking forward to the fight as much as I was dreading it.

And that was what I had needed to see. The rage, the hatred, the fear and uncertainty that I had felt for days suddenly evaporated as if it'd never been. Romulus Reese really wasn't worth the time or effort to hate. He was broken, diseased; dead inside. If anything I pitied him.

Chloe...

At the thought of my beloved, I felt a resurgence of my determination and it was just in time. The signal blew, an air-horn held aloft in Markus' hand, the look on my face changed, reflecting the pity I felt for him, and Romulus' expression flipped from smug to enraged as he saw it.

"Don't you fucking dare," he roared and flung himself at me.

It was amazing. I was calm, *finally*. The fear and rage that he had worked so hard to build in me with his actions had all been holding me back. It really was just a matter of finding a way to remain calm and in control. The sound of his bare feet pounding across the grass was loud in the clearing. The breeze rustling through the trees and the sputtering hiss of the torches and fires used to light the ring equally loud. The Pack sat in silence. This was not for their entertainment, this wasn't a gladiatorial style battle to please the masses. They knew what was at stake now. This was a moment for honor and solemnity, and as such, it was met with a determined silence in their observation.

I swayed to the side and stuck out my foot as Romulus lunged at me, one massive fist leading. If he had struck me it would have been a terrible blow but he missed me by the proverbial mile and I couldn't help but smile as he tripped and sprawled in the dirt. Before I could react he rolled and sprang to his feet and I was suddenly on the defensive. Punches and kicks seemed to fly at me from every direction and it was all I could do to keep ahead of him. A glancing blow struck my shoulder and I spun with it, pivoting on my foot and sending my elbow flashing out and up as I completed the tight turn.

My elbow smashed into his face so hard that he was lifted bodily from his feet, legs flying out as he turned almost horizontal in the air and I drove my elbow down, smashing his stomach with the bony joint and driving him into the earth beneath our feet. The air was driven violently from his lungs as his back met the ground and I dove in for the kill. Or I would have except for the fact that he spun, still gagging and unable to draw breath, and lashed out with one foot which caught me across the side of my head and sent me flying several feet until I landed heavily on the grass. I was dazed for a moment by the force of the blow but rolled quickly to put some distance between us.

We both climbed to our feet, snarling and spitting blood to the side when the air-horn went off again signaling the start of the second round and I grinned.

The Pack stirred, shifting almost as one as we began our change. The scent of blood was in the air and the wolf *loved* the smell of blood. The silent Pack began to yip and cheer, slowly growing from the quiet crowd into a fevered mob. I grew in height and bulk. My arms became longer, reaching almost to my knees which bent backwards with a sickening cracking sound as my feet grew longer. I stood up on the balls of my feet, heels in the air as my claws dug into the ground beneath me. I still held the advantage in speed, finishing my transformation before Romulus was even half way through with his and I leaped at him, covering twenty feet in a single bound, arms outstretched, hands reaching for his throat.

He howled and ducked to the side, spinning faster than I expected and kicked me out of the air with a blow like a sledge hammer. I felt at least one rib crack under the impact and I flew through the air, tumbling end over end until I landed on the grass just beside one of the fire-pits with a heavy crash and a groan from some of the observers.

"William!" I heard Chloe shriek and a second later a choking sound as Lucinda jerked on her leash again.

Not going to be that easy, motherfucker, I thought, growling low in my throat. *Come on... come on you son-of-a-bitch. Come at me.* I stayed down, rising slowly to one knee as Romulus stood tall and stalked his way toward me. My chest hurt like hell from where he hit me, which just proved that I was right when I thought that one solid blow would be all he would need to end me. His strength was monstrous, even by our higher than human standards.

He stopped near me, arrogant and overconfident. He reached down and lifted me into the air by my throat, holding me easily aloft with one hand. That was when I lifted my legs, planted my toes into his chest and kicked down as hard as I could, drawing ten deep gashes through his flesh with the sharp claws on my feet. He howled and dropped me, hunched over to grasp at his chest and stomach. I scrambled to my feet and reached low, bringing my hand almost from the ground up and slashing my claws right across his face. The impact sent him tumbling like a top and he sprawled on the ground.

The howl he had let out when I kicked him was nothing compared to the ear shattering shriek that left his throat as my claws raked across his face, digging deep into his cheek and when he stood again the gaping, bloody socket of his left eye gave evidence to the true reason for his scream. I felt a surge of satisfaction at that. Even if he still managed to defeat me he wouldn't last long as

Alpha. He had lost too much support and eyes didn't tend to regenerate after that much damage to them. A half blind Alpha would never be tolerated for long.

The air-horn went off a third time and I backed away several paces as Romulus fell to the ground and began to change again. *Ten minutes*, I thought as I, too, began to change into my wolf form. *Seems like it's been longer than that.*

My breath came in heaving gasps, streaming from my mouth in a visible cloud in the rapidly cooling evening air, each lungful burning my throat like a cold fire. Wolf-kind are stronger and faster and have greater stamina than humans, but I don't care who you are, fight with the intensity that Romulus and I were fighting with and you would feel like keeling over too.

Romulus lunged at me again, snarling viciously and I leaped to meet him. We collided in midair, a heavy thud that echoed throughout the clearing and finished the job of breaking my fractured rib completely. My jaws snapped at his bloodied face and we both rolled away from each other only to join together again, smashing into each other like linebackers. The minutes wore on as we circled and leaped, bit and pawed at each other but we couldn't find an advantage. Romulus had the greater strength but I had speed and two working eyes. I tried to keep to his left in his new blind spot and he circled tightly keeping me in sight as best he could. No matter what I tried I couldn't move fast enough to keep out of his sight and my mind began to work feverishly, analyzing the situation, searching frantically for a solution.

I paused for a moment as a thought occurred to me and in that moment he lunged again. I had been fighting like a wolf, but I had a human mind. It was time to use it. That time, instead of lunging forward to meet him as I had been, I ducked, letting him fly over me and my teeth flashed once. I bit down on his hind right leg as he passed me in the air and spun, following him until he hit the ground. My teeth ground down tightly, blood filling my mouth and he howled in pain as I jerked my head hard from side to side, breaking his leg with a wet snap that echoed throughout the clearing.

The Pack had gone silent again. The only sound now was that of our harsh panting and his pained whimpers. Off to the side I could hear Chloe muttering to herself. I circled him slowly as a low thump reached my ears. The Pack stomped their feet. Once. Again. Then again, and again, and again, faster and faster until the frenzied drumming of their feet on the wooden bleachers became a constant rumbling roar of thunder.

I stopped, breathing hard and stared down at Romulus just as he lifted his head to face me. I lunged forward, my teeth flashing a final time and a gout of blood erupted from between his jaws as I simultaneously crushed and ripped open his throat with a single, vicious shake of my head.

I changed slowly back into my human form and stood as tall as my broken ribs would let me. Blood stained my mouth and ran down my chin and chest all the way to my groin as I turned to face the Pack.

"My name!" I roared, "Is William Reese! And from this night forward, I am your Alpha!"

The responding roar, pouring forth from the throats of two hundred and fifty wolves, was so loud that I was sure the sound alone split the night sky and the cloud cover that had been so constant broke apart, letting the first rays of the full moon illuminate the clearing.

Chapter 20

Chloe

Lucinda dropped my leash and went forward, stalking across the field in her impossibly high heels, a swing in her step. Remus stood beside me, his face unreadable as he stared at his brother's cooling body and I sympathized, I really did, but as the moonlight washed through the field I could feel a hum in my body.

"Remus," I gasped, clawing at the buckles of the collar at the back of my neck, "Remus!" he stirred and looked at me, "Get it off!" I pleaded and he shook himself as if waking from a dream. I bowed forward as my skin shivered in the most disconcerting way imaginable.

"Just let it happen Chloe," he murmured and the collar fell away. I bent at the waist, hands on my knees and closed my eyes, going very still. I breathed, calmly, in and out, one after the other, slow and steady and I can't really describe it. I slipped my skin, but didn't. It was as if I stared my wolf in the eyes and we came to an understanding.

I was in control.

I swallowed and looked across the field and my wolf and I knew rage as one. Lucinda was attempting to hang off of William as if she had some sort of claim and though William leaned away, she was not relenting. I marched across the field, came up behind them and gripped Lucinda by her hair. I pulled her backwards off of William with a snarl and my lover looked at me dazed.

"Hands off my mate, bitch," I snarled.

"You little bitch!" Lucinda exclaimed and she swiped at me, a glancing slap across my face. I pulled hard on her hair, yanking her off her feet and sending her tumbling away across the grass.

"Challenge declared and accepted!" someone shouted, almost gleefully, and I heard William shout.

"Sharon, *no!*"

I would deal with her later, right now, Lucinda was rolling to her feet and the air horn blasted and she lunged. I side stepped her easily. She lunged at me again, I put the requisite amount of space between us, grabbed her and followed through, bringing my knee up into her face, using her hair as a hand hold to drive her head down as I drove my knee up.

She snarled and I threw her to the ground and put some more space between us. I felt my wolf growl and the sound rumbled out from between my lips unbidden but not unwanted. I snapped and snarled at Lucinda, who was struggling to her feet in her strappy gladiator heels. She looked at me, crimson staining her face from her nose that I had bloodied and she was afraid. I could see it in her eyes, scent it on the breeze. A bitter tang of sour sweat overlaying the rich earthy forest smells.

Lucinda and I circled one another for what seemed like forever and the air horn blared again. She smirked, a slow grin spreading across her lips and I cocked my head to the side. Her smile slipped, melting away as I let go my humanity and felt the fur flow. My wolf and I were in agreement. This was how this would end. With *both of us* in the driver's seat.

My body was unfamiliar, but not terribly so. My arms a little longer, my legs a bit thicker. Lucinda's coat was as black as her heart but mine resembled the sun through a misty morning. I didn't ponder it long because she tackled me, her arms around my waist, driving me back.

I linked my hands and drove both of my elbows down with as much force as I could between her shoulder blades. The Pack gasped and there was a sickening crack. A sharp sound, a broken howl of pain emanating from Lucinda as her arms fell away and she face planted in the grass.

I kept my balance, barely, and breath heaving looked at the sky. William's words echoed back to me, "*Among Wolf-kind, you haven't won if your enemy is still breathing.*"

I didn't want to kill anyone. Life was sacred, so incredibly sacred. I looked down at Lucinda who looked up at me, fear in the one eye

I could see. She was paralyzed. It was evident and I knelt by her. I gripped her head between my monstrous hands and closed my eyes, giving it a swift twist and a jerk. The snapping sound was loud and awful and I felt it reverberate up my arms. It made me sick and my stomach lurched as I let her body fall, threatening revolt but I managed not to retch or vomit in front of the Pack.

I let the wolf have her way then, shifting completely and Remus was right. It felt incredible. Beautiful and freeing but I couldn't stay this way. I wasn't done, the wolf was telling me with thought and feeling that I needed my voice. I needed to speak to my people and seal this. I came back to myself, crouched beside Lucinda's cooling body, tears gathering in my lashes. I closed my eyes and turned my head so I wouldn't have to look at what I'd done, what I'd had to do.

"Chloe," William's voice, his scent wafted along the breeze. His hands gently gripping my upper arms in a reassuring touch, as he held me up. I turned to him and open my eyes.

"I'm not done," I whispered and the look in his eyes was equal parts sympathetic and empathetic. I rose to my feet, a bit shaky at first and looked out over the throng of the Pacific Northwest Pack. The clearing was silent, its inhabitants in one varying form or another, mute.

"My name is Chloe Young, daughter of Mathias Young," I called out. I looked from one wolf-kind to another to another and finally settled on Sharon's ashen face.

"I swear to you, I will do everything in my power to protect you, to help our Alpha lead you, and to be here for you. I will learn and be a good Alpha Female for this Pack but don't you *ever* mistake my kindness for weakness. You come at me, you come at my Mate, you will find out just how very *unkind* I can be. Am I understood?"

My proclamation was met with weighted silence. William was a warm presence at my back, and slowly, one by one, the Pack began to kneel. I tucked myself into William's side and looked up at him. He looked down at me and as our gazes met, I said what I had been longing to ever since I'd woken up in Romulus' gilded cage.

"I love you, William Reese," and the tears threatened to spill. He cupped the side of my face and smiled, and it was everything I could do to maintain the appearance of control, when all I wanted to do was fly apart. Have a meltdown so I could pick up the shattered pieces and move on, stronger in the places I'd been broken.

William dipped his head, his warm brown eyes, so beautifully flecked with amber, full of emotion. His lips touched mine, a bare whisper of a touch through the blood that still coated him. I didn't care. I drew from the strength he offered me to get me through this moment, in front of our people. He drew back from the kiss and smiled at me and all I wanted was for him to take me *home*.

CHAPTER 21
William

Home...

That was all Chloe wanted right at that moment. I could feel her desire as clearly as I could feel my own and I smiled quietly, aware of the ghastly image it must've been with the blood still smeared across my lips and chin, but I nodded and handed her my coat as Nora brought it up. I draped it over her shoulders, impressed that she had been so calm facing the entire Pack nude as she had, and tugged on my pants as quickly as I could.

Things always seem to happen really fast right after a huge event, like two Alpha challenges in a single night, for example. People were milling around in small groups. Largely they were discussing my fight against Romulus but a good portion were in awe of Chloe's battle with Lucinda, of her control and her ability to stave off her change, her *first* change. That was huge, that was monumentally *huge*.

"Markus, we need to get out of here," I muttered and Markus snapped to attention.

"Yes, Alpha. Follow me."

He led us through the crowd, easily redirecting those that attempted to greet us or introduce themselves. Nora and Brent ran interference at our backs. I didn't really hear what excuses they gave, I wasn't exactly paying attention. My focus was on the tiny shape of my mate pressed against me.

We somehow got through the crowd and into Markus' Jeep. Chloe and I sat in the back, seat belts be damned, with her leaning against my chest and my arms wrapped securely around her. I barely even noticed the pain from my healing broken ribs.

"Alpha," Markus called from the front and I reluctantly pulled my gaze away from Chloe to meet his eyes in the rearview mirror.

"What is it, Markus?" I asked.

"You understand things are going to have to move now, correct?" I nodded even though he wasn't looking at me. "I understand."

"The Pack is going to want to see some leadership. Some decisions need to be made on a few members as well."

"Remus and Sharon," I said with a low growl and he nodded. "What the fuck did that old bitch think she was pulling tonight with that challenge crap?"

Markus shrugged. "I long ago gave up trying to understand how that woman's mind works. Sharon might not have survived her captivity as intact as we thought."

"That doesn't excuse her. Find out why she did it, I'll decide what needs to be done with her later."

"Umm... actually, Alpha. It's your mate who should make that decision..."

I blinked, surprised for a moment before I cursed quietly to myself. I had totally forgotten that. This was going to be even dicier than I had thought. Chloe was the Alpha Female of the Pack. That meant that, while the entire Pack deferred to me as the Alpha, the women deferred to her first. And as the Beta Female of the Pack, Sharon could be in a significant amount of trouble.

"We need teachers," I told Markus and he nodded. I suspected he was already considering that very thing. "Chloe needs a crash course in Pack structure and politics and I will leave it to her to decide how to dispense with Sharon. Remus is going to be another issue entirely. Request another meeting, set it for tomorrow night. All members not immediately leaving Seattle are required to attend."

"As you command, Alpha." There was a gentle smile on Markus' face and I couldn't help but return it. Despite everything that had gone wrong, something went right at least. I was the new Alpha and I had Chloe back with me.

When we pulled up outside my house I got Chloe out of the Jeep and the door unlocked. By the time I turned back to wave Markus off, it was to see his tail lights vanishing back up the drive toward the road.

The old Wolf had a good head on his shoulders. He certainly knew when he wasn't needed. Chloe followed along as I led her up the stairs, through the library and up to my room with its master bath. I settled her on the closed lid of the john and turned on the shower. It was scalding hot as I jumped in, quickly rinsing Romulus' blood from my face, neck and chest. The water that poured down the drain was a muddy pink mixture of blood and dirt; I didn't want to touch her with that. She deserved better. She deserved *everything*.

I climbed back out, leaving the shower running to find Chloe still wrapped in my coat and still sitting on the toilet where I'd had to leave her. She was shaking, so minutely that I wouldn't even have been able to tell if I hadn't put my hands on her shoulders.

"Sugar?" I whispered, and when it didn't immediately garner her attention I tried again, "Chloe, look at me."

When she lifted her head, her eyes were overflowing with tears, they streamed down her cheeks making tracks in the lingering makeup and dirt smeared across her cheeks. "I'm s-s-sorry," she stuttered, brokenly. She wiped at her face with her hands, smearing yet more dirt across her fair skin. "I'm sorry, I didn't want to fall apart."

"Shh-shh-shh," I shushed her. "You don't have anything to apologize for," I whispered and gathered her into my arms, holding her close.

"I don't think I can get used to that. I don't think I can get used to k-k-killing someone."

"And you shouldn't," I told her. "We aren't monsters, Sugar. We aren't beasts that kill indiscriminately. We're half human, half wolf. Romulus lost the human half of himself, if he ever even had one, and that's why he needed to be put down. We're wolf-kind. And sometimes that means law of the land, so to speak, survival of the fittest… Sometimes we have to end someone and you should never get used to it. If you could end a person's life, even someone that deserved it, and not feel anything I would be very worried about you, and so would the rest of the Pack."

She nodded but appeared to have lost the ability to speak. She choked and gasped, sobbing almost uncontrollably for a time and I simply knelt beside her and held her, offering what strength and support I could.

I knew enough from the first time I was forced to take a life, there was little I could do to make her feel better. All I could do was be there for her and let her work it out herself. When it was my time, Markus had taken me to a bar where I'd gotten blind drunk and had played pool for eight straight hours.

Eventually, her sobs subsided and I carefully pulled the jacket from her shoulders. She loosened the death grip she had on it, letting it slip away. I caressed her skin, reveling in the warmth of her, letting my hands glide softly down her arms as I carefully inspected her for injury.

Aside from a few minor scrapes that were already well on their way to healing, she was physically fine so I pulled her to her feet.

"You got water on your jacket," she mumbled and I stifled a laugh.

"I think the jacket will survive. Let's get you cleaned up, Love."

"Mm-hm," she hummed, nodding and I led her under the spray. She gasped quietly as the strong jets of water pounded against her skin and I grabbed her body wash and squeezed out a generous portion onto my hand. I pulled her out of the spray and rubbed my hands together before I started to cleanse her. I started at her throat, gently rubbing the wash into her skin and let my hands glide down over her shoulders and down the length of her arms, back up to her upper chest. She moaned quietly as I rubbed the soap into her breasts and trembled as I worked my way down her body.

I tried not to frown, I didn't want her to worry or be concerned with anything other than relaxing. I could see each rib clearly and her arms and legs felt thinner than they had been the morning before Rom bit her. I didn't like it. She seemed so frail beneath my hands and I trembled, fighting back the urge to curse Romulus with every breath. I'd already killed him. There wasn't much else I could do.

I was kneeling at her feet, working the soap into her calves when her hands landed on my shoulders and I looked up at her. She said nothing and neither did I, she simply combed her fingers through my hair, slicking it back from my face, a thoughtful look on her own. I smiled at her, turning my attention back to her legs.

From her calves I moved up to the back of her thighs as she sighed quietly above me, the tension slowly leaking out of her. I smoothed my hands over her ass, spreading the soap across every inch of her skin until I stood and worked my way up her back to her shoulders.

I reached up and pulled down the shower head, using it to rinse the soap from her body. Somewhere in cleaning her off she had closed her eyes and simply stood there, her arms at her sides and her head tilted back, whimpering in pleasure and maybe a little impatience every few moments.

"Almost done," I told her and put the shower head back before I reached for the shampoo and squeezed some out on top of her head. With one arm I reached around her waist, pulling her close to me until our bodies were pressed together. Her arms went around my waist, and with her head still tilted back I used both hands to massage the shampoo into her hair, running my fingers through the length of it, massaging her scalp, taking my time until she was practically limp in my arms.

I rinsed the shampoo from her hair and simply held her for a while, breathing in the scent of her. Peaches and sunshine, once again the scent of the Chloe I had fallen in love with. I couldn't imagine my mate without the scent of peaches clinging to her skin…

I didn't know how she felt about me now. I mean, I knew she loved me, but I didn't know what she *needed* from me, so I simply held her. Ignoring the erection she must have felt pressing against her belly for the time being. God, I ached to love her right now. Wanted to kiss her, caress her; bury myself deep inside her. But I waited. Waited to see what she would do, what she wanted, for her to tell me what she needed…

"I love you, William," she murmured against my chest and a shiver ran through me as her lips brushed lightly across my skin.

"I love you too, Chloe. I can't lose you like that again. I fell apart for a minute there," I admitted, and her arms came up and wrapped around me tightly. I grunted slightly, doing my best to ignore the stab of pain that ran through my chest. It was nothing compared to the pain I had felt when Romulus took her from me. Nothing like the kick to the gut I felt when I realized, fully, that I was in love with her, and that she was gone.

I don't know when it happened. I don't know how. Next thing I consciously remember was our lips pressed together, tongues dueling in our mouths and she moaned quietly into me as one of my hands slid up her body to squeeze her breast. I ran my thumb over a rapidly hardening nipple and her breath caught in her throat.

"I love that," I said, grinning against her lips before I let my mouth trail down her throat.

"W-what?" she stammered.

"How responsive you are. For example, if I do this…" I leaned down and ran my tongue across her left nipple, flicking the hard nub with the tip and she jerked against me.

"Or this," I sucked her nipple into my mouth, pinching it gently between my teeth as my other hand slipped between her legs.

I slowly slid two fingers inside her and her finger nails dug hard into my shoulders, a loud moan escaping her. I rolled my eyes up the length of her body where she stared down at me where I knelt at her feet.

"Don't you fucking *dare* tease me, William," she growled breathlessly. "It's been two weeks since I've had you inside me. I need you, I need you now…"

"Your wish," I groaned, "My command." I reached around her and lifted her into the air, getting to my feet, my hands gripping her ass tightly. Leaning back she braced her shoulders against the shower wall. Eagerly, she reached down and positioned the head of my cock at her entrance.

I thrust up into her slowly, sliding all the way in and then just held her for a moment, reveling in the feeling of her body against mine, letting us both enjoy the sensation of being so close to each other after our time apart.

Her body felt even hotter than before in my arms, heat

practically radiating off of her and I groaned as I felt her muscles clamping down on me in a rhythmic pattern as a small orgasm slid through her.

I wanted her in my bed, I wanted to wrap myself in her completely, for *hours*. But the idea of interrupting what we had just started to get us to the bed struck me as unthinkable. Chloe rocked her hips against me, her breasts heaving with every breath and I moved to meet her. Every thrust into her ground her clit against the base of my cock and it took only a handful of minutes before she stiffened in my arms, coming even as I emptied myself inside her with a quiet groan.

I withdrew from her hot, grasping cunt, moaning quietly and set her back on her feet. We said nothing as we rinsed off again and stepped out of the cooling shower. We dried each other with the decorative towels I kept hanging on a wall rack in comfortable silence and when we were done, Chloe tied her hair back loosely out of her face with a spare hair tie of mine that'd been left on the vanity. She took me by the hand and led me to my bed where she pushed me down onto my back, now more than capable of physically challenging me if she so chose.

I heaved myself completely onto the bed and settled, just looking at her. Yes, she was thinner, the effects of not eating properly while she was stuck with Rom, but beneath that, I could see a new and even greater strength. The muscle hidden just beneath her incredibly soft skin was taught and powerful, her entire body now lean and lithe with controlled strength.

She crawled across the mattress, slinking toward me until she took my cock in her mouth, stroking me quickly back to life with her lips and tongue and as soon as I was completely hard she finished crawling up my body, dragging her breasts across my leg and groin and up my stomach until she was straddling me before she slowly lowered herself down onto my dick.

I pulled her close to me as she started slowly sliding her body up and down my length. When I started to move to meet her though, she pushed down on my stomach and sat up, pressing me into the bed shaking her head. Sweat already dewed her face and her breasts and throat were bright with that flush that I found so attractive on her.

"Nuh-uh," she moaned and ground herself onto me. "You don't move. Just lay there and let me do this, let me love you." What could I do? I smiled and nodded and she started to move again, her hands planted on my chest for balance. She bit her lip, so goddamned alluring, before throwing her head back with a throaty gasp. She was just so *beautiful*.

I ran my hands up her back until I reached her hair and found the hair tie she used to hold it back. A quick, gentle tug and her damp, fiery locks were falling around her face, just brushing the tops of her breasts as she moved.

I promised I wouldn't move, as difficult as that was becoming. However, I never promised I wouldn't touch her. With every movement of her hips I felt a greater and greater desire to thrust up into her, to meet her descending body with upward momentum on each stroke. To distract myself I let my hands explore her smooth skin. Up her thighs, feeling the muscles bunching and lengthening as she moved, across the swell of her ass and up her sides to cup her breasts in my hands.

I could hardly stand not to move. I threw my head back, squeezing her breasts tightly and we both moaned loudly as she started moving faster above me. I gave up holding still and grabbed her hips, thrusting up to meet her with every motion and in moments I was seeing stars with how hard I came.

"Oh God, I love you Chloe," I groaned as I emptied myself into her *again* and her body suddenly clamped down on me, her breath catching in her throat, body shaking erratically as she came apart above me. She suddenly threw herself down on my chest *and bit me*.

The shock that ran through me then was nearly as strong as the orgasm that had shaken me mere seconds before. She bit my chest, just to the left of center, her teeth breaking the skin and gripping the muscle beneath, but instead of the sharp pain I would normally have associated with such an attack, I felt a wave of indescribable pleasure run through my body.

And an equally powerful sense of relief. *Yes*, Chloe loved me. She loved me as a human, but now it was obvious that her wolf loved mine, that she accepted me wholly as her mate.

Moments later, calmed, and with the sweat drying on our skins she pulled her teeth from my flesh, licking my blood from her lips. She looked down at me with a wide eyed expression etched across her face, her hair a wild and messy tangle, framing her face.

"Was that?" she asked and I nodded.

"Your wolf seems to think I'd make a good mate for you," I said amused, no, *joyful.* "You just marked me like I marked you."

"I don't even know what happened... I was..." she stopped a moment and flushed again. "I was coming and I just suddenly had this overwhelming urge and I just bit you. It was like it wasn't even me."

She slid off of me and curled up against my right side with her head on my shoulder, our legs tangled together. She gently placed her hand on my chest over the rapidly healing imprint of her teeth in my flesh.

"I know why you did it," I murmured against her hair. She tilted her head and looked questioningly up at me.

"I already marked you. Your body holds a print of my teeth, telling everyone that you belong to me. And since your change, your wolf didn't like that you hadn't marked me, knowing that you felt the same for me too. There was nothing to tell other wolf-kind that I'm spoken for. It was only natural for you to mark me in return." She considered that for a moment before I cupped her cheek in my hand, bringing her attention back to me.

"I belong to you, Chloe Young, mind, body, and soul. And you belong to me."

That got a smile from her and before I knew it her lips were pressed to mine again and she was pulling me on top of her.

"Come show me what that body can do," she whispered huskily in my ear. I smiled and I took my time and showed her.

Chapter 22
Chloe

William chuckled and I gasped as the sound vibrated through my body. I opened my mouth to say something glib and his head darted down, his mouth capturing mine in a deep, soul lifting kiss. I sighed out around that kiss in pure contentment and felt William's fingers twine with mine. He raised both my arms above my head and pressed them into the pillows and sheets.

His hips rocked against mine, his cock growing stiff between us, the friction a pleasurable thing that stoked the fires of my desire for him even higher. He pulled his mouth from mine and I tried to follow it with a cry that sounded petulant.

"You know we're going to have to sleep at some point," he said softly, teasing. I opened my mouth to retort, but the smart-assed remark I had primed disappeared into a gasp and throaty moan as he sank his cock deep into my body. He felt so good.

We stared each other in the eye from inches away, and while the last two times we'd made love tonight had been almost frenzied, desperate, and primal. This was something else. This was something softer, gentler. This was the meeting of two souls that were so madly in love with the other they wanted to become one being and *stay* that way for as long as possible.

William's eyes slipped shut and he brought his forehead to mine. My body glowed, hummed with a gentle pleasure as he slipped in and out of me in a slow and even rhythm that felt like we could go on this way forever.

His hands left mine, stroking down my arms, as he held himself aloft so as not to crush me or cause discomfort. I cupped his face between my hands and brought his mouth to mine, twining my arms around his shoulders holding him to me as we made love for who knows how long.

When we came, it was a kinder, gentler thing than the orgasms previous. The pleasure radiating out from my center, gently lapping at my edges before washing back in. William smiled down at me, his eyes closing and his head turning to the side as if my gentle cry of release was the sweetest music he'd ever heard. Several deep strokes more and he bowed his head and took his own pleasure.

My body throbbed and pulsed with soft afterglow and I swore it was in time with my beloved's heartbeat. He carefully vaulted my leg and drew me into his side as we panted and gasped and lay completely spent and satiated in the circle of each other's arms.

"I love you Chloe Young," he murmured again and it struck me...

"Reese," I told him and felt his head jerk as he looked down at me, I didn't have the energy to look back though.

"What?" he asked.

"Reese," I panted, "You love me, Chloe Reese."

William said nothing, simply squeezing me tighter against himself, a deep and contented sigh escaping from him. I smiled.

"I still want a wedding, a human one. It's every little girl's dream to get married one day. Our wolves may be cool with a couple of bites and there you have it, but it's important to me..." I confessed and swallowed hard, nervous; afraid he would dismiss the idea as silly or that he would patronize me like my father would whenever I told him something was important to me. I waited to be... discounted, marginalized, but it didn't happen. Instead, William squeezed me again, gentler this time and kissed the top of my head with love and tenderness.

"Whatever you want, Sugar. I'd do anything to make you happy." I snuggled closer, relieved and we were silent for a time.

"I'm glad he did it," I said somberly. William was silent, and very still beneath me. "I'm glad he did it so we didn't have to choose, so you didn't have to..."

"I wouldn't have, not if you didn't want it. We are extremely long lived, Sugar. It's not all sunshine then moonlight runs either but you know that. *I am so sorry* that *this* was your introduction to this life. Nothing but pain and blood." He sounded so unhappy and it made my heart ache for him.

I huffed a small laugh, "It was a rough start, but we're together now. I know the truth," I sighed out and reveled in the sensation of his fingers sliding up and down my spine in their gentle caress.

"There are so many things I should have, *could* have done better."

"I love you, William Reese. That is what your choices; good, bad, or indifferent have led us to. Something beautiful and something *real*. I need to hold on to that." He gave me a gentle squeeze and kissed my hair again.

"Sleep, Chloe," he murmured and I could hear the weariness in his voice.

"Promise not to let me go," I said and I knew it sounded weak but I didn't care.

"Never again, Sugar. Never again," he solemnly vowed and with a final contented sigh, I slept. We both did, and we slept *hard*.

I opened my eyes to a murmur of voices. I was still safe and secure in William's arms, both of us covered by the bed's crimson sheet, but we had a visitor. Markus leaned against the metal railing that acted as a safety measure at the top of the spiral stair leading down into the Library. I was really going to have to look through there sometime soon. I wondered what gems were hidden on those shelves...

"Welcome back, Girly." Markus grated, chewing on a toothpick in the corner of his mouth. I wrinkled my nose a bit at the slight hint of mint I caught from all the way across the room.

"What time is it?" I asked sleepily.

"'round two o'clock." I sat up sharply clutching the sheet to my chest. William let me go.

"The meeting! I have so much to learn, I have so many questions!"

"Calm your tits, Princess," William said laughing and I whirled, frowning and punched him lightly in the arm. "Owe! Hey! You know that hurts a lot more with your new strength," he chided but I just glared at him.

"It's not funny! I'm responsible for something like two-hundred people and I don't even know what we *are!*" I said forlornly.

Markus laughed, "You picked a fine mate, Boy. I like her. Get dressed you two and meet me in the kitchen. I'll make breakfast. I figured you'd need a minute so I set the meeting for tomorrow night to give you time to recover. Junior there always tries to do too much at once." Markus gave a gusty sigh and left the room waving over his shoulder. I felt my shoulders drop and chewed my bottom lip thoughtfully.

"We have a lot to do, don't we?" I asked and William sat up beside me.

"Yeah, but we'll do it together. Come on, let's get dressed. Markus will set us straight. It's the Arbiter's job to keep the Pack's Alpha appraised. We'll be getting a crash course in politics today I expect."

"Your father was the Alpha, don't you know a lot of it already?"

William smiled, "Some but not everything. Father tended to play his cards close to the vest."

I slipped out of bed and stretched, expecting that delicious sort of soreness from a night of great sex. The kind that left you begging off anymore the next day lest you really hurt yourself and trashed your ability to walk. There wasn't any. Like not at all. None. Huh, there might be some advantages to this whole wolf-kind thing.

"Get dressed, Chloe, before I bend you over the end of the bed and fuck you again," William was looking at me like I was something good to eat and I grinned.

"Well aren't you just a big bad wolf?" I teased.

"Don't tempt me woman," he said, the edge of a smile kissing his full lips. God I wanted to tempt him, was ramping up to do just that, but Markus' voice called out from the kitchen at the far end of the house.

"Keep it in your pants Junior! Better yet, both of you find some pants and get your asses out here! I don't have all goddamned day."

William and I laughed and found clothes, which for him were a pair of jeans that hung dangerously low on his hips and for me was another of his oversized tees. I led the way down the stairs, William's hands resting lightly on my shoulders as he followed. The touch reassuring and comforting. At the door leading into the living room I paused, frowning at the sight of the door which was leaning against the wall, off its hinges.

"Was that like that last night?" I asked.

William was looking me over, "I told you I lost my shit for a minute there, Love," he said softly. I took one of his hands from my shoulder and kissed his palm softly, bringing a gentle smile to his lips, before I continued leading the way to the kitchen.

We sat at the table and my stomach growled at the bacon and sausages Markus had frying. He expertly flipped a pancake and winked at me.

"Yet another domesticated wolf?" I asked with an arched brow and they both laughed for a moment.

"What do you want to know first, Sweetheart?" Markus asked.

I chewed my bottom lip, "Give me a biology lesson," I said bravely. "What am I? I mean, I know the basics, but..." I hesitated, searching for the words I needed but coming up empty.

"Spit it out, Honey," Markus said kindly and I sucked in a deep breath and let it out slowly.

"If William and I ever have children will they be like Romulus? Because if the answer is yeah, I need to keep up on my birth control. I don't know if I could do it."

Markus set his spatula down and looked over to William whose expression was one of worry as he looked me over. Markus cleared his throat, "Well, first off you're limited on your options for birth control. As far as I understand it, and yer gonna wanna check with one of the females of the Pack on this, birth control pills and the like are just like any other drug we take. Not exactly effective due to our ridiculously high metabolism."

I felt myself blanch and shot a nervous look to William who shared it with me. We hadn't used protection last night. Markus laughed.

"Boy, you didn't pay any attention to the Beta's did you?" he asked.

"Shut it, Old Wolf. Do we need to be worried?" William reached for my hand and I gave it to him.

Markus let out a gusty sigh and turned back to cooking, to save the food from burning, "Chloe, you just went through your first change last night and even though it was the damnedest thing I ever saw..." I cut him off.

"Wait, why was it 'the damnedest thing'?" I asked frowning.

"You're a natural Alpha, girl. Only once or twice in a lifetime do you come across someone who has the fortitude to control their first change like you did last night. It's not supposed to happen. Even so, it *was* your first change and a wolf-kind's hormones go all kinds of screwy with the first change. I think you're safe. That being said, conceiving ain't the hard part for us. Blood Born wolf-kind are rare Honey.

"Even if a female wolf-kind conceives, they got nine full moons, nine changes, to go through. Gotta have a certain amount of control to carry to term. You could do it. After last night, I'm damn sure about that," he nodded and started plating up the food. William got up and moved around the older Arbiter, setting the table and pouring glasses of orange juice.

I sat back in my seat and tried to wrap my mind around it and felt a little selfish for tackling that problem first. I mean, I had over two-hundred and some odd people to take care of with William... I frowned.

"So if William is Alpha, and the one to lead us all, what *exactly* is it that I do as female Alpha?"

Markus grinned, "Well as Alpha Bitch," he laughed outright at the look I gave him. "Don't glare at me, I didn't come up with the title. That was long before my time. Anyways, as Alpha Bitch it's pretty much your responsibility to make sure that the Betas are properly educating the newly Moon-Forged and that the Blood Born kids are being properly brought up. You're the Pack's social worker. Also, you're a big part of the Pack's legal system. Both of the Pack's Alphas preside over any wolf-kind on wolf-kind criminal proceedings.

"Violence among the Pack isn't tolerated, despite the brutality of the Challenges for succession. The human world ain't equipped to deal with us, so we have to police ourselves. It's the Alpha's, as in both William and you, it's your job to oversee any criminal proceedings when it comes to doling out Pack law. I deal with the civil law angle when it comes to the Pack's dealings." Markus stopped talking and stared at me.

"What?" I asked.

"Eat, or do I have to go back to the biology lessons?" he asked.

I ate, and listened to him as he continued to fill me in. I felt like I should be taking notes. There was so much to learn. Finally, he leaned back and sighed.

"You need to think about how you want to deal with Sharon and Remus too," he said. I stood and started clearing our plates, rinsing them and putting them into William's dishwasher.

"Do we really have to do anything?" I asked softly.

"Do you wanna look weak?" he shot back and I frowned.

"Haven't enough of y..." I stopped myself, "Haven't enough of *our* people died already?" I asked, sadly. My hands shook as the memory of the loud crack of Lucinda's neck echoed in my ears.

"You need to come from a position of power you two," Markus said and heaved himself to his feet. "William knows the law, no decision has to be made *right* now. But one does need to be made so y'all better be thinking about it."

He got up and stretched and went for the stairs but he turned and looked back at William over his shoulder, "You best take her for a run tonight, Boy. Show her what it is to be wolf-kind without all the blood and the teeth." He fixed his eyes on me, "There are good things about what we are too," he promised as his parting shot, then he disappeared down the stairs.

I looked at William who was smiling and I felt myself frown a little.

"What?" I asked.

"Oh, you're going to like this. Come on," he stood and held out his hands to me and I took them. He drew me in, wrapping my arms around his waist and walked me to the steps, him moving forward, me walking backwards. I laughed slightly.

"Where are we going?" I asked softly.

"I think Markus has the right idea, Sugar. We need to take a mental break, and you need to see the fun side of being wolf-kind. We're going for a run."

I smiled up at this man, this impossible man who I had grown to love so much in such a short time and the way his beautiful brown eyes sparkled, I just couldn't and wouldn't deny him anything.

"Okay," I agreed and yipped, shrieking a laugh as he bent and threw me over his shoulder. He slapped me on the ass.

"Quiet, woman! With your high pitched noises and girly sounds."

"You love my girly noises," I chided with a wicked grin turning my lips.

"Too fucking right I do," he agreed and he carried me down the stairs and out front of his house into the early autumn twilight.

Chapter 23
William

My house sat on the edge of a great deal of forested land, perfect for wolf-kind who loved to run, and I'd yet to meet one that didn't. The wolf in us enjoyed the woods, loved the forests and mountains and absolutely *loved* to run. If you were a couch potato sort before being bitten, you wouldn't be afterward. The wolf wouldn't let you.

"So, is there a plan here? Or were you just going to carry me around like a sack of potatoes all night?" Chloe asked from behind me as I walked toward the trees. I reached up and swatted her ass again and she gave an adorable little yip.

"Patience, my love." She growled and I laughed for a moment before I relented and stopped to set her back on her feet. She got her balance easily but winced a touch as her bare feet touched the cold, damp earth.

"Okay, Sugar," I said as we reached a large tree that stood at the very edge of my property. The house was a distance away, a good hundred and fifty feet at least; I had never really had occasion to measure the distance, but it was a good estimate in my opinion. I leveled Chloe with a salacious little grin and ordered, "Strip." She gave me a strange look and then looked around for a moment.

"You mean get naked, out here, where anyone could see?" she asked.

"That shirt won't survive the transformations and will only get in your way. Plus there aren't any neighbors for a mile or more in either direction, so come on, get naked." I followed up my words with action, loosening my belt and kicking off my oversized jeans as they fell off my hips. She eyed me for a moment and licked her lips, I think unconsciously, before she pulled off the shirt she had stolen from one of my drawers. A wave of gooseflesh washed over her skin as the cool air hit her.

"Okay!" I said and clapped my hands together once, sharply. "Let's not waste any time, I'm as chilled as you are. So do you remember how you felt when you went through the hybrid transformation last night?" The moon hadn't yet risen. We could have waited, with the moon still full she would change far more easily, the urge would help her find the triggers she needed, but the faster she got used to making the change voluntarily the better.

"How so? Scared? Angry?" she asked. The words were a bit sharp but I could tell she was simply concentrating. Her eyes were closed, nipples hard in the chill air, something I tried very hard not to focus on, as much as I wanted to.

"No, the wolf and you, working together. That sense of control and power. The joy of joining with the animal and being one... *that* feeling." I was intimately familiar with my own wolf. He and I had come to an understanding a long time ago. Unlike Chloe, I wasn't a natural Alpha. I'd fought the change for a long time. I'd hated it. I'd been almost feral in my wolf state for a while before I finally came to terms with the death of my family and the new life that was laid out for me. Yes, I had been a troubled youth as a new wolf-kind, and I was still young by my people's standards. But, I was at least considered old enough to lead them, if I could hold onto it. The next few months would show the Pack what kind of a leader I would be, and if they were comfortable letting me *continue* to lead.

"William?" I startled, jumping slightly at the sound of Chloe's voice. I had lost myself for a moment in my memories and when I focused on her again, I saw that she was looking at me with a naked concern in her expression, with her body language. Her hands fidgeted at her sides, smoothing her palms along her bare hips and she shifted her weight on her feet, almost swaying from side to side.

"Sorry, Sugar. Lost myself there for a second." I could tell she wanted to ask but I pushed on, not really wanting to discuss it yet. I didn't want her to worry so I changed the subject before she could ask.

"Anyways, search for that feeling. There are two levels, as you already know. Hybrid and full wolf. I can't exactly explain to you how those feel, it's different for every person, but you'll know them when you feel them. We're looking for full wolf right now. There will be time later to practice with the hybrid transformation."

She looked like she wanted to question further about my trot down memory lane but after a moment, she closed her eyes again, her lips set in a firm line. I reached out and gently brushed my thumb across her lips, causing her to smile slightly.

"Don't tense up," I whispered. "Just feel for the wolf, listen for her... tell her we're going to play. She should like that." Her shivering and fidgeting slowly subsided. After a minute's time, she stood stock still, almost like a statue. The change started swiftly after that. Her body shifted and melded, flesh and bones rearranging themselves in a single fluid movement. One second she was there, and the next my Chloe was gone, and in her place stood a beautiful tawny wolf, fur white, tipped in a golden red reminiscent of Chloe's fiery hair. She reached nearly to my waist standing on all fours, eyes as brilliantly blue as they were in her human form and now flecked with specks of amber as mine were. I smiled and buried my fingers in her thick pelt, massaging her neck.

She opened her mouth and yawned wide, tongue stretching out showing two rows of wickedly sharp, gleaming white teeth, before she closed her jaws and settled back on her haunches, tail wagging happily back and forth across the dirt. If a wolf could grin, she did it, tongue hanging out one side of her mouth in an entirely canine expression of pure joy.

I couldn't help but smile myself, bending to kiss the top of her head. She really was a natural! The change had been seamless and almost silent, the barest whisper of sound as her body shifted its natural shape. I stepped back from her and she whined a touch, but it was time I joined her.

I closed my eyes and triggered my own change. It wasn't nearly as smooth or as quiet as Chloe's had been. There was a sickening sound of bones snapping and rejoining, flesh tearing and healing as my body changed its shape and Chloe let out a startled yelp, rising up to all fours as if she were ready to run away.

It's okay, I told her. *I'm fine, my love.* Not in words, you understand. Wolves have a complicated and purely instinctual method of communication. Wolf Packs in the wild have been observed coming across an obstacle or prey to hunt and the entire Pack has silently reacted, even the ones toward the back that couldn't possibly have seen, heard, or smelled whatever it was the lead wolves encountered.

Body language is an impressive thing and wolves have taken it to an entire comprehensive system of communication with very little vocalization required. Still, I gave a little bark, and stood up on all fours, spinning in a circle and wagging my tail happily, to show her that all was well. I looked like your typical grey wolf, grey and tawny brown; black marking my thick, insulated fur. Standing next to her I was physically much larger than her, as we were in our human forms. I nuzzled her shoulder and licked at her ear affectionately for a moment before I took a few loping strides into the woods.

I stopped and glanced back over my shoulder at her before she started following me, hesitant at first but then with greater speed as I started running ahead of her. Pretty soon she was keeping up and we ran.

The average Grey Wolf has a top running speed of about thirty-one to thirty-seven miles an hour. We were not typical Grey Wolves. We didn't have anything even approaching natural strength or speed. We were both much stronger and much faster. So as we ran, we covered a lot of distance.

We chased each other through the woods, leaping over fallen trees and plunging through thick brush and vegetation, the ever darkening gloom of night did little to impede our vision and our noses more than made up for any diminished visibility. I was constantly having to nip at Chloe's flanks to keep her on track as she found herself distracted by gopher dens, animal scents, game trails, unique, *at least to her*, tracks and so on. In the woods there was no end to the scents and things to investigate and as a new wolf she was *fascinated*, drawn to all of them.

I let her play, but kept us moving steadily onward until I finally caught the scent I was looking for. A sharp, heavy, mineral odor. Like wet stone.

Roughly twelve miles from my house right on the border of the

Olympic National forest lay the Sol Duc Hot Springs Resort. I led her to the edge of the property, belly low to the ground in a silent crawl forward as I peered intently at the area. Early fall meant the summer tourist season was over and while the place wasn't empty, it was more sparsely populated than it would have been at the height of summer. Still, there were people around and I kept a wary eye and nose out for anyone wandering the grounds. The resort may be owned and operated by Pack, but the guests were all, usually, very human.

Satisfied there were no guests present, I straightened and loped out onto the property, leading the way away from the swimming pool, instead moving toward the naturally heated mineral pools. The pools were very man made and ranged in temperature from the high eighties up to a hundred and four degrees.

I picked one in the middle range, shifted to my human form and slid into the water with a quiet groan. "Come on in, Sugar," I said and waved to Chloe where she stood, still as a wolf, at the edge of the pool. "We'll chat for a bit and relax."

She shifted back and almost shrieked, gasping as the cold air hit her skin. She leapt into the gently steaming water, plunging to the bottom of the pool in a crouch.

"Holy shit," she sputtered as she came up, wiping water out of her eyes and sweeping back her hair. "That was a little more intense than I expected!" she admitted and I winced, apologetically.

"Yeah, sorry about that. I forgot, the wolf's fur is so well insulated. It can be a real shock going from one shape to the other when the conditions are like this. You get used to it after a while. At least a little bit."

"Thanks for the warning," she drawled sarcastically.

"Hey, honest mistake."

"Yeah, yeah. So what are we talking about?"

"Well what do we need to figure out, overall?"

She drifted over and sat beside me, leaning back against the side of the pool and I made sure to ignore the way her breasts just broke the surface as she considered. I make no apologies for how badly I wanted my mate right then, but I needed to focus, so I pushed all thoughts of lust as far away as I could and concentrated on the issues at hand.

"Remus, Sharon... my father," she said the last with a disgusted sneer. She gave me a sidelong look and a small smile turned her lips again, the kind of smile that I had come to love more than any other. Just the tiniest turning of her lips, as if she had a secret. I mentally dubbed it her 'Mona Lisa' smile right at that moment but kept silent on the subject.

"It might be a good idea if we learned a little more about each other too," she heaved a substantial sigh, "I mean, you look twenty-five but by your own admission, you're in your seventies and I know almost nothing about you to be this crazy in love with you."

Her admission made me smile, "You know the important parts," I told her and slid over until we were touching. I pulled her around so she was straddling my lap and gave her a gentle kiss. "The rest is just window dressing, but we'll figure it out as we go."

"Alright," she sighed and leaned her head against my shoulder. There was silence for a moment before she spoke again in a small sounding voice. "What about kids?" she asked and I fought the urge to heave out a huge sigh. I really didn't know how she would take that and I didn't really know how it would have been intended myself, to be honest. When I'd been human, I'd wanted children. As a wolf-kind, I'd let that dream go a long time ago...

"I'm not exactly ready for children at this point," I said uneasily. "With the Pack such a mess, there's a lot of work that I need to focus on to get us back on track. I'm not sure if I could handle worrying about children at the same time."

She nodded against my neck. "I'm really worried our kids would be like your brother... Like Rom."

I did sigh that time. "I can't say they wouldn't be. Blood Born are more aggressive. That's not always a bad thing, but there does seem to be a higher chance of them being like Rom. Remus is a different case. He seems to have better control of himself overall at least." I shrugged and frowned to myself. "I don't know what to tell you, Sugar. I can't make any promises. All we could do is try to show any kids we might have, the love and attention they'd need and teach them to be good people. Dad never did show the twins much affection that I saw. Maybe that had something to do with Rom being so horrible. Or he might have just been broken from the start. It's hard to say, really."

She sagged into me, molding herself against my body and I simply held her for a long time as we each lost ourselves in our own thoughts. She'd wanted kids, her asking about it this much proved that to me. I wish I could say her fears were unfounded, that Rom was one in a million just like human kids, but he wasn't. Blood Born just tended to be more animal, more wolf than human... whether they came from two Moon Forged parents or not. Sociopathic tendencies manifested more with the Blood Born than with human children, it was my people's real curse. Our true tragedy.

After several minutes, Chloe stirred a bit. "What about you?" she asked and I frowned.

"What do you mean?"

"Well, I know you like art. I know you're good with your hands and you make sculptures. I know you like to read. And you *really* like the color red. I know you are freaking phenomenal in bed," I laughed, and her voice gentled, grew more serious, "What else do I need to know about you William Reese?"

"Hmm..." I thought for a minute, really considering the question before I spoke. "Well, I've come to appreciate the smell of peaches a lot more since I met you," I said. I could still faintly detect the scent of peaches around her. Even through the strong odor veil of minerals given off by the geothermic water we lounged in.

"I like movies, and music. I love this park, camping, hiking, all that. I'm an outdoorsy kind of guy, I guess you could say."

"Nothing wrong with that. You don't like cities?"

I shrugged and she whimpered slightly in protest as I rocked her in my arms. I smiled that she was so comfortable and answered her question, "Not that I dislike cities. They're just so... loud, and they stink. There's so many people crammed into such a small space and all those tall buildings and concrete, and asphalt... It's like there's no air. It's claustrophobic and there isn't enough green. Not enough good dirt beneath my paws, too much steel and glass." I shuddered slightly and shrugged again but I made sure to only use the shoulder her head wasn't resting against. "I just prefer woods, and mountains, and open spaces."

"Is that the wolf in you, or were you like that before you were bitten?" There was a touch of concern in her voice.

"You're not going to suddenly have huge personality shifts, Chloe. It doesn't exactly work like that. Yeah, even as a kid I didn't much care for living in the city." I hadn't thought about my life before being wolf-kind so much in the last several years, as I had in the past few days. I held her tightly for a moment. "You know we're stalling, right?" I said in a quiet murmur.

She shook her head.

"Not yet," she said, shifting her weight against me, grinding herself against my dick, which obligingly responded to the attention. The water only came up to my chest where I sat on the submerged bench and I slunk down to put more of us under the water. She was starting to shiver slightly as the cold air touched the now damp skin of her upper body and she gave a contented sigh as we sank beneath the warm water. She turned in my lap so she was sitting with her back to my chest, my length nestling into the crack of her beautiful ass again and she leaned back, resting her head on my shoulder as my arms came around her.

"What about your dad?" I asked, finally. It was still a difficult subject, but it was probably going to be simpler than the other issue we had hanging over our heads that we needed to hash out.

She groaned and pressed her face against my neck. "What about him?" she said her voice muffled.

"You know he's not going to be happy about this. Not even a little."

She frowned and let out a disgusted snort.

"And?" she asked. "What the hell do I give a fuck what he thinks about it? If he can't get his head out of his ass that's not my problem." Her anger masked her deep hurt and I considered how best to continue; this *needed* to be talked about. Likely Mathias

Young was already looking for his wayward daughter and that could pose a problem for our Pack.

"But if he doesn't pull his head out of his ass then he is going to continue to kill our people... You're his only daughter, Sugar. Mathias Young has burned down the world of wolf-kind for far less in the past. We may be forced to kill him," I pointed out and she nodded, just slightly.

"I know," she sighed, quiet, broken, her beautiful lilting voice heavy with sorrow, the tang of salt mixing with the minerals of the spring. She wiped at her face and I pulled her back cuddling her closer.

"As much as you might hate him, he's still your father," I pointed out gently and she tensed in my arms.

"I don't want him to be. That man on the phone... I just don't want him to be."

"No choice in that, Sugar." I pressed a kiss to the back of her neck and she sighed again.

"We'll figure it out later. For right now, can you promise you're not going to send out a hit team to kill him or something?" she asked. "At least not until we have more information?"

I chuckled, though there was no real humor in it. "It doesn't exactly work like that but yes, I won't be going out of my way to hunt *the* hunter of Hunters. Not without a very compelling reason." Of course keeping Chloe safe and by my side was a very compelling reason... Her nodding again distracted me from the thought.

"Alright, what about Sharon and Remus? What do we do with them?"

I didn't really know what to say at first. Well, that's not exactly true. I knew what to say. I knew what *the law* said. I just wasn't sure I liked it or wanted to do it.

"Pack law is very clear, Remus assisted in the murder of the pack's Alpha. And *worse*, he actually revealed the Pack's location to one of the most effective hunters we have ever seen. Whatever else he may be, your father is *very* good at what he does, and he now knows that we occupy this territory, all because of my brothers' selfish political machinations." I brooded on that for a while, but

Chloe, ever inquisitive, didn't let me brood for very long.

"So what does Pack Law require? I can't imagine it's anything good."

"According to Pack Law, Remus should be executed on the next full moon. There's a ceremonial weapon, meant for exactly that purpose. As Alpha at the meeting tomorrow night, I would be expected to pass sentence on him and on the next full moon, kill him in front of the local Pack with a silver edged weapon."

"Local?" she paused and held up a hand for a moment to stop me. "Never mind, we'll get back to that later. They would really expect you to kill him? Your own brother?"

"He's no brother to me except that we lived together under the same roof. He and Romulus were both older than me and they *did* teach me a lot, they *did* help me when I first came to the family, but that was only at Father's behest. Chloe, Sugar, he helped *kill his own father* and he betrayed the entire Pack. Patricide is the mother of all sins to our people, not only did he do that, he committed treason to do it. All of those are capital crimes... and I am the Alpha. If I can't carry out a sentence as it's decreed by Pack Law, who's to say I won't bend or bow on other issues? The Pack could lose respect for me and I could be deposed pretty quickly if that happens. You've seen the fights of succession..." I didn't want to be fending off challenges every full moon. That was a pretty damned good way to get dead in a hurry and I had everything to live for right here in my arms.

Chloe was silent again but she was fidgeting, shifting her weight slightly and kicking her leg in a most distracting manner as it caused her ass to shift side to side just slightly in my lap. I moved my hands to her hips and held her tightly, keeping her still.

"If you keep doing that we're not going to finish this discussion before I bend you over the side of this pool and fuck you," I whispered in her ear and she turned to look at me out of the corner of her eye with a mischievous smirk.

"You say that as if it's a bad thing," she said but she obligingly stopped kicking her leg. "Would... would it be impossible to show any leniency to Remus?"

"He hasn't shown much to indicate that he deserves it. He helped kill Father. He helped keep you captive." I paused and thought about that. "Though he did bring you to see me. And did he help you with the change?"

"We discussed it while I was eating. We stopped and got food right after we left the house the other day," she said and I felt a profound sense of relief wash over me.

"He also kept me alive before that. When I wouldn't eat he went out of his way to give me these protein shakes," she said and my relief twisted sharply into an even greater feeling of despair. Pack Law was very clear. Even if I felt a sense of gratitude toward Remus for helping my mate, I couldn't just suspend his sentence and let him stay free.

"Couldn't you make him leave?" she asked and the proverbial light bulb went off over my head even as a sense of dread filled me out from my center.

"Theoretically..." I muttered, considering the idea.

"Why theoretically? You either can or you can't, right?" her fingers wound around mine as she idly played with my hands beneath the water.

"True, though it isn't entirely that simple. You don't understand it yet, but you'll learn. To a wolf, at least to wolf-kind, the Pack is *everything*. It's supposed to be at least. The Pack is your family, your life, your support. Without a Pack a wolf is in trouble. I could order Remus to leave. I *could* banish him from the Pack. But he might not agree, he might ask for the executioner's blade instead."

"What?" she sounded confused. "Isn't the Alpha's word as good as Law? If you order him to leave how could he refuse? How could he ask to die instead?"

"He could request death in place of losing his Pack. Omega, that's a wolf without a Pack, is the worst punishment that we can hand down. Sure he gets to live, but Omega is no kind of life for us, Love."

She was silent for a moment after that statement, the finality in my tone giving her a brief pause. "Is it really that horrible?"

I nodded. "It can be. To Blood Born even more so as they've

never known anything other than the Pack. As Moon Forged, we were human first. We spent time without a Pack. We *could* return to that, if we really needed to, although the wolf inside us wouldn't be thrilled by it. But Remus? He might not be able to handle something like that. It's really difficult to say. But it may just be the best option given his crimes. I'll think about it," I promised. I knew she didn't understand, that she wouldn't or couldn't understand but I was pretty sure that she was right. Omega was a fate worse than death and for what Remus had done, I wanted him to suffer.

"What about Sharon?" she asked, interrupting my thoughts on my brother. I hummed quietly as I considered that, letting my hands slide up her sides from her hips until I was gently cupping her breasts. She made a deeply contented sound and relaxed further against me.

"You have to make that decision," I said. "As the Alpha Female it's your job to police and pass judgement on these things."

"What judgement am I passing, exactly?" she asked, a touch breathlessly as I kneaded the soft flesh of her breasts in my hands. She moaned quietly and arched her back for a moment as I pinched her already hardened nipples. "I mean, what did she do, really? What was so awful?"

"When you attacked Lucinda, were you challenging her for the role of Alpha? Was that your intent?"

She let out another quiet moan, dragging out the word, "Noo-o-o. No, I wasn't thinking about the fact that she was the Alpha Female. She just pissed me off the way she was trying to hang off you like that. I mean, she'd been doing the same to Romulus just before the fight and his body wasn't even cold yet and there she was, trying to rub herself against *my* mate." She stressed the word 'my' with a fierce anger that made me practically beam with pride and a feeling of all-encompassing love for her swelled in my chest. I nipped her shoulder near the mating mark I'd left and Chloe gave a throaty gasp.

"That's what Sharon did. It wasn't a challenge, and for her to say that, in front of the entire Pack, forcing the issue? That was not within her right to say. But the whole Pack heard it, and there was nothing else to be done by that point. She forced the issue, was trying to get you killed. She figured it was your first full moon. She figured you wouldn't be used to it or be able to control it and she was counting on Lucinda killing you." I growled, angry at the very thought of what could have happened.

"She put my mate in danger for her own petty vindictive bullshit and I will not stand for that type of behavior in my Pack." Without realizing it I had changed my tone dramatically, using a forcefulness that was typically reserved for dealing with hard headed individuals in need of leadership and guidance and without thinking, or possibly, even being aware of it, Chloe responded to it.

"Yes, Alpha," she said, the wolf in her reacting instinctively to the voice and word of her Alpha, her body going limp in submission against my own.

I took a deep, steadying breath. My hands had grown still on her body and I forced myself to resume my gentle massage of her flesh.

"Sorry," I muttered, contrite. "I didn't mean to get so intense."

"It's okay. I kind of like it," she murmured, sheepish and I caught a glimpse of that sexy as hell flush painting the tops of her breasts from over her shoulder.

I chuckled quietly against her hair. "So you have a few options, but only a few really. Pack Law dictates no interference when it comes to a Challenge, it doesn't really have anything to say about creating one from nothing. Really, if she hadn't opened her mouth, by Pack Law you would have had your ass whooped by Lucinda, and would have had to show deference as her Beta before the crowd and it would have been done."

She arched her back slightly again, opening a space between us and reached behind her to grasp my dick with one small hand, stroking me slowly. "Deference, such as?" she asked.

"It's very difficult to think when you do that," I groaned and it was her turn to laugh at me.

"Says the man who has been playing with my tits for the last five minutes."

"I happen to enjoy your tits," I said.

"And I happen to enjoy this." She gave my dick a tug and my

eyes slipped closed of their own accord. Damn she was good at changing the subject.

"You would have had to grovel for forgiveness." I gasped as she tightened her grip and groaned. "As for Sharon, your choices are to have her marked and demoted. Remove her as Beta, but we'll have to choose a new Beta quickly to fill in her usual role. Preferably someone close to us and supportive of us as both a couple and as Alphas of the Pack."

"Okay," she sighed and continued stroking me, her hand gliding lightly across my skin. She put almost no pressure on the shaft, her fingers just loosely circling me but on the up stroke her thumb ran across the head and sent a jolt of pleasure through my entire body that only a bonded mate could do.

"And my second option?"

"Have her leave the Pack entirely, make her Omega."

She paused, her hand becoming still for a moment before she resumed moving. "And that would be an extreme reaction which would be seen by the Pack as personal and not in keeping with the role of a leader. I would probably lose what little respect I've gained so far and I'll have an uphill battle getting that back. Right?"

I nodded and let one hand slide down her body until my fingers rested on her pussy, gently parting her lips. "You've got a pretty good understanding of things already, my love," I told her.

She gasped and pushed at the floor of the pool with her feet, lifting her ass so she could position me at her entrance. "Alright that's enough politics for tonight, now stop talking and get inside me."

I can be many things. Contrary. Stubborn. Difficult. Even a bit stupid on occasion. One thing I very rarely was? A complete and total idiot. She didn't have to tell me twice and I slowly thrust up into her as she slid down the length of my cock. When her ass settled against my stomach again I was buried all the way inside her and I couldn't help but groan at the sensation of her body wrapped around me. She didn't push herself up. She simply shifted her hips, grinding her body against mine, keeping me buried to the hilt in her grasping cunt the entire time. She braced her hands on my legs, her head back against my shoulder, mouth gaping in a silent cry.

I came first, sometime later. I felt it boiling up inside me until I couldn't hold it back anymore and I pressed her down against me, holding myself fully inside her as I pulsed and twitched within the tight grip of her pussy. She moaned quietly, her muscles contracting around me as she joined me and her nails dug hard into my arms where she held onto me.

We sat for a time, not separating from each other in the pool until I was forced to shake myself hard to avoid falling asleep, drowsy with afterglow.

I tilted my head forward and kissed her neck, gently nipping at her skin with my teeth until she shifted against me causing us both to moan slightly.

"As good as it feels to just stay here inside you, Sugar," I said. "We need to get back to the house." She nodded, sleepily, and pulled away from me. Climbing out of the pool, we shifted quietly back to our wolves and started the journey back home.

If I could have smiled a human smile I would have. As the thought occurred to me I realized that it just felt right. Our home. It had been just my space, my house, for so long and now it was indelibly marked in my head as Chloe's home as well, as *ours*, and as we trotted off into the night there was no doubt in my mind, whatsoever, that it would be a better home for having her in it.

Chapter 24
Chloe

"This is seriously becoming my favorite way to wake up," William said, voice deep with sleep, but still bright with a smile. I laughed and let him slip from my mouth.

"Seriously, I could live with this every morning, don't stop," he said and I grinned up at him, stalking up the length of his body giggling.

We made love for a good portion of the morning, both of us pointedly ignoring what needed to be done under the light of the moon later that night. I didn't want to bring in our reign with punishments and by handing down sentences. It seemed wrong, tyrannical, and I shuddered inwardly at how much it felt like *Rom* and what he would do.

Every time I had the thought that I really didn't *want* to be the Alpha Bitch of our Pack, I got this pervading sense of disgust from my wolf and she was right. The situation was far from ideal, but I could and would do this. William needed me by his side and it was either me, or to have let Lucinda remain and there was *no* way I could have let the Pack continue to suffer under that special little cuntcake's crazy.

What Sharon did needed to be punished according to the Pack, but according to me, I felt like she was about to be punished for doing them all a favor. I tipped my head back under the shower spray to rinse my hair when the thought occurred to me and I bit my lower lip.

Was I sure that wasn't what Sharon had in mind when she'd done it? I mean it was pretty obvious that Remus had a bunch of ulterior motives that were a freaking mystery to the lot of us, but still, ulterior motives none the less. How could I be sure that Sharon hadn't had the same? I suppose I could just ask her and hand down punishment accordingly.

I sighed, and washed again, even though I didn't really need to. I just was enjoying the hot water too much.

"Chloe!" William called from out in the kitchen and I smiled; I couldn't help it.

"Yeah!"

"Come and eat! Markus is here so put on some clothes!" I laughed. I knew the man was here, I'd heard him. I rinsed and shut off the tap and spent several minutes more luxuriating in the feel of the plush bath towel against my skin. I slipped on the dress that had been in the bottom of my bag. It was almost too light for the cooling weather here but I was running painfully low on clothes, let alone clean ones.

It was a baby doll hi-lo dress, a white affair, reminiscent of a tank top at the top with elastic below the breasts. The dress fell to my knees in front and my ankles in the back and was cute as hell. The sheer white fabric edged in delicate lace. I dried my hair, gritting my teeth at the whine of the hairdryer and looked at myself in the mirror.

I looked like me, except I was different. More sure of myself in my stance. My hair a touch longer than it'd been; where before it'd barely brushed the tops of my shoulders, now it was about two inches past.

"Chloe?" William appeared in the mirror behind me and my heart gave a sharp ache at just how beautiful he really was to me. "You okay?" he asked.

"Heavy is the head that wears the crown, Boy. Bad enough she's been wolf-kind all of a couple of weeks, throw in being Alpha Bitch on top of that, I'm kind of amazed y'all are holding it together." Markus grumbled from behind William, just out of my sight.

William's generous brown eyes roved me from head to foot, a gentle, appreciative smile curving his lips which made me smile in return, a deep bloom of pleasure opening inside me at the thought of being pleasing to him. God I was so stupidly giddy in love with William Reese it was mind boggling.

Markus chuckled and appeared over William's shoulder, "Look

at you two all moony eyed," he stated and let out a gusty, mocking breath.

"I'm fuckin' starving, get your asses out here," he gruffed, and William bowed his head, laughing. I took Williams hand and we followed the Arbiter down to the kitchen.

"You boys have been busy," I said gratefully. A platter of turkey sandwiches and a bowl of fruit sat on the counter, along with three different freshly opened bags of potato chips in three different flavors.

"Oh! My favorite!" I declared going for the sea salt and vinegar. William's eyes sparkled when I sneezed at the sharp vinegar tang.

"You knew that didn't you?" I asked popping a chip into my mouth and smiling at the pucker it caused. I always had to giggle at that feeling.

"Yep," he said and went for the sour cream and cheddar, my second favorite.

"Tell you something you didn't know," I spoke around a mouthful of crunchy chip.

"Now this I gotta hear, I put that dossier together myself." Markus slid into a seat and leaned back.

"Mmm, when I was ten and won second place in that martial arts tournament, I didn't quit after that, my dad wouldn't hear of me in second place for anything ever. Honor student, you name it and I was in it. No, my dad got me a private instructor, the best of the best. Lucinda really didn't stand a chance." My tone was weighted with regret and both men stared at me silently for a full minute before Markus started to laugh.

"Sharon did us all a big damned favor," he said, and I felt my shoulders drop.

"You have no idea," I said quietly and I looked at Markus, "Do you think that was her intent?"

"No, Sugar," William set his chips aside and pulled me into a firm embrace.

"Kid's right, Sharon ain't a schemer like Rem. I think she fully expected you to die." Markus shook his head.

"Well I'm going to ask her anyway, in front of everyone."

"Why?"

"Because, I want to know from her, I want to know why and I want to understand it before I start off passing judgement on something I know nothing about."

Markus beamed at us. "This Pack may be headed for a rough road-a-ho in the near future, what with Rem exposing us like he did and with Chloe here being the daughter of The Hangman. It's a good thing we've got leaders with a level head. We may just survive the trouble ahead with you two at the helm."

I cuddled into William and he held me close as we traded a weighted look of concern. Markus smiled and nodded to himself.

"That look right there, that tells me without a doubt you two are the right ones for the job," he said.

Something occurred to me, "Why do you call him that? My father?"

"What the Hangman?" Markus asked. William went very still at my back.

"Yeah."

"It's the weapon he uses, Sugar. He favors a silver coated length of piano wire, a garrote." William's voice was so somber, full of such sorrow that I instantly regretted asking. I opened my mouth to apologize for asking and stopped, all three of our heads jerked in the direction of the stairs as the door opened downstairs.

"Hello! It's me Nora!"

All of us visibly relaxed as the young – well, young *looking* girl came up the stairs. The heavy mood of the moment before evaporating when she smiled across the room at us. For a Goth girl she sure seemed happy.

"Alphas," she greeted and grinned. I frowned. I doubted I would ever get used to that.

"Come on, let's eat," Markus grumbled. We all four sat down at the table.

"What brings you here?" I asked Nora.

"Well, Markus called and said you have some, ah, delicate questions about female wolf-kind anatomy."

I blinked, "Thanks?" I said to Markus who was shaking with silent laughter.

"Don't mention it!" he wheezed trying not to lose his shit completely. I smiled sweetly at him.

"Right, so birth control, apparently medicine isn't an option so what is? Please don't spare any details." I gave Nora a sphinx like grin. *That* wiped the smile right off his face.

"Boy, grab some food, I'll grab the beer and we best go *outside* and leave these women to it, you get me?" William grinned and tortured Markus a little.

"I don't know Markus, I'm pretty comfortable," he said and Markus gave him a baleful look.

"Go on you two. He's right, I have questions and she's here willing to provide answers..." didn't have to tell them twice. They took half the small mountain of sandwiches, fruit and chips with them and trouped down the stairs and out into the afternoon's failing light.

"IUD works best for us, multiples aren't uncommon for our kind, but no, it's not like we have a litter of puppies in wolf form or anything. In fact, you have to be strong enough to resist the shift or you risk losing the babe or babies before you can carry to term. We have a wolf-kind doctor; we call the Pack doctor a Galen after some Roman doctor guy from way back when," Nora explained after we heard the door shut behind the boys. She picked up a sandwich and smiled. "That about cover it?" she asked.

"That about covers what I wanted to know for now, thank you." We ate in silence for a few while I considered what she said.

"How do I get an appointment with the Galen?" I asked.

"Consider it done, I'll make it happen," she swallowed and I nodded.

"What does 'marking' someone mean?" I asked. She went really still and sighed.

"Let me guess, Sharon?" she asked. I nodded.

"Is that what you're going to do? Mark and demote her?" I stared at my half eaten sandwich.

"I don't know, I'm considering my options but in order to do that, I need to know exactly what they are..." I trailed off and fixed her with a look. She chewed silently, a war on her face.

"Please don't make me order you," I said gently and sat back in my chair. Nora blinked at me, surprised and twisted her lips back and forth in thought.

"It isn't pretty, but it isn't Omega either." She said 'Omega' like it was a dirty word, I filed that away for later.

"So to mark one of us, is essentially to brand one of us, here," she pointed to her shoulder, "The brand is done with an iron made out of silver. It hurts, and when it heals it scars because, well, silver... That and as far as I've heard it, the silver particles left behind during the branding process makes it so it heals human slow and makes it itch like a mother when it does finally heal over. The scar lasts for *years* and as long as it's there, the wolf-kind in question can't formally challenge for a fight of succession until the last vestiges of the scar fade away. If it ever does."

"So we can heal wounds made with silver?" I asked.

"Human slow, and like I said, the scars can last forever. And if the wound is a mortal one made with a silver weapon? That's it, we can and we do die. Topically we can wear silver, but after about a day the site welts up and itches like a mother and it takes days for that shit to go away.

"Like any allergy, some wolf-kind are worse and some better. Alphas tend to be more resistant to the allergy. Some Alpha's, I've heard, are barely slowed down. That's rare though and those are only natural Alphas which are rarer still. Ingesting silver is no good. Like really dangerous. We vomit like the worst case of food poisoning ever and it can eat our insides. It's a bad way to die."

Nora chattered on and I did my best to listen. I had a lot to think about and I wasn't really sure how on board I was with the potential to *brand* someone. I mean, my God!

"You okay Chloe? You look a little green," Nora looked at me with some concern.

"I'm fine, this is all really new and some of it is just so damned..."

"Brutal? So archaic it makes your teeth hurt? I know," she

heaved a gusty sigh, "But, it's just how things are, how things have always been done," she shrugged like that made *any* of this okay.

"Thank you, Nora," I murmured.

"Got any mind to who her replacement is going to be?" she asked.

"None. I don't know the Pack, have no idea who would be a good candidate versus who wouldn't." I turned and looked out the window.

"Well, you could always let the Pack decide," she said and I snorted.

"What? Like they picked Romulus for Alpha?" I asked and Nora grinned.

"Yeah, sometimes you need to go on more than just instinct." I felt a whole hearted surge of agreement from deep down inside and had to chuckle.

"What about you?" I asked. "Any interest in the position?"

Nora gave me a tight lipped smile, "I'd be honored," she said simply and the 'but' hung in the air between us so tangible it was almost a visible living thing.

"But?" I prompted.

"But, there are those that are stronger that would Challenge me for succession."

"Got a better candidate you can name?" I asked.

"No," she said honestly.

"If you're named tonight, you have an entire month before you'd have to meet any challenges, correct?" I asked.

"Yes," she said warily.

"Why do you think you would lose a challenge for succession?" I asked. Nora shifted uncomfortably.

"Me and Brent, we're Blood Born like Rom and Rem, but we didn't really get the mean streak. We were born and raised by two Moon Forged parents, they're in the Albuquerque Pack down south. Anyways, our parents weren't exactly fighters. They don't really train the females to fight either. Wolf-kind can be sexist that way.

"There are a lot of Moon Forged females that have drifted into this Pack that were military before they were forged, they know how to fight, they've been trained for it. They wouldn't make a good beta, not like me who was born into this, but Lucinda didn't exactly bother to impress proper Pack etiquette, you know what I mean?"

I pinched the bridge of my nose between my eyes, "Just how big of a mess is this Pack?" I asked.

"Look, William's dad was a good Alpha when it came to securing the pack from threats from the *outside*, but he was shit at dealing with the Pack internally and Lucinda may have been the biggest and baddest bitch on the block, but she was a shit Alpha Bitch and the last Alpha didn't do anything to fix it. It's pretty much all been Sharon and the Arbiter holding things down."

Of course. I sighed and opened my mouth to speak but the front door opened downstairs and Markus called up, "Girls! It's time to go, let's get to it."

"I'm nominating you, Nora, that is, if you trust me."

"As my Alpha wills it," she said dubiously, a glimmer of fear in her eyes.

"I do, I also will that you be here every day from today until the next full moon so I can train you, hopefully being wolf-kind will give you an inside edge on the learning curve." I said and we both got up.

"Okay," she said but she didn't look sure. Damn it. If it wasn't one thing, it was another. I followed Nora downstairs and William smiled a little wanly at me.

Neither of us wanted to do this, yet here we were, just the same.

CHAPTER 25
William

I didn't feel much like talking on the drive. It didn't seem like there was a lot to talk about anymore. We'd been doing nothing *but* talking, *when we weren't fucking*, for far too long already. Markus seemed to catch the vibe and drove silently. I sat shotgun with Chloe clutched in my lap, staring intently out the passenger window at the trees drifting by. Fuck the seatbelt laws. I wanted her close, and you went days and sometimes weeks without seeing a human cop or state patrol out here.

I really wasn't positive what to do about Remus. And I really wasn't looking forward to it.

"What'd you mean last night when you said 'local Pack'?" Chloe asked suddenly and I turned my attention from the window to her.

"With a Pack as large as ours we can't all remain in the same area for long. Hell, we've already lived in Washington longer than we have almost anywhere else. With how slowly we age, we have to Pack up and move every so often to keep people from getting suspicious. Most of the Pack lives scattered across the country, typically going about their human lives. The Moon Forged do at least. Like I said, they can do without the immediate support of the Pack better than Blood Born can.

"There's usually two or three that stick together as a sort of small Pack unit for support and to help keep each other out of trouble and under the radar. We have several events throughout the year where the extended Pack members will fly or drive in for a week or two spending time with the Pack as a whole."

"So local Pack would be just the ones that lived in Washington?"

"Just the ones that live on the Olympic Peninsula."

"How many is that?"

"Fifty or sixty?" I said in a questioning tone to Markus who nodded without saying anything or taking his eyes from the road. "Fifty or sixty," I said to Chloe with a touch more confidence in my tone. "And even that number fluctuates any given week."

"How are you supposed to keep track of all this?"

"Years and years of practice and lessons. You'll learn, my love. Try not to worry overly much about it right now, okay? It's really not something you need to concern yourself with right this second. You'll have time to get all this straight."

She chewed on her bottom lip for a moment before she gave a short nod.

"So today we're expecting in the fifty range as far as attendance goes?" she clarified and Markus gave a growling agreement.

"Somewhere around there," he said. "The vast majority of the Pack left yesterday. They've got their regular lives to get back to. This situation with the Alpha succession has thrown everyone's usual schedule severely out of balance. Jobs still have to be held though, so they couldn't stick around any longer."

"I'll help go over all of this with you later, Chloe," Nora offered from the back. "It really isn't as difficult as it seems. One thing you have to remember is that you'll probably never know where each individual member is at any given time. It's just too big and constantly shifting and fluctuating. All you need to know is that even if we don't have all their locations, we do have all of their phone numbers and we can contact any of them at any time. That's how we get everyone here for emergency meetings like the Alpha's death. Phone trees and coded email blasts."

Chloe and Nora quietly discussed things as we traveled the last few minutes' worth of miles to the clearing. I was starting to get tired of that damned clearing. I think I had seen it too many times in the last few weeks as it was and nearly every time it was because something terrible had happened or was going to happen. Father's death, Chloe's attack, the fight against Romulus, and Chloe's battle with Lucinda…

Yeah, I really hate this damn clearing.

Next to me Chloe looked up and slipped her hand into mine,

twining our fingers together. "I hate it too," she muttered and I blinked for a moment.

"Did I say that out loud?" She nodded and I frowned. *Pull it together, idiot. Now is really not the time to lose your shit.*

"When are they bringing Remus?" Chloe asked and I gave her a sidelong look.

"They who? Who would bring Remus?"

"Well the..." she trailed off floundering for the word she wanted. "Guards or whatever the wolf-kind equivalent would be. I mean he had to have been taken into custody or arrested or something to get him to show up here tonight, right?"

Understanding dawns clear and bright on even the most overcast of days, as father used to say. That light of understanding went off and everything made perfect sense all of a sudden.

"No, no, he wasn't captured or arrested or anything like that. He'll be here of his own accord."

She gave me a look that clearly suggested she thought I had lost my mind and I frowned at her. "What?"

"Seriously?"

"What?" I was getting confused again.

"You honestly believe that Remus would just show up here, knowing he's going to be basically on trial for patricide, regicide, and treason? He probably high tailed it out of the state while we were on our way home from the fights of succession."

"Chloe, wolf-kind don't work that way," I said gently, "If he ran we would hunt him and he would die in a very slow, very unpleasant manner. He knows that he's in trouble and the wolf won't let him just run. He'll face his mistakes head on. Besides, if he ran, aside from us hunting him down, he would basically be declaring himself an Omega. No one would voluntarily do that."

She still looked dubious but let the matter drop and turned just in time to see Sharon walk into the clearing, her head held high as if she owned the forest and I couldn't help the turning of my upper lip into a hate filled snarl that bared my teeth for just a moment at her. I had counted Sharon as one of my best friends and biggest supporters. And while she might have supported me, she didn't support my mate and in my eyes that was almost worse. An outright betrayal.

She didn't react to me and walked on to stand to the side of the clearing, hands clasped calmly in front of her. The bleachers, still standing after they had been erected for the succession challenge, quickly began to fill. Stands meant to hold nearly three hundred people looked woefully empty with a paltry fifty butts in the seats but within half an hour everyone had arrived... except for Remus.

Chloe kept glancing at me. I could see her out of the corner of my eye. We stood between the stands, looking down the length of them toward the trees. Chloe stood to my right and Markus stood on my left with Brent and Nora behind us. Four of us stood still and calm, just staring ahead in a show put on for the wolves in attendance. We had to look as if we were calmly in control. Chloe didn't quite fit that but she was new to the whole thing, so could be excused.

She looked over at me again and opened her mouth. "He'll be here," I interrupted before she could say anything. I turned my head slightly to look at her and gave her a small smile. "Listen, I can already hear him."

She frowned but a moment later closed her eyes and cocked her head to the side slightly, straining to focus her new senses to hear what I had already heard. Footsteps. Deep, heavy footsteps. Approaching with no sense of urgency. A calm measured cadence of foot falls on the rich forest floor.

Thump.

Thump.

Thump.

Thump.

He stepped from between the trees and paused for a moment at the very edge of the field and across the expanse between us. Our eyes met. I think that he knew then what I intended to do for his shoulders sagged the smallest bit as if a heavy weight had just settled on him.

The quietly talking wolf-kind in the stands fell into silence as Remus started across the clearing. He walked with the same pace he'd used on his way in, the measured, even step of a man that knew everything that stood before him, and who knew that he deserved what was going to happen to him.

"William," he said curtly as he stopped a few feet from us. He didn't speak loudly but everyone in the stands would easily be able to hear him. He glanced at Chloe and greeted her as well. "Chloe, you're looking better already than the last time I saw you," he said in a polite tone.

"I've been eating better," she told him and a small smile tugged at his stony features. He glanced back at me and I fought to keep my face an emotionless mask. Now was not the time for an Alpha to be emotional. Remus reached out and opened the left side of my loose jacket, just enough to see the scarred over bite mark on my chest and his face split again into a satisfied smile before he looked up at me, meeting my eyes with a steady gaze.

"Congratulations, William. You took one hell of a risk marking a human. I'm glad to see that it's paid off for you."

"Thank you, I wish these circumstances were different, Remus–"

"But they aren't," he said, cutting me off. "I know. Let's get on with it. There's no sense in dragging things out."

He took a step back and let his hands drop to his sides, waiting calmly for my sentence. Markus waved one arm, motioning to a group of young men standing before the stands on my right. They came forward, bringing with them a small but heavy table carved from a solid chunk of redwood and two boxes made of a similar material. The men carrying the boxes did so as if they contained live ordinance that could go off at any moment and their hands were covered by leather gloves that reached past their wrists. Overkill, I thought. But they were scared of what the boxes contained, and I couldn't honestly say that I blamed them. I wasn't thrilled about it myself.

I took a step closer to Remus, raising my voice slightly even though it really wasn't necessary for me to be heard. "Remus Reese," I said. "You have committed crimes against this Pack that are unforgivable. You conspired to kill our previous Alpha, our father, with your brother Romulus. Worse, you conspired with The

Hangman, the worst of the Hunters, and revealed to him the location of our Pack. In the months ahead, hard decisions will need to be made. It is uncertain if the Pacific Northwest Pack can even remain in the Washington Territories any longer, knowing now that the Hunters know where we are.

"You have jeopardized the lives of more than two hundred of your own kind, who are precious few already, for your own selfish reasons. According to Pack Law there is only one punishment for your crime. Death, at the next full moon."

Remus nodded. "I accept my–"

"I'm not finished Remus Reese," I cut him off and he blinked in surprise. "Pack Law dictates that your punishment should be Death at the hands of the Alpha. However, I, as Alpha, reserve the right to adjust sentences as I see fit." A quiet muttering spread through the crowd as people began to wonder where I was going with all this.

"Remus, you're a smart guy. You're driven and methodical. And despite everything you have been more of a brother to me than I would usually be willing to admit," I added the last with a glance over my shoulder at Chloe who gave me an encouraging smile. "You helped Chloe, and me, when you didn't need to. So I won't be ordering your death today, Brother. I won't bring in my reign over this Pack with any more of my family's blood. But you can't stay with the Pack."

The mutterings grew louder as some people started to figure out where I was going with this and Remus had gone white, all the blood draining from his face as his mouth dropped open.

"No," he whispered, hands beginning to shake at his sides. "William, no. Kill me. Don't do this. Don't do this, William. William!" As he spoke I turned and opened one of the boxes and reached within it to remove the item that had so frightened the men that carried it to our side.

It looked like a craft stamp, a simple handle of highly polished wood and set within the flat surface of it was a band of metal in the shape of the Greek symbol Omega.

The mutterings in the audience grew even louder as those that hadn't realized it yet, finally figured it out.

"I can't William," Remus said. "You know I can't. Blood Born need a Pack. Blood Born *need* a Pack!"

"Remus." My left hand grasped his shoulder and I held the brand loosely in my right, my arm hanging at my side. "Remus, look at me." The panicked expression on his face was difficult to see. Remus Reese had always been the calm and level headed one. The one that rarely showed emotion, and to see him breaking down at the mere sight of the brand…

He looked at me and I smiled at him as kindly as I could. "I love you, Remus. You *are* my brother, and I can't kill my brother. There's been enough death in this family already. Do you understand me? There has been enough death already."

His shaking slowly stopped and he squared his shoulders looking me in the eye with a determined steel once more returning to his gaze.

"Jacket," I murmured and he lifted his left hand, pulling aside his jacket to reveal his bare chest.

In silence, as everyone stilled to watch, I lifted the metal brand. Markus lit his zippo and I held the silver to the flame. It seemed to take forever for the metal to heat, but finally, satisfied it was hot enough, I pulled it from the fire.

I pressed the Omega symbol against Remus' chest, in the same place where Chloe had bitten me. The instant the silver touched his skin there was a loud hissing sound, like meat touching a red hot frying pain and a wisp of smoke rose up from his skin. The stench of burning flesh assaulted my nose and I gritted my teeth.

Remus let slip a strangled cry but clenched his jaw tight and remained otherwise silent for the five seconds that I held the brand against his flesh. When I pulled it away there was an angry black burn left behind on his skin in the perfect shape of the Omega.

"Remus Reese is dead," I said quietly. My grip on his shoulder was one of the only things keeping Remus on his feet, the other being sheer stubborn will. "Do you understand me, Remy?" He raised his eyes from the burn on his chest.

"I understand, William."

"You need to be gone by sundown tomorrow, Brother."

"Remus was your brother," he said. "Remy Dulcet is an only child."

I sighed, already feeling drained and lost. "Be that as it may, Remy, Remus Reese is dead, and you, Remy Dulcet, can start over somewhere else. Remy Dulcet *can* make amends where Remus would never be able to."

He said nothing, but held my eyes, the deep obsidian of his gaze boring into mine with a frightening intensity.

"Return to our territory without an extremely compelling reason, and you face the death penalty that I spared you tonight," I said to finish off the ceremony.

"I understand," he said. "Take care of him, Chloe," he added before he turned and slunk off into the night. I could still here his footsteps for some time as he left and eventually I felt a hand land on my shoulder and turned to look at Markus.

"Ya did good, Kid," he muttered, voice pitched low so only we would hear him. "Omega might seem like a fate worse than death to him right now, but you gave him all the tools he needs. He'll figure it out, Remu– Remy is a smart man. He'll be fine."

"I hope so, Markus. Because if he doesn't, I just sentenced him to a slow torturous wasting existence when a swift death would have been kinder."

Chapter 26
Chloe

I watched Remus thrash through the underbrush and listened to William and Markus speak on it. Deep, dark storm clouds of pity and remorse swamped me. The raw, naked pain and even fear that had flickered across Remus' features made an indelible mark on my heart even as the brand had pitted and melted his flesh.

A weighted silence filled the clearing and I turned my eyes toward Sharon. She wasn't looking so certain anymore and I couldn't say I felt bad about that. The way she'd carried herself into the clearing had left me angry and I had decided on the same fate for her, but seeing Remus? Well that had softened my position some.

Honestly though, none of the options before me were that great. Both required a brand and I really wasn't sure I could go through with such an intentional act of cruelty. I swallowed hard. A big part of being a leader was doing things you didn't want to do. Another part of being a leader was never asking of anyone that which you weren't willing to do yourself.

As reviled as he was, I was my father's daughter in some of the more important ways. The ones that really counted. Having a backbone was one of those ways. I was also my mother's daughter. Even though she'd died when I was young, she'd taught me understanding. To look beyond the surface. Past the color of people's skin, past their clothes or where they lived or how they were raised. I tried very hard to do that here even though Sharon wouldn't afford me the same courtesy.

She stared at me, her lips compressed in a thin line of contempt and I just had to ask her, "Tell me why I don't afford you the same fate, Sharon."

She visibly paled but held her ground, "I..." she closed her mouth, opened it again, closed it again and finally snarled, "Why don't you just do whatever you're going to do?"

"Because I don't want to," I told her honestly. I looked out over the assembled crowd.

"I don't want to burn you, I don't want to fight you, and I don't want to start my reign of leadership with punishment and pain. There's already been enough blood spilled on this hallowed ground," Sharon scoffed and I turned my eyes back to her and cocked my head to the side.

"But part of being a leader, part of being an *effective* and *good* leader, means doing things you don't want to do all the time." I let the silence roll through the glade and settle in.

"Pack Law demands that I either banish you as Omega, or that I mark and demote you. There's another option though," I said; a sudden stroke of brilliance really. The wolves murmured to one another and Sharon looked at me puzzled.

I needed to cement my status with these people, *my people*, I needed to impress upon them that I wasn't weak. That I knew how and that I would lead them. That I wasn't afraid and never would be.

"What are you talking about?" Sharon demanded, scowling.

"Chloe..." William's voice held a thread of confusion twining with a thread of warning.

"How about it Sharon? Do you think you could do better leading this Pack than I could? Do you think you're more Alpha than me? That's your third option. You could Challenge me for leadership of this Pack, right here and right now and I could do the same damn thing I did to Lucinda to you the next full moon. I'll let you think about it. Go ahead and take a minute."

I locked gazes with her and her eyes widened. Rather quickly Sharon's eyes only got wider still, as she realized I was dead serious and she went down on one knee, "No Alpha, I won't challenge you, I... I don't want to challenge you."

"Looks like you have some self-preservation after all," I uttered and heaved a great inward sigh of relief. I hadn't been bluffing, I would have killed her the next full moon, I just really, *really*, didn't want to.

"You won't be challenging anyone else anytime soon either," I said. "Sharon, I pronounce sentence. You will be marked and demoted. Nora will take your place as Beta of this Pack. Do you agree to this pronouncement or do you wish to Challenge me? Last chance."

Sharon looked up at me and the look was of pure venom, "I don't wish to challenge you, Alpha. I agree to your sentence."

"Good deal," I said with a raised brow and plucked the brand Markus indicated out of the box. It was a straight line with two shorter diagonal hash marks through the longer line's center. William made to take it from me and I shook my head. He gave me a proud little smile and I gave him a brave one in return.

Sharon didn't take her brand quietly, not like Remus. She screamed long and loud and my heart broke a little. I made sure to brand her in a place that could easily be covered, figuring she was going to hate me no matter what I did.

"This matter is done, closed, do you all understand me?" I demanded.

"Sharon is not to be treated any differently than any other member of this Pack."

"I don't need your weak pity!" Sharon snarled.

"That's where you're wrong, Sharon. Don't you ever confuse my kindness for weakness because I swear to God, I swear *on my mate's life*, it will be the last thing you ever do! That goes for all of you!" I clasped William's hand and looked up into my beloved's eyes. We both turned as one to address our Pack and shouted in unison.

"I am the Alpha!"

CHAPTER 27

William

It took a while to get through everything after that. Not all night, thankfully. But definitely a while. The brands were taken away and Sharon stalked from the meeting with her head bowed noticeably in comparison to how she arrived on the scene earlier.

I pulled Chloe away from Nora where they were discussing plans for the next few days. Nora needed to set up lessons for Chloe, as well as give her a rundown on her responsibilities as Alpha Bitch of the Pack. She came willingly and I folded her into my arms, breathing in her scent and taking a great comfort from her body pressed against mine. Without thinking, her arms had slid inside my jacket and her hands stroked softly up and down my back sending tingles through my skin wherever she touched me.

"I hope that feeling lasts forever," I muttered without meaning to. She tilted her head back and gave me a questioning look, but I just smiled and shook my head. "Don't worry about it. Just a stray thought." I smiled and kissed the end of her nose, laughing as she made a face and scrunched her nose up as if she wanted to sneeze for a moment.

"So, how'd I do?" she asked in a quiet murmur and I pulled her tight.

"You did great, Love. I'll admit to almost suffering a coronary when you asked if she wanted to Challenge you, but it was brilliant. Excellent work."

"Little gushy fer my tastes, but he's right," Markus added. He walked up behind Chloe and she turned in my arms so she could see him. "Ya did good. Now let's get the hell out of here. The wife's waitin' fer me and I want to get home already."

I started and looked at Markus in an entirely new light. "You're married? Why didn't I know that?" I asked, surprised.

Markus laughed and gave Chloe a wink. "There's a lot that you don't know about me, Kid," he said. "The sheer tonnage of things that you don't know would knock you senseless."

Chloe laughed and followed behind him as the old wolf started walking away.

"Hey!" I followed after them and took Chloe's hand as we walked. She twined her fingers through mine but I was busy glaring at Markus. "That's really not fair, you old dog," I called after him and he just kept laughing. Laughter was something I think we needed a lot more of around here and I was content to be the butt of his joke if it put such a smile on my mate's face.

Markus dropped us off outside the house after spending the entire drive fending off, or outright ignoring me pestering him about his wife, and we went in and upstairs, undressed and slipped into bed, both of us unconscious before we even knew it.

When I woke, my eyes opened and I stared up at the vaulted ceiling above me, feeling somehow out of place. Something was different. There was a feeling I had that I just couldn't place at first, something I didn't usually wake up feeling on an average day in the life of William Reese.

Chloe was sprawled across my chest, her arms thrown around me and her right leg lying across my hips. Her skin felt soft and warm against mine and my body told me how much it enjoyed her presence.

But that wasn't it. To be perfectly honest I had woken up with a woman in my bed more than once. I'm in my seventies and certainly not a saint or a monk. So a beautiful woman in bed with me, not the unusual thing. Maybe it's because she was my wife, for all intents and purposes?

No, that wasn't it either.

I pulled her closer and breathed in the faint scent of peaches and sunshine that I associated so strongly with Chloe Reese. Holding her in my arms, her body pressed against mine, I felt more relaxed and content than I had in a long time.

My eyes popped open again, I hadn't even realized I had closed them.

That was it. Content. I hadn't felt content in longer than I could remember. Every day I woke up facing training, combat; the harsh life of a wolf-kind. As son of the Alpha, with two powerful brothers to worry about, I was always watching my back, all the time.

I didn't have to watch my back anymore. Well, okay, yes, I still needed to watch my back. But I was the Alpha. My mate was the Alpha. We were an Alpha pair and I could honestly say that I was completely in love with her. When exactly had that happened? I chuckled quietly to myself. It'd probably happened somewhere between threatening to rape her and when she said 'shut up and fuck me', I just hadn't noticed.

"What are you laughing about?" a sleep filled voice asked from the level of my chest. I tilted my head down, looking into her beautiful amber flecked blue eyes.

"I was just wondering when exactly it was that I fell in love with you." She smiled and stretched languidly. As her leg shifted across me and her breasts slid against my chest, I wasn't at all surprised that my dick started to grow harder beneath her thigh.

"And that thought causes you to get a hard on?" she asked, moving her leg down and taking me in hand.

"No, you sliding your body against mine does that."

"Damn right," she muttered and pulled me over on top of her. Her leg came up, thigh rubbing against my side as she opened herself for me. "So when did you conclude that you fell in love with me?" she asked.

I braced myself on my elbows and kissed her gently, resisting as she tried to pull my hips closer to her. The head of my dick just brushed against her and she pulled more insistently at my hips, lifting her own towards me.

She growled, frustrated, and I smiled against her lips.

"I realized it, I think, somewhere between threatening to rape you and when you said–"

"Shut up and fuck me already," she growled and I laughed again as I let her pull me forward and slid into her with one slow thrust.

"Yeah," I groaned. "That was what you said, more or less." Chloe laughed breathlessly against my neck and rocked her hips against mine.

We had a lot to do still. The Pack was still a mess. The Hunters still knew that we had taken the state as our territory. Nora and Brent would be there soon to start going over things with Chloe and I had promised that I would stick around to help, so we were going to talk in my workshop while I finished the tree that I needed to dismantle and ship out to my client by the end of the week. We had time for this though.

I slowly pulled almost entirely out of her, until just the head of my dick remained, splitting open the swollen lips of her pussy before I plunged back into her, driving a loud moan from her lips.

At the moment I was much more concerned with the pleasure I could bring to my mate and myself than I was with Pack politics and lessons. I was happy, and they could wait for just a little while.

Epilogue
Remus

Omega. He made me an Omega. A wolf without a Pack. I was alone. Truly alone for the first time in my life. A life far longer than my appearance suggested. I didn't look much older now than I had when William was bitten by my father back in the sixties.

How long could I live if a Hunter didn't catch up to me? How long would I live if I didn't die in an accident? Centuries. I had centuries of being alone ahead of me. Centuries of isolation with no Pack, and no family and no brother to stave off the madness that had taken Romulus.

So I did what I was told, since I had nothing else to do. I ran.

Highway 101 stretched for more than one thousand five hundred miles from Tumwater, Washington, and ended at the East Los Angeles Interchange. Right then, Los Angeles sounded like a good idea. William was right, I didn't like it, but he was. I couldn't stay with the Pack that had been my home, my family, for my entire life. My twin was dead at my brother's hands.

My head almost spun from the insanity that had become my life. I hadn't even had enough time to empty or list the apartment Romulus and I had shared in the city before I'd needed to leave. I had just enough time to Pack a small bag with a few changes of clothes and a few personal effects that I really didn't want to lose. Then I was on the road.

My heart burned in my chest almost as fiercely as the brand on my skin. The cool fall air did little to help the burning sensation as it flowed past me. I needed to get out of Washington. For a while if not permanently.

There are few things I truly enjoyed in the world. Sex was one, violence another; when it was deserved. Romulus enjoyed violence for the sake of violence, and that was part of what got him killed. I loved my twin. He was my blood, my other half, but he was dangerous, broken... crazy. My hands tightened on the grips and the roar beneath me surged louder for a moment before I forced myself to relax.

I had never been without a Pack. I had never been without my own kind around me and I could find more, true; but I was marked. I was an Omega. I would never be welcomed by another Pack. It was rare that an outsider was welcomed into a Pack, even without the stigma of my new status hanging over me.

I flicked the turn signal with my thumb and pushed against the bar, leaning the huge Harley into a gentle course correction until I had slid across the freeway and into the far left lane.

Ahead I saw a sign indicating that I was entering Oregon State, just as the sun began to near the horizon.

There you go William, I thought. *Out of the territory before sundown, as promised.* Behind me, the men that had been assigned to follow me and ensure that I left, pulled off the road and disappeared and I returned my focus to the front as I gunned the throttle and roared off into the gathering dusk.

I wondered how far I could run. How fast I could go. How much time would it take for this Omega to run from his past? And for an Omega, was there even truly a future to run to?

THE MOON FORGED TRILOGY: BOOK II

OMEGA'S RUN

AJ DOWNEY | RYAN KELLS

Hunter's CHOICE

A.J. DOWNEY

Prologue
Hunter

Sharp grinding pain caused my eyes to water. My left leg and wing were useless to me. I was trapped. Unable to do anything for myself, too weak to make anything other than a piteous call that would likely go unheeded.

I closed my eyes and lay still and waited for death. Thousands of years of living and this is how I would go. In the middle of a stretch of asphalt, the cold rain pattering down on me while heartless humans passed me by in their nice warm cars, tsking under their breath at the poor bundle of floundering feathers in the road.

Idiot.

I was an idiot, pure and simple.

I wailed my frustration as my heart pounded against my delicate ribs. Each beat sending a fresh lance of pain through my broken wing, a sympathetic sharp pang echoing in my leg.

Who would have thought I would die like this? It was shameful. Ridiculous even.

A sharp sound, footsteps, I swiveled my head to take in a pair of worn, brown work boots jogging across the highway. Gentle hands in thick leather closed around me and I screeched. In as much pain as I was in, I couldn't help it. I was turned and as I was I looked into the most beautiful eyes, deep and soulful, the color of the sea meeting a storm swept horizon. They were surrounded by pale milky skin and wisps of hair I swore was spun copper.

For a moment I thought it may be Bébinn, come to fetch me to Annwn, but the pain she wrought when she plucked me from the grit of the modern highway told me otherwise. I fought her, I couldn't help myself, but she took me from the road and got into a vehicle and that was all I could remember for some time...

Chapter 1
Jessamine

"You name this one yet?" Charlie asked me, and I shook my head.

The Barred Owl had been under my care for a couple of months, his left wing and left leg had been broken, thankfully both had been simple fractures. He was on the mend and due for release as soon as I could get his atrophied muscles built back up.

I couldn't bear to name him, it wasn't so simple... he wasn't like the other owls under my care. He was different somehow. Big for a Barred Owl for one, and the way he watched me move through the old barn we used as an Aerie, well it bespoke an intelligence far beyond any ordinary owl.

No, I just couldn't name this one.

"Well now, maybe that just means you're finally growing up Jessamine!" He winked at me and I gave an indelicate snort, wrinkling my nose in distaste, I shook my head violently, strawberry blonde bangs flopping into my eyes, pony tail dragging against the rugged green canvas material of my Carhartt jacket.

"N...n...n...n...nnnnever!" My stutter was horrible but I forced the word out through it anyways. Most of the time I chose to remain silent. I carried a notepad and pen on a string around my neck for when communication was absolutely required.

Charlie had fashioned a cover out of leather so that I could replace the note pad in it whenever I needed to. He'd spent so much time on it. Tooling a Barn Owl into its medium brown leather surface by hand. The loop that held the pen was sturdy and once he'd gifted it to me, I'd worn it every day since.

That had been when I was eighteen, it was a parting gift when I'd gone off to veterinary college. I'd lived here with my aunt and uncle, well my mom's aunt and uncle, she didn't have any siblings, since I was seven. Charlie was as old as my aunt and uncle who had recently retired to Arizona and a warmer climate. Not Charlie though. Nope, he would live and die around these parts and his tribe. The Quileute of the Olympic Peninsula in Washington State.

I went around the large open interior of the old barn, cleaning cages, feeding my charges and checking on the newer birds. I worked full time at a veterinary hospital in Port Angeles about thirty minutes from my aunt and uncle's property.

It was my property now, for all intents and purposes, just not in name. They wanted it to be, but I had refused such a generous gift. They had it in their wills it would go to me, but even then, I'm not sure if I would be ready to really own it, even though I had been operating it for years.

Moonchild Owl's Haven started when I was nine, with a sick Spotted Owl my uncle and I had found while mushroom hunting. We had no idea what we were doing, but we couldn't just leave the poor thing. So we took it to the vet, and insisted on learning.

A local bird sanctuary, The Northwest Raptor and Wildlife center took us on as volunteers. We had done things almost all wrong with the Spotted Owl, who by the grace of some higher power and Jaye Moore, the director of the Raptor Center, had lived. Despite having bungled the initial care of Hootie back then, I had fallen in love with the cause almost instantly and my uncle and I had been willing pupils under Jaye. We had learned everything there was to learn about caring for all types of birds from her, but for me, it had always been about the owls. I'm not sure why.

When I was thirteen, my uncle and I applied for the necessary permits to become a wildlife rehabilitation facility. My uncle and I had spent every summer renovating the old barn on the property, from the age of nine to thirteen, to get it ready to house any injured owls. We won the permits and had rehabilitated quite a few owls from then until now. Only three in that time had become fixtures. Their injuries necessitating a permanent residency under my care.

I went to the back wall of the barn and looked up at the almost life sized tree artfully burned into its raw wood surface. Leaves bearing the burned in name of every owl we had ever helped hung on brass hooks from the many branches. It was a project my uncle and I had started from day one.

"What're you going to put on his tag if you don't name him?" Charlie asked as I looked over the tree. I shrugged my shoulder and turned, he was watching the bird with a curious look on his face, the bird though; he was watching me.

He was more brown than white, his patterning dappled and streaked in such a way as to remind me of the light falling through the trees. His beak was the color of bone, not yellow like a lot of the Barred Owls around. His eyes though, they were limpid pools of darkness, large and oddly expressive, and followed me as a man's would. Drinking me in as I moved about the barn. There was something there, something I couldn't place, but he, he was like no other owl; be it Barred, Barn, Spotted or any other species I had housed under my roof.

"Odd feller ain'tcha?" Charlie asked absently. The bird turned and looked Charlie in the eye and Charlie shuddered as if he'd gotten a sudden chill. I clapped twice and Charlie looked at me.

Throughout my childhood, Charlie, my Uncle and I had developed a series of hand signals for me to let them know what I was up to. My Aunt had never grasped it, but it was like our own sign language. I signed out that I was cleaning up and calling it a day out here and that he should do the same.

I had never bothered learning ASL, American Sign Language, what was the point out here where my world was as small as it was? Where no one else spoke it? I didn't venture to the city very often and my note pad and pointing sufficed more often than not.

Was I lonely?

Yes, sometimes, but that was my lot in life. Besides, I had Charlie, and my owls. They were like my feathered children and I loved each one, choosing a name, growing attached and crying with a sense of loss at every release. Some would call me masochistic, and to some degree I suppose that was true, but you can't do what I do and not feel. That would simply be barbaric.

I stopped in front of my unnamed Barred Owl's cage, Charlie

ducked out of the barn and into the ever present light drizzle outside. I considered the owl who cooed softly at me, another odd occurrence. I sighed and looked around to make sure that Charlie was good and gone from hearing range.

"W-what's your n-n-n-n-ame fella?" I asked softly.

When it was just me and the owls, away from human judgment, my stutter was much less. Psychogenic they called it, as opposed to neurogenic. It meant that there was nothing neurologically wrong with me or my brain to cause the stutter. No, mine was all in my head on a psychological level due to trauma. Not something I liked to think about or talk about.

The owl cocked its head almost all the way 'round upside down, like they do sometimes, and considered me. It gave a familiar broken call and I smiled. That was where my initial love of owls had come from.

When my Aunt and Uncle had plucked me out of the temporary state custody I'd been in, I'd already been self-conscious of my speech by then. Aunt Margie and Uncle Dave were a childless couple by fate, not design. So when Uncle Dave's niece, my mom had gotten into... trouble, and could no longer handle taking care of me, Aunt Margie had insisted that she and Uncle Dave come to the rescue. It was the kind of people they were and I loved them for it.

Unfortunately for me, going from life in the city to life here on the Olympic Peninsula was a lesson in culture shock. It was so *quiet* here at night, and the animal sounds from out there in the dark, terrifying at first. That was, until Uncle Dave told me the broken hooting I was hearing was an Owl, and he pointed out a ghost of a bird in one of our trees.

He told me that there was nothing to be afraid of, that the owl was just saying 'Welcome to the neighborhood,' that she just had a stutter like me. I think it was his attempt at telling me not to let my stutter get me down, that the animals didn't but I was way beyond a small pep talk at that point.

The big Barred Owl hooted at me questioningly and I smiled. He was just so *odd*. It made me wonder about him even more. I pursed my lips in thought and rejected the notion of going into his enclosure for now. As human as his mannerisms were, he was still a bird of prey and as such pretty dangerous and unpredictable. I smiled at him and backed away. He ruffled his feathers and hunkered down on his perch, blinked and watched me go. He would be ready for release just as soon as I could get him back into flying form, so a month or more down the road.

I slipped out into the mist like rain, shutting and securing the old barn door behind me. I looked out over my small side yard at the two story Cedar shake sided house that had been lovingly built by my uncle for my aunt. I had taken over the master bedroom on the second story when they had cleared out. A small deck jutted out from the floor to ceiling windows to either side of the French doors.

I traipsed across the gravel drive and mounted the steps to the small deck two at a time. I wiped my boots carefully on the mat before letting myself in to my bedroom.

I took off my boots just inside the doors on the slate entryway before it transitioned into carpet. I took pains to keep the outdoors where they belonged and not in my house. I stepped into my rubber soled sheepskin slippers and padded across the floor to the bedroom door. My bedroom was technically on the side of the house, rather than the back or front. I took off my coat as I went down the stairs, hanging it carelessly on the banister as I passed into the kitchen. I set about making myself and Charlie some dinner, boiling water for hot tea.

After a time, he came in through the back door. I scowled and pointed at his boots. He laughed and took them off. I scowled again at his holey sock where his big toe poked through as he took a seat at the marble kitchen counter.

"That big, Barred bastard, is about ready to go into an aviary," he grunted, and I smiled. The Barred Owl wasn't exactly native to the Pacific Northwest and was forcing out the much rarer and endangered Northern Spotted Owl, both by killing the slightly smaller owl and by interbreeding with it. To quote the villain of the movie Braveheart, "If we can't get them out, we'll breed them out."

In Charlie's world Barred Owls were interlopers, forcing the

6

native Spotted Owls from their rightful territory. I'd imagine, being Quilleute, hell, being Native, gave Charlie a stronger opinion than most about the subject, and rightfully so. Still, Charlie was like me, a firm believer that every creature great and small deserved to live with as pain free an existence as possible. The world was harsh enough without us adding to it.

That's not to say we were vegetarians or anything close. We did have a deep respect for what we ate and as I dished up the salmon steaks and green beans we bowed our heads in a moment of silence, paying our respects to the creature we were about to consume.

"Gotta mend the south aviary tomorrow if you're gonna start working that big Barred, getting him ready to fly." He spoke around a mouthful of food and I rolled my eyes while simultaneously giving him a thumbs up. He laughed, knowing exactly what it was I meant. He didn't apologize for talking with his mouth full, he just shoveled more into his maw and chewed with gusto.

I cooked, he cleaned. That was the deal around here. I poured us some steaming mugs of blackberry tea and added a generous amount of honey to both while he rinsed dishes and loaded the dishwasher. He'd be heading home in his big old Ford pickup soon. I'd told him he should just move into the downstairs room but he'd have none of it. Swearing he'd live on the res and die on the res which was a good forty minutes away.

I sighed and went into the living room, adding logs to the ravenous potbellied stove in the corner.

"Well, Jessa-my-girl, it's time for me to haul my old bones back to the res." Charlie stretched and dropped into one of the seats at the little dining nook. He laboriously began pulling on his old boots.

"You going into town tomorrow?" he asked. I swiped across my neck once, our sign for no. It was my day off, but he already knew that.

"All right then sweetheart, you going to help an old man get that aviary up and running?" I shrugged and raised three fingers and pumped my fist up and down twice, holding imaginary jesses. He raised an eyebrow. Right now we had five birds, three of which needed exercise which is what I'd just told him.

"Well, when you're done you know where to find me at." He grumbled and I smiled sweetly. I went over and gave him a hug. He went out the back door and around the house, boots crunching on the gravel drive. I closed the door and a moment later I heard his old Ford grumble to life.

I sighed and doused the lights on the first floor after setting the coffee pot for the morning.

Sometimes there weren't enough hours in a day. Today had been no exception. Still, the birds and Charlie were fed and tomorrow was a new day. I shuffled up the stairs, leaving my coat behind and put myself squarely into a hot shower. As I climbed into bed I could hear the big Barred Owl all the way from the barn, his call clear and loud. Scientists call it the "Who cooks for you! Who cooks for you all?" which I thought was funny. It didn't sound like that to me. To me it sounded like all was right in my world.

A.J. DOWNEY

HEAVEN, HELL & THE LOVE IN BETWEEN

Chapter 1

The ivy of despair had taken root in my chest months ago. There was nothing specific that had happened, that I can remember, that brought on my depression. I didn't lose my job, or a boyfriend, no one had died, still, it had taken root within me somehow, and as the days grew shorter and the rains had come the vines had grown, constricting my heart within my chest, blocking out all light and anything that was good, and warm, and comforting. Things I had once taken great pleasure in doing, the restoration work I did at the museum, painting, the theater... all of it suddenly seemed dull and I just didn't know what to do with myself.

Some of my acquaintances had stopped calling, I call them acquaintances rather than friends because true friends wouldn't give up on someone simply because they were feeling blue, even if that blue period lasted longer than a few days or weeks... would they? No. I don't think so. Roxanne, my oldest and longest friend, my best friend, had not given up on me. She'd said to me: "Gracelyn, I'm here for you. No matter what, you just call me." I had smiled and we had hugged but I didn't know how to quantify what it was that I was feeling.

I was sad, all the time, but I didn't know why I was sad. I hurt for no reason, cried for no reason, and I was tired all the time for *no reason*. I had finally gone to my doctor who had diagnosed me with depression. She'd given me pills, which I dutifully took, but they didn't help. I felt lost and adrift and therapy wasn't an option, not only was it not covered by my medical plan, you had to have a problem to work the problem out, didn't you?

The heels of my boots clicked sharply against the pavement as I made my way home to my apartment. The January wind bit along the exposed skin of my face and I scrunched down further into the collar of my black winter pea coat.

I had no problems, I grew up in a loving home, raised by my grandparents after my parents had passed in a bad car accident... which is something I had come to grips with a very long time ago. While I had not been popular in school growing up, I hadn't been unpopular. I'd had friends, gone to college, gotten my Masters in Science of Historic Preservation and was certified by The Academy of Certified Archivists and was working on a dream project preserving historical artifacts from an archeological dig. I mean what was more exciting than preserving artifacts from a Viking raid in Scotland?

I turned and clacked up the steps to my building and let myself in. I lived in a modest high rise apartment in a relatively quiet neighborhood... well as quiet as any neighborhood in New York could be. It was relatively close to the museum I worked out of, only two subway stops away. I could walk if I wanted to most days and I did, the life as an academic isn't exactly an active one so I walked to and from work and ran two or three times a week to stay in shape. It was getting harder and harder to resist the call of the subway though as all the joy in my life slowly leeched away worse than the color out of a painting left too long in the sun.

I unlocked my apartment door and closed it heavily behind me, locking the deadbolt and leaning against its worn surface. I dropped my purse and tote bag in the entryway and my keys into their dish on the little hall table I kept near the door. I hung my coat and scarf on the back of the door and before I did anything, unzipped my riding style boots from knee to ankle and toed them off.

"I'm home." I called to no one in particular. I lived alone. Hence why it didn't really matter if I left all my stuff in front of the door. I padded in my tights clad feet to the kitchen and opened the fridge, then closed it with a groan. Who was I kidding? I wasn't hungry. I used to enjoy cooking for myself but not since the black ivy of my depression started choking the life out of me last year. I went into my bedroom and undressed, hanging my black blouse, and deep green skirt, and jacket back in their places.

I peeled out of my tights and underwear after casually flipping my bra into the dirty laundry basket. The tangle of undergarments sulked on the top of the pile and I let them as I padded across the hall into my bathroom. I let the shower heat up, pulled some towels out of the linen cupboard and climbed in, letting the hot water beat my tense shoulders into some semblance of submission.

Today had been meeting after meeting with the walking wallets that were funding our project. I hated dealing with the suits with a passion, my time was better spent in the lab with the tools of my trade, brushing dirt away, recording details and small discoveries about whatever artifact happened to find its way to my worktable. My day had been especially frustrating due to the fact that what currently occupied my worktable was the hilt and a good third or more of a genuine Viking blade, circa the tenth century. That's right, the tenth century... you know it gets exciting for a history nerd like me when you start dropping into the lowest double digits before the word century.

I plucked the hair band off the end of the long golden braid hanging over my right shoulder and worked the strands of my dishwater blonde hair out of their thick rope. The water against my scalp felt good, but maddeningly I remained numb and indifferent, which frustrated me. I scrubbed my hands over my face and stuck it in the shower spray, huffing out a sigh. It was late, I was tired and all I wanted was my bed so I decided to make some seriously quick work of this shower, lathering my hair and rinsing it quickly, I skipped the conditioner and used my honey and milk body wash equally as quickly in a quick head to toe lather with my bath poof. I rinsed well and shut off the water, reaching for a towel.

The storm of a meltdown was brewing, I could feel it in my chest, and behind my eyes. I didn't want to cry, I didn't want to be alone and yet I couldn't help it, the tide of emotion was rising and I was about to be swamped. I wrapped the regular sized bath towel around my hair and twisted, straightening up and flopping it back turban style on my head. I used the bath sheet to dry my body, starting with my face before finally wrapping it around myself twice below my arm pits and tucking the corner tight so it wouldn't slide off.

I wiped a streak in the steam coating my bathroom mirror with my hand and looked at myself. Cornflower blue eyes stared back at me, high cheekbones and a narrow chin bracketed a full mouth above and below. I was pretty by the generally accepted standard but I had never relied on it. I valued brains over looks and didn't have time for people that wanted to base their opinion of me on my packaging rather than what I had to offer in the intellectual department. Sometimes it got lonely, okay most of the time it got lonely, especially after the black ivy of despair moved in on me. I used my Tuscan honey lotion on my hands, arms, and legs and wrung my hair tightly one last time with the towel before letting it down. It was a tangled mess of snakes and there was no way I could sleep on it this wet, so I brought out the brush and hair dryer.

I shouldn't have skipped the conditioner. The brush snarled painfully in my locks and the sharp pain in my scalp brought the sting of tears to my eyes and that did it. The floodgates opened, the tide rose, crashed into my careful walls and decimated them with the force of a tsunami. A tsunami that pretty much poured out my eyes.

God damn it, I couldn't do anything right!

I cried my tears and dried my hair, brushing through the snarls and the pain on autopilot. Once dry I pulled it over my shoulder and braided it quickly to keep it from being a nightmare in the morning. I tossed the towels into the dirty laundry once back in my room and slipped a satin and lace nightgown over my skin. All of my sleepwear is sexy, an indulgence, my underwear is much the same. It was something Roxy had talked me into trying. An attempt to drag me out from beneath my black cloud. At the time it had been a marginal success, but they'd just rolled right back in again.

What was wrong with me?

I crawled into bed beneath my thick down comforter and lay in the fluffy marshmallow softness of my bed. The tears welled hot and immediate and spilled over. I just wanted this to end so badly. I wanted the hurt to stop, I wanted to sleep forever. Nothing helped, not my friend, not my work, not the pills. I felt like I was going mad and the fight, well the fight to just get out of bed in the morning was becoming harder and harder. I just didn't know how to cope with these feelings, and I didn't know how much longer I could live like this. So I sobbed into my pillow and hugged another to me, helplessly caught up in the storm of my emotions. I don't know how long I lay this way, weeping brokenly, alone in my apartment, but eventually, I fell asleep.

About the Authors

A.J. Downey is a born and raised Seattle, WA native. She finds inspiration from her surroundings, through the people she meets and likely as a byproduct of way too much caffeine. She has lived many places and done many things, though mostly through her own imagination. An avid reader all of her life, it's now her turn to try and give back, entertaining as she has been entertained. She blogs regularly at *http://authorajdowney.blogspot.com*

If you want the easy button digest, as well as a bunch of exclusive content you can't get anywhere else, sign up for her mailing list right here: *http://eepurl.com/blLsyb*

A California native and avid reader, for Ryan Kells, making the transition from reader to writer was simply the next logical evolution. He enjoys a number of genres from paranormal suspense to dystopian post-apocalyptic. All of his work contains a romantic spin with a decidedly erotic flair.

www.facebook.com/authorajdowney
www.facebook.com/authorryankells

Second Circle Press